With considerable force, *Rapido* rammed the *yawara* stick into Wiggins' stomach. With a strangled cry, the bodyguard reeled backwards, only to be hit in the face by another blow from the small Texan. With blood gushing from his nose, Wiggins whirled round, and ran headlong into the wall.

Looking at the converging bouncers, but paying no attention to the commotion elsewhere in the room, *Rapido* pointed elsewhere . . .

The bouncers received a shock!

* Awaiting publication at Corgi Books

The Return of Rapido Clint and Mr. J.G. Reeder

J.T. Edson

CORGI BOOKS

THE RETURN OF RAPIDO CLINT AND MR. J.G. REEDER

A CORGI BOOK 0 552 12440 0

First publication in Great Britain

PRINTING HISTORY

Corgi edition published 1984

Copyright © J.T. Edson 1984

This book is set in

Corgi Books are published by
Transworld Publishers Ltd.,
Century House, 61–63 Uxbridge Road,
Ealing, London W5 5SA

Made and printed in Great Britain by
Cox & Wyman Ltd., Reading, Berks.

For Mike Codd, who consistently produces excellent artwork for the jackets of our books.

Author's Note

Once again, we wish to thank Ms. Penelope Wallace for her kind permission to bring back her father's best loved detective, Mr. J.G. Reeder.

To save 'old hands' from repetition, but for the benefit of readers new to our work, we have included certain background information regarding Alvin Dustine '*Rapido Clint*' Fog – known later as 'Cap' – the organization operated by Mr. J.G. Reeder and various terms about which we have frequently received requests for clarification in the form of Appendices.

We realize that, in our present 'permissive' society, we could use the actual profanities employed by various people in the narrative. However, we do not concede a spurious desire to create 'realism' is any excuse for doing so.

Lastly, as we refuse to pander to the current 'trendy' usage of the metric system, except when referring to the calibres of certain weapons traditionally measured in millimetres – i.e., Walther P-38, 9mm – we still continue to employ miles, yards, feet, inches, stones, pounds and ounces, when quoting distances and weights.

J.T. EDSON,
Active Member, Western Writers of America,
MELTON MOWBRAY,
Leics.,
England.

CHAPTER ONE

WHY DON'T YOU GET
THE CHOPPER?

'I'M right pleased I let you talk me into coming here instead of going to the Alhambra, 'specially as Haysoff Spades'd called in sick and won't be showing tonight,' declared one member of the audience, crossing the foyer towards the exit of the Interstate Vaudeville Theatre in Fort Worth, Texas, at the conclusion of the Monday evening per-. formance. Tall and burly, in his early thirties, with close cropped blond hair upon which he was setting a tan coloured J.B. Stetson hat that had a Luskey Roll crease in its crown, his ruggedly good looking features were reddened by the sun rather than tanned. Like his Texas drawl, his features were suggestive of Teutonic and most probably Germanic origins. 'That was what I'd call a pretty good show, but the fancy pants dude's they've got for their head he-hooper comedian was *way* too fast for me. Way he kept on spitting out his quips one straight after another, a man'd be like' to think's how he was in one hell of a hurry to finish his act and get off on his way someplace.'

'He for certain wasn't letting no flies settle on his tongue, Dutchy,' conceded the man to whom the comment was made, displaying the usual disregard of ethnic origins frequent amongst Texans.[1] The Stetson he was donning had obviously begun its long life as white, with a Denton Pinch crease, but the passing of time and exposure to the elements had turned it a greenish-grey hue. Matching the blond in height, but considerably older, he had the lean and leathery look indicative of long hours spent out of doors in all kinds of weather. While not otherwise given to displaying his emotions, there was

---

1. *In Texas, any man of Teutonic origins tended to be given the sobriquet 'Dutchy' regardless of whether he came from Holland, Denmark or Germany.*

something in the blue eyes of his oak brown face which suggested a dry sense of humour. 'But I reckon's how he's got something and's like' to go far as a "comedic-alian" should he start to think a mite about where-at he is and who-all he's playing to.'

'You reckon so, huh?' inquired the burly man, his attitude implying he regarded the opinion of his companion as worthy of consideration.

'That I do,' confirmed the second speaker, with the air of supplying information of great importance. 'Fact being, while we was back of the stage through the "entry-misserion" and you was lolly-gagging with all them fancy lil dancing gals, that's what I told Bob O'Donnell over a cup of coffee in his office.'

'*Coffee?*' the blond challenged.

'Well, I do admit it *looked* more like Limey tea without milk and didn't taste over much like Arbuckle's,'[2] the older man admitted, his accent implying he too had been born and raised in the Lone Star State.

'Would it have tasted like *sourmash?*' 'Dutchy' queried dryly.

'*Sourmash*, with *Bob O' Donnell?*' the older man gasped, but his next words indicated that his disbelief over the question had not arisen from the fact that he knew the possession and drinking of alcoholic beverages was illegal under the 'Volstead Act'.[3] 'Why it was best "Kaintuck" bourbon no less!'

'Which's against the law of these United States, I've heard tell,' the blond remarked. 'But I'm no snitcher. Anways, what'd you tell him?'

' "Bob", I said,' the elderly Texan replied. ' "Why don't you tell that young Hope feller to haul back on his reins a mite and give all us good folks in the 'order-inance' a chance to

2. *'Arbuckle's', range term for coffee. Derived from this having been the brand name of the product seen so frequently throughout the Old West that most cowhands never knew any other kind was available. However, if a hand on a ranch was referred to as an 'Arbuckle', it implied he was useless and the boss had sent off Arbuckle's coffee premium stamps to pay for his 'extraordinary' services.*

3. *An explanation of the term, 'Volstead Act' is given in;* Footnote 1, APPENDIX TWO.

12

keep up with all them right funny things I reckon he was spouting. Kind of 'reminder-ate' him's how this's Texas, it's high summer and hotter'n the hot place. Us folks ain't going nowheres, but've come in here to 'ree-laxative' 'n' be made happy. We don't want to have to go chasing after words, no matter how 'commer-ical'. Hell, Bob," I said. "Way he was going on, you'd've thought's how he was holding a 'contest- ical' with us having to guess what he was saying." '

'And what'd Bob say to that?'

'Allowed's how he'd been thinking along them "pre-zactical" same lines his own self and aimed to drop by 'n' tell that young Hope feller to slow down a mite.'[4]

If any of the people leaving the theatre had been listening to the conversation taking place between the two men it would have presented puzzling aspects to them. For one thing, it implied they were allowed to go backstage during the intermission. This was a privilege granted to very few who were not in some way connected with the entertainment business, and neither of the men looked to have that distinction. Furthermore, the elderly Texan apparently not only had access to Robert 'Bob' O'Donnell—who was head of the Interstate Vaudeville Circuit and of considerable importance in theatrical circles throughout the whole of the United States—but had proffered advice which had been acted upon. Yet, although the impresario was far from being a snob who sought to remain unapproachable to all but those of influence, there was no visible sign of why either had been accorded such preferential treatment. Certainly nothing in their appearance gave the impression that their acceptance could have been caused by one or the other possessing wealth or high social standing in the community. Their attire was that of ordinary working cowhands visiting what was still known as 'Cowtown'—because of its long standing association

4. *Although there is no mention of the suggestion having come from Sergeant Jubal Branch, it was passed on by Robert 'Bob' O'Donnell. Taking the advice, the comedian in question learned a most valuable lesson about timing his 'delivery' to suit each particular audience which helped take him to the top of his profession. See,* Chapter Six, THIS IS ON ME, *Bob Hope and* 'Vaudeville', THE AMAZING CAREERS OF BOB HOPE, *Morella/ Epstein/Clark.*

with the cattle business which, despite the growing prominence of the oil industry, was still a major factor in the economy of the Lone Star State—for an evening of relaxation and entertainment.[5]

Although he had not been inside to see the show, one person at least on the sidewalk could have explained the matter. Of medium height, skinny, with sallow, sharp and unpleasant features, he was cheaply dressed in a brown three-piece suit, grubby white shirt and multi-hued necktie with a knot hardly larger than a pea. Having earned his living since early childhood by illicit means, generally specializing in picking pockets, Hubert 'Fingers' Kretzmer had good cause to know Jubal Branch and Hans 'Dutchy' Soehnen. They were sergeants in the Texas Rangers and, as such, were regarded as men of considerable consequence throughout the State.

Even though Kretzmer had not started his usual depredations on the property of the crowd, he had every thief's reluctance to being brought into contact with peace officers of any kind even if—as was the case with the two Texas Rangers—they did not have specific jurisdiction in that particular locality.[6] Deciding neither sergeant had seen him and letting out a sigh of relief, he began to slouch away with the intention of finding a safer area in which to ply his illicit trade. However, just as he had got clear of the crowd, he felt a large hand descend upon his shoulder. Trying to pull away, still without looking to his rear, he was gently yet firmly swung around.

'What's up, Fingers?' Dutchy Soehnen inquired, with what sounded like pained disappointment, and he lowered his hand from the shoulder he had grasped. 'Way you started to light a shuck as soon's you saw Jubal and me, a man'd be like' think you wasn't friends with us no more.'

'I ain't done *nothing* wrong!' the pickpocket protested, looking around nervously, regardless of the fact that for once he was completely innocent of offense.

---

5. *How ranching became a major factor in the economy of Texas is told in:* GOODNIGHT'S DREAM, FROM HIDE AND HORN *and* SET TEXAS BACK ON HER FEET.

6. *The jurisdictional authority of various types of law enforcement agencies in the United States is described in:* Footnote 2, APPENDIX TWO.

'Whenever did you?' Jubal Branch inquired and, moving forward with his companion, he helped to ease their captive into the recessed doorway of a store adjacent to the theatre. 'And there ain't no call for you to be looking for ole Lightning. Even though he's the best danged bluetick coonhound ever sired, I never take him with me to the "thee-hater" on account of he will start up howling along of the music.'

'I wouldn't try taking a greaser stand off, though, on account of him not being to hand to run you down,' Soehnen advised, a timbre of menace underlying his seemingly amiable words. 'Jubal and me had us a meal down to the Cattlemen's Hotel afore the show and, with the size of the steaks they serve inside us, we wouldn't take kind at all to having to chase after you.'

'Been working hard?' Branch asked, his manner apparently solicitous.

'No I ain't!' Kretzmer asserted and, although his abstinence from crime resulted from not having been granted time to start, he adopted an air of self righteous co-operation. 'We all know you don't have no *right* to, but you can put your hands through me happen you're so minded.'

'Why thank you most to death,' the older sergeant replied sardonically. 'Would you do the "honour-ablies", Dutchy?'

'It'd be a *privilege*,' Soehnen declared, aware that his companion's mispronunciation of words had started as a ploy to appear less shrewd and intelligent than he was and had now developed into an unshakable habit.

Working swiftly, with the deftness of long practise, the blond sergeant set about searching Kretzmer. He found no weapons. Nor, knowing the man with whom he was dealing, had he expected to. Being an arrant coward, the little pickpocket always whined when he was caught instead of offering physical resistance, unless the victim was elderly, infirm, or an obviously weak and helpless woman. However, although there were other things which he might have been expected to have in his possession, these too were absent. Failing to find them, in addition to checking the conventional pockets, Soehnen ran his fingers around the bottom of the jacket and over the loosely fitting vest without detecting bulges to indicate stolen property had been concealed there.

'Looks like he's clean,' Branch assessed, watching his companion step back and give a shrug.

'I wouldn't go so far's to say *that*,' the burly blond replied, wiping his hands on his sides as if wishing to remove something unpleasant from them. 'But he's not toting muggle,[7] nor anything harder, and he's not packing anybody else's belongings.'

'I told you I hadn't done nothing *wrong*,' the little pickpocket pointed out. Then, encouraged by the knowledge that neither peace officer had a reputation for subjecting criminals to rough handling except in justifiable self defence, he allowed his indignation to prompt him into continuing, 'There's some 's might reckon you should've *better* things to do with your time than pushing 'round innocent folks like me.'

'Day you're *innocent*, that's the day I start voting Republican,' Branch drawled and eyed Kretzmer quizzically. 'So what's these *better* things you reckon's how Dutchy 'n' me could be doing?'

'Maybe you've got something to tell us about whatever new kind of meanness good ole Hogan Turtle's boys're doing these days?' Soehnen suggested.

'I don't know *nothing* about what they're doing,' Kretzmer replied hastily. 'Nor want to!'

'Nothing at all?' Branch queried.

'Not a single god-damned thing!' the pickpocket insisted. Then, wanting to remove any impression which he might inadvertently have give the peace officers about his ability to supply information on the illicit activities of a man whose family had been very prominent in the criminal circles of Texas even before independence was won from Mexico in 1836,[8] he continued with the first thing that came into his head. 'Why don't you get the Chopper?'

---

7. 'Muggle', one name for a marijuana *cigarette*.
8. Some informatioin about two earlier heads of the family, Colemen and his son, Rameses 'Ram' Turtle, can be found in: OLE DEVIL AND THE CAPLOCKS—*which, along with other volumes of the* Ole Devil Hardin *series, covers aspects of the struggle by Texans to obtain independence from Mexican domination*—SET TEXAS BACK ON HER FEET, BEGUIN-AGE *and* BEGUINAGE IS DEAD!. *Their respective influence is also described by inference in:* Part Four, 'Mr. Colt's Revolving Cylinder Pistol', J.T.'S HUNDRETH *and* THE QUEST FOR BOWIE'S BLADE.

'The Chopper?' Branch repeated quietly, darting a glance at his companion. 'Now why do you reckon we should start looking for *him* in particular?'

'Is he around?' Soehnen demanded and there was no longer any trace of the sardonic mock friendliness in his voice. 'Or even in Texas?'

Regardless of where he might serve in the United States, no peace officer would consider with equanimity the possibility of the criminal to whom Kretzmer had referred being in his bailiwick!

Although he had only struck once in Texas, 'the Chopper' was a very successful professional killer. As he never tried to conceal his guilt, but invariably advertized it through the local newspapers, he had numerous successes elsewhere to his credit. For all that, despite every Federal, State, County and municipal law enforcement agency having tried to discover it, his true identity remained unknown. Such was the excellence of his ability as an organizer, that even those clients known to have employed him and who could be induced to talk about him, could not supply a lead traceable to him. Nor were informers, who could almost always ferret out secrets, any more productive, in spite of a large reward being offered. Every piece of information which it was hoped would direct the search to him had petered out at what was obviously a low level of the chain he had created through which customers could make contact. Only one thing was known for certain and even this was far from helpful. He was a master of disguise and, so far as was known, had never adopted the same one twice. While it was assumed he could not be bulky in build, despite having appeared to be on occasion, descriptions by witnesses had established only that he was neither exceptionally tall nor noticeably short.

'Now how would I know a thing like *that?*' Kretzmer asked, silently cursing himself for the impulse which had led him to mention that particular name. His manner was far from convincing, even though his next words were true. 'I've never even so much as laid eyes on him!'

'But you know *something*,' Branch insisted.

'Not me!' the pickpocket denied vehemently, but again without being able to give an appearance of veracity.

'Do you know something, Dutchy?' Branch asked, sounding

as if shocked by a thought which had just struck him. 'Did I know such just *couldn't* be, I'd think good ole Fingers was a-fibbing!'

'Never, for shame!' Soehnen gasped, in well simulated horror and disbelief.

'My eyes ain't's good's they used to be—and never was,' the older sergeant remarked to his companion. 'So do you mind who-all was in the "order-inance" tonight, *amigo*?'

'I saw Tobe O'Reilly, Jimmy Tillet, Fernando Robles 'n' Wee Willie Wolf,' the younger peace officer replied, aware that the other had excellent vision and guessing what prompted the question. 'Fact being, now you've called it to mind, there was a whole slew more fellers who, should everybody have their rightful rights, ought to be in our "Bible Two".'[9]

'Now that's what I call "hinter-tresting",' Branch admitted and his pensive mein was not entirely assumed.

On having noticed there were a number of prominent criminals in the audience, knowing the theatre to be very popular on account of the high quality of its entertainment, the elderly sergeant had considered it was no more than a coincidence they were present. Attending the 'first night', even of a show which would be changed at the end of the week, had a cachet which was not restricted to the honest and wealthy. Law breakers also sought to attain the sense of superiority which arose from being able to boast of having attended a performance as early in its run as possible.

Given the suggestion aroused by Kretzmer's comment, Branch was beginning to envisage another possibility, and he did not doubt it had also occurred to his companion!

If a crime of magnitude was known to be in the offing, particularly one which was the speciality of the Chopper, prominent criminals—even if not involved personally—felt it advisable to ensure they had an alibi capable of standing up during the subsequent investigation. Furthermore the Chopper, without giving the identity or time selected for the

---

9. *'Bible Two', also sometimes referred to as the 'Black Book'. A list of wanted fugitives from justice supplied to the Texas Rangers. Brought up to date and published annually, the sobriquet originated from the claim that it was read more frequently than the real Bible by members of that organization. J.T.E.*

18

demise of his victim, was in the habit of issuing a warning of his proposed activity so that such precautions could be taken. Knowing it was coming, but not where, to whom, or—even if having hired him—when he would strike, they would take care to keep themselves on public display as much as possible until it was done.

All of which, both sergeants realized, pointed to there having been a special significance behind what the pickpocket had hoped was nothing more than a distraction and irritant for the way they were treating him!

It was a thought no peace officer worth his salt would ignore!

The first problem was how to elicit whatever scraps of information Kretzmer had gathered!

Although the pickpocket had never been a regular 'stool pigeon' motivated by monetary gain, more through fear of the consequences of discovery than out of any loyalty to his fellow law breakers, Branch and Soehnen had the experience to apply a persuasion calculated to make him tell what he knew.

'How many of 'em are still around, Dutchy?' the older sergeant inquired, nodding towards the street in a pointed fashion.

'Most all of them,' the blond peace officer reported, after having stepped away far enough to be able to see the front of the theatre.

'I thought they might be, in the "circum-stanticals",' Branch claimed. 'What say we take good ole Fingers out there all friendly-like and, making good 'n' sure they can hear, thank him right kindly for telling us all we wanted to know?'

'Why sure. And I've got a ten spot here to give him for doing it,' Soehnen assented, taking out his wallet and extracting a bill of that denomination from it. 'Like they say, the labourer is worthy of getting paid.'

'*Paid*!' Kretzmer yelped in alarm. 'I didn't tell you *nothing*!'

'You know that and we know that,' Branch pointed out, seemingly with commiseration. 'Trouble being, will those jaspers out there know it?'

'Or the Chopper, comes down to a real sharp point,' the younger sergeant supplemented, 'when word gets to him—as you know's well we do it will—as how we was heard to say we

19

didn't even know *he*—even if we don't name names—was in Texas.'

While Kretzmer could not by any stretch of the imagination be termed intelligent, he was able to appreciate the full ramifications of the conversation. Even when he was under the influence of *marijuana*, which he was not at that moment—the interrupted foray to pick pockets having been intended to procure the wherewithal to purchase a supply—he was never courageous. Being 'cold turkey', he was even less inclined to valour. Therefore, realizing how a course of action such as had been suggested by the sergeants could be misinterpreted, he felt as if an ice cold hand was running up and down his spine. On hearing of what would appear to have been a betrayal for financial gain, which was sure to happen, the Chopper would take reprisals of a most painful and, eventually, a fatal nature. He had done so on three previous occasions when he had considered he had been endangered in a similar way by stool pigeons.

However, the little pickpocket knew all too well how he could avoid being placed in such dire peril!

Should Kretzmer supply the little information he possessed, the code by which the two sergeants operated would ensure he was allowed to go on his way without having been seen in their company.

'Time's a-wasting!' Soehnen briskly, when satisfied the pickpocket had thought over the situation to its full. 'Let's get going!'

'Hold hard!' Kretzmer gasped, backing further into the doorway. 'I can't tell you *much*, but you can have all I know. The word is that the Chopper's got his-self a contract here in Cowtown and you know him. He allus lets the biggies know when he's going to make a hit on their range.'

'And he let *you* know?' the blond sergeant inquired dryly, aware the man he was addressing had never by any stretch of the imagination qualified as a 'biggie' in criminal circles.

'You know he didn't!' the pickpocket asserted, deciding this was no time for self-aggrandizment, especially as it would not have been accepted by his well informed audience. 'But I know one of Tobe O'Reilly's boys real good and he told me's the word'd come.'

'Has Tobe got any notions on who-all's going down?' Branch inquired.

'Billy didn't say so,' Kretzmer replied, then realized what

20

could have been implied by the question. 'Hell, you don't reckon's how Hogan Turtle'd need to bring in the Chopper should he need anybody taking out, do you?'

Before either sergeant could reply to the question, there was an interruption!

Two shots from a heavy calibre weapon cracked somewhere on the other side of the street!

CHAPTER TWO

ALL HELL'LL BREAK LOOSE

LOSING their interest in *Hurbert* 'Fingers' Kretzmer, Sergeants Jubal Branch and Hans 'Dutchy' Soehnen, without needing to consciously think of what they were doing, reacted instantly to the sound of the shots. As they were swinging around, each was instinctively reaching with his right hand towards where he carried a weapon in concealment. Nor did they require an extensive search to locate part of what they needed to know. On the opposite sidewalk, almost facing their position, although his equally prosperous looking companion showed no sign of being injured, a well dressed man clearly had been hit by at least one of the bullets and was going down.

Each of the sergeants was already starting to arm himself by the time they emerged from the recessed doorway of the store into which they had taken the pickpocket to be interviewed. Reaching swiftly beneath the rear of his ancient looking and loosely fitting open brown jacket, the elder brought an obviously well used ivory handled Colt Civilian Model Peacemaker revolver from its holster inside the waistband of his Levi's trousers.[1] Almost as quickly, Branch having moved with a rapidity which was vastly different from his leisurely speech and actions in normal times, Soehnen extracted from a shoulder rig on the left side a big black Government Model of 1911 automatic pistol manufactured by the same company.

While crossing the sidewalk, Branch and his companion allowed the weapons to dangle by their right legs so as to be less conspicuous. Working with the swift and unflurried speed which told of long practice, each took out his silver 'star in a circle' badge of office and suspended it from the breast

1. *Details of the various types of Colt Model P of 1873 revolver, more generally known as the 'Peacemaker', are given in various volumes of the* Floating Outfit *series.*

pocket of his jacket in plain view. Sprinting across the street, having taken the precaution of letting themselves be identifiable as Texas Rangers and, therefore, legally entitled to ·be armed in public, they sought for and received the information they desired about from where the shots had originated.

'Down that alley there, Rangers!' yelled the companion of the victim, clearly recognizing the official insignia they were displaying.

While going in the direction indicated, Branch and Soehnen were not too surprised by the number of uniformed and well armed officers belonging to the Fort Worth Police Department they saw converging from both ends of the street. If a hint of the Chopper being in town had reached the municipal law enforcement agency, even though it had not been passed on to their Company of the Texas Rangers before they left headquarters that evening, there were sure to be patrols out in strength to try· and catch him. Knowing the shots would be heard and attract attention from more than just themselves, this was one reason they had considered it most advisable to exhibit their own official status by wearing their badges in plain view.

Regardless of the presence of reinforcements and the danger that some of these might misinterpret their actions, in spite of the precaution they had taken to indicate they too were peace officers, the sergeants did not slow down. This was not because they doubted the ability of the local lawmen to handle the situation, or because they resented the possibility that their Company might have been left in ignorance of the information. Nor were they motivated by a desire to steal the credit which would certainly accrue to whoever apprehended such a notorious criminal. Instead, they were acting as their considerable experience in such matters suggested was for the best. All the uniformed officers were still some distance away and they were well aware how quickly the Chopper, if indeed it was him, was credited with being able to effect an escape after having brought off a kill. Therefore, they intended to commence the pursuit more promptly than would otherwise have been the case.

Arriving at the mouth of the alley, Branch and Soehnen saw a vague figure moving through the gloom towards the other end!

Realizing the danger and aware of the kind of man they might be up against, the sergeants skidded to a halt. However, although they brought their weapons into alignment, they did not immediately open fire. Being conscientious and experienced peace officers, despite adding to their peril, they wanted to be sure it was the Chopper—or whoever else might have done the shooting—before taking offensive action of any kind. Having estimated from what they had heard that a handgun of some kind was used, with the distance separating them, they considered the risk was justified.

'Peace officers he—!' Branch yelled, beginning the traditional command for a fleeing person to halt by indicating his official status.

Before the announcement could be completed, or either sergeant was able to take any kind of action, the figure swung around. However, it soon became apparent they had made a terrible error with regards to the way in which he was armed. There was the harsh chatter of a heavy calibre automatic firearm being discharged. Coming so close together, the red spurts of the muzzle blasts appeared to be a single long flare. From what happened, it was obvious the muzzle of the weapon was being turned in a horizontal arc while the firing was taking place.

Caught in the veritable torrent of flying lead dispatched along the fairly narrow confines of the alley, neither Branch nor Soehnen was able to get off a shot in reply. Instead, feeling the savage impacts as more than one bullet struck each of them, their weapons flew from their hands unfired. Blundering backwards helplessly, they fell on to the street.

*   *   *   *   *   *   *   *

BY the time Sergeant Brendon O'Toole of the Fort Worth Police Department arrived with half a dozen dark blue uniformed patrolmen where Jubal Branch and Hans Soehnen were lying, another five had come from the opposite direction. Shrilling loudly from the surrounding streets, police whistles announced that more officers would be converging as quickly as they could.

If either of the Texas Rangers had been able to see, they would have known their summations were correct with regards to the municipal law enforcement agency having heard that the Chopper—or some other, almost equally dangerous, criminal—could be in town. While O'Toole was

24

armed only with a big Colt Model of 1917 revolver in his massive right fist, there were two Winchester Model of 1912 riot guns and three Winchester Model of 1894 carbines[2] in the hands of the patrolmen. Because of Fort Worth's history, which had included more than a few gun fights between peace officers and outlaws, the Police Department wisely based its policy upon that of its predecessors in the—as it was then called—office of the town marshal. Any time it was suspected officers might be up against a criminal known to be armed and who would not hesitate to shoot, they were instructed to supplement their mandatory and basically defensive hand-guns with weapons offering a greater range and fire power.

Pausing briefly, having already recognized the two Texas Rangers and warned the patrolmen who were with him not to open fire, O'Toole needed only a single glance to tell him the worst. Each had been hit in the torso by four bullets of comparatively heavy calibre. While Soehnen was still just alive, the experienced sergeant knew it would be a matter of minutes rather than hours before he joined Branch in death.

'Stay with 'em, Jones, Ramairez!' O'Toole barked, forcing himself to put aside thoughts of grief and concern for the two men who were his old and trusted friends. For all that, some trace of his emotions showed in the timbre of his Irish brogue. 'Have somebody call for an ambulance. The rest of you, come with me and come careful. The bastard we're after's got a Tommy gun, or I've never heard one!'

Followed by the patrolmen, with the exception of the two he had named, the sergeant made for the mouth of the alley. In spite of the sound having been distorted by the walls of the buildings on each side of the alley, he was sure he was correct in his assessment that the Texas Rangers were shot by a Thompson submachine gun. Therefore, he knew—particularly if it should be the Chopper they were after—he and his party might soon be going up against a cold blooded

2. *A lineal 'descendant' of the Models of 1866 and 1873, which established the reputation of the Winchester Repeating Firearms Company, the Model of 1894 was one of the first they manufactured to handle the more powerful 'smokeless'—as opposed to 'black'—powder cartridges. Furthermore, its carbine variety is said to have been sold in greater numbers than any other shoulder arm designed for the civilian market and not to fulfil a military contract.*

killer armed with a weapon capable of rapid fire far beyond the capacity of any firearm they were carrying. Against this, the burst he had heard directed against Branch and Soehnen suggested that even if a fifty round drum magazine had been used instead of the more common twenty cartridge 'box' type, a good many of the load had been expended. Therefore, unless they allowed time for an exchange of magazines to be carried out, they would have the advantage of numbers and fire power.

Passing swiftly through the alley, O'Toole glanced in each direction along the street he had reached. Two more patrolmen were hurrying from the right and one pointed, yelling they had seen somebody making for the gap between two buildings at the other side and to the left. Without waiting for them to come up and give further information, he strode rapidly in the direction indicated.

Caution dictated that O'Toole looked before committing himself and the harness bulls to going around the corner. Peering beyond the end of the building, he found the light from the street lamps on either side barely entered the area. In spite of this, his first impression was that the open space between it and its neighbour was completely devoid of human life. However, he was too experienced a peace officer to rely upon this being the case. Instead, he decided to make another inspection with the aid of portable artificial illumination.

'Get ready to go in shooting!' the sergeant ordered and his left hand lifted free the powerful electric torch which was suspended from his black Sam Browne belt.[3]

Having given the order, even though his big Colt was equipped with a double action mechanism which normally precluded the need for it to be cocked manually, O'Toole drew back the hammer with his thumb as an aid to accuracy

---

3. *Designed at the instigation of General Samuel J. Browne (1824-1901) of the British Army, because he had lost an arm in action and needed the extra support when carrying his weapons—a pistol when on horseback, or a sword if dismounted—the type of belt to bear his name originally had one or two light shoulder straps running diagonally acorss the chest from left to right. The basic 'Sam Browne' belt became popular for uniform wear by various law enforcement agencies in the United States. Although the shoulder straps have now gone out of favour and are no longer fitted, one was still used at the time of this narrative.*

and speeding up firing the first shot if necessary. With that precaution taken, he switched on the torch and directed its beam in a sweep of the alley. For a moment, he thought the area was deserted. Then there was a movement and slight rustling sound from between two of a row of trash cans put outside by the occupants of the building on the left.

'This's the police!' the sergeant yelled, his voice echoing hollowly from the walls on either side. 'Come out with your hands empty and above your head!'

'Don't shoot sir!' replied a voice which gave the impression of more than a quavering of alarm.

'We won't, so long's you do what I said!' O'Toole promised and, having drawn a conclusion from the accent of the speaker, he went on for the benefit of the patrolmen who had fanned out across the mouth of the alley with weapons held ready to take whatever action might prove necessary. 'Hold your fire, all of you. It isn't him we're after, I'm thinking!' Having delivered the warning, he raised his voice and directed it once more into the alley. 'Show yourself the way I told you!'

'Yes sir, boss!' the voice assented, making the first two words run into one so they sounded as, 'Yassuh' and gave added strength to the sergeant's supposition.

As O'Toole had expected, on rising from his place of concealment with empty hands raised high above his head, the speaker proved to be a Negro. Of slightly more than medium height and slim, although black and with an understandably worried expression, his features were Nilotic rather than Bantu in their close to European lines.[4] Bare headed, with crinkly very short black hair, he appeared to be somewhere between twenty and forty years in age. Although many of his race tended to dress loudly, he was wearing a dark brown three-piece suit, a navy blue shirt, dark green necktie and black shoes.

'Who're you, boy?' O'Toole asked, advancing followed by the patrolmen.

---

4. 'Nilotic'; possessing the physical characteristics of the people originally native to the Nile basin. The Masai of Kenya and Tanzania are probably the best known representatives of this ethnic group. 'Bantu'; pertaining to one of the many Negroid nations such as the Zulu, Bechuana, Xhosa, Damara, Swahili, Kikuyu, Wa-Kamba, etc., of Central and Southern Africa.

'Billy-Sam Cornridge, from New Orleans, sir,' the Negro replied, running his gaze from one to another of the peace officers and looking worried. 'I ain't done nothing, honest to the Good Lord. I was just passing through here looking for a crap game I'd heard was—!'

'Did you see anybody coming through here?' the sergeant interrupted.

'I for certain sure did, sir,' Cornridge confirmed with feeling. 'That's why for I was hiding 'tween them trash cans!'

'Pete, take the boys with the carbines and riot guns on through 'n' see if there's any sign of him. The rest of you stay with me,' the sergeant ordered and, after he was obeyed, gave his attention to the Negro again. 'What did the feller look like?'

'I dunno, sir,' Cornridge claimed, rolling his eyes until the whites showed starkly against the black of his face.

'You *dunno?*' the sergeant growled.

'I for certain sure don't, sir!' Cornridge affirmed, politely and yet definitely. 'Any time I sees somebody a-coming whose carrying a Tommy gun and with what looks like the hoods them gentlemen of the Ku Klux Klan wears over his head, that's when I figures's how it's safer not to look even twice much less stand anywheres in this way. So I ducked down a-twixt them trash cans until I was certain sure he'd long gone on by.'

'So you'd don't know which way he went when he left the alley, huh?' O'Toole stated rather than asked.

'No, sir, I for sure don't,' the Negro replied. 'Like I said, I just kept myself all scrunched up twixt 'n' 'tween them trash cans while he went on by lickerty-split like the Devil after a yearling. Then, just's I was figuring I could get up 'n' be long gone, I heard you police gentlemen a-coming and, not knowing it was you, I reckoned I'd best stay put until I found out who-all you might be.'

'And you don't know whether he took off right or left, huh?' the sergeant asked, hearing the patrolmen moving restlessly to his rear.

'No, sir,' Cornridge answered. 'I'm sorry I can't be of mo—!'

'That's all right, it wasn't your fault,' O'Toole interrupted and, deciding the Negro could not supply any further information he went on, 'Get his name and address, Burgherof, in

28

case we should need to talk to him later. The rest of you, come with me.'

Having given the order, the sergeant set off along the alley. Knowing the Ku Klux Klan were no longer active in Texas, despite what Cornridge had said, he felt sure they were not involved in the shooting. On the other hand, whoever had gunned down the three men opposite the Interstate Vaudeville theatre—even if it was the Chopper, for once operating without a disguise—he might have donned a hood to avoid being recognized. In response to the question he flung over his shoulder, one of the patrolmen who had seen the suspect crossing the street replied that the light had been too poor for them to make out such details as the hood. In fact, they had not even seen the Thompson submachine gun and, as it had not been found by the rest of the officers, assumed he must have carried it by his side.

Wanting to be involved if his companions should catch up with whoever they were after, especially if it was the Chopper, Patrolman Burgherof hurriedly scribbled the address he was given in his noteback. Then, telling the Negro to wait until somebody returned, he ran after the others. Glancing back as he went, he saw that Cornridge was leaning against one of the trash cans and concluded his instructions would be obeyed.

'Not hide nor hair of him, Sarg,' "Pete" reported, as O'Toole and the rest of the patrolmen, with the exception of the one left with the Negro, joined the advance party on the street at the end of the building. Gesturing with his carbine in each direction, he continued angrily, 'He was out of sight afore we got here and there's not even any of our other boys around here's might've seen which way he went.'

'He sure moves quiet!' commented a harness bull carrying a riot gun. 'We stopped's soon's we got out here, but couldn't hear him running off.'

'He's not likely to chance doubling back,' O'Toole assessed. 'So pair up with the boys's're only toting handguns 'n' spread out through the next few alleys. Just keep one thing in mind, though. We all know he's dangerous 'n' what he's toting; but, happen you come on somebody, make good 'n' sure it's him and not some civilian, one of our boys, or from the Sheriff's Office, afore you start throwing lead.'

*   *   *   *   *   *   *   *

'WE couldn't find him, sir,' the burly sergeant reported bitterly. 'It seemed like the ground'd opened up and swallowed him once he'd got through that second alley.'

After having passed through the gaps between the buildings which the man they were hunting could have reached in the time available Sergeant O'Toole had decided reluctantly he and his party were achieving nothing. Returning to the area in which the multiple shooting had taken place, he had found senior law enforcement officials of his own Department and the Tarrant County Sheriff's Office were present along with reinforcements. Glancing around, he had concluded everything was being dealt with as he would have done if he had remained on the scene. The three victims of the unknown assailant had been removed. Officers were still questioning members of the audience and those known to have criminal records had been segregated. He was describing his activities to Chief of Police Stanley Madison and Sheriff Francis Everard.

'You can't be blamed for that,' asserted the head of the Fort Worth Police Department, and the senior law enforcement official for the county nodded concurrence.

'How about Jubal Branch and Dutchy Soehnen?' the burly non-com inquired, although he felt sure he knew what the answer would be in the case of the first Texas Ranger he mentioned.

'From what I heard, Jubal was dead,' Madison replied, his voice showing that he too had strong feelings which went beyond it having been just fellow peace officers gunned down. 'Dutchy was alive when they put him in the ambulance, but the intern with it said there wasn't much hope.'

'It's a bad business all 'round,' Everard stated sombrely.

'The worse we've had in Cowtown for many a long year,' the Chief of Police supplemented. 'I've tried to let Benson Tragg know what's happened to them, but so far I've not been able to reach him. Seems the telephone wire to his headquarters's down and we can't get through on the radio.'

'God damn all these new-fangled contraptions, Jubal would've said, even though he was allus quick enough to use whatever of 'em was needed,' O'Toole growled. 'He was one smart lawman.'

'That he was,' Madison concurred, deciding Sergeant Jubal

Branch of the Texas Rangers would not have wished for a better epitaph.

'All hell'll break loose when Maj' Tragg gets the word,' O'Toole claimed, after a moment of silent tribute had followed the tribute from his superior.

'There's nothing more certain than that,' the Chief of Police agreed, also knowing the intense loyalty Major Benson Tragg gave to the men under his command. Even at such a moment, remembering its composition, he found himself wondering why so many very experienced sergeants came to be in one Company. However, putting aside the question, he went on, 'Nobody in the crowd, not even the feller who was with the first victim, got so much's a glimpse of the killer.'

'If only we could find *somebody* who did!' Everard said, almost plaintively, being more politician than lawman and willing to allow the more experienced professional peace officers to handle matters, although the situation demanded his presence in accordance with the rules laid down by Tarrant County.

'We *had* somebody,' the sergeant replied, his tone a mixture of embarrassment and annoyance. 'Only we don't have him no more!'

'Who was it?' Madison asked.

'How'd he get away from you?' the sheriff demanded in the same breath.

'It was *my* fault,' O'Toole admitted, never one to shirk, or try to pass elsewhere, the responsibility for an error of judgement. 'We come on this black feller hiding in an alley. Whoever did the shooting'd run right by him, but all he could say was he'd got a hood of some kind over his head—!'

'A *hood*?' the sheriff interrupted.

'That's what he said,' the sergeant confirmed. 'From what he reckoned, him being from New Orleans by his account, the hood made him think of the Ku Klux Klan and—!'

'We haven't had any Klan trouble hereabouts—!' Everard put in, but was not allowed to continue.

'And, seeing the jasper was carrying a Tommy gun,' O'Toole continued, as if the comment from the sheriff had never been made, 'he didn't reckon it'd be safe for him to look too close.'

'I don't reckon any darkie would under those circumstances,' Madison judged. 'What did he say he was doing in the alley?'

'Just passing through, looking for a crap game he'd heard tell about,' the sergeant replied.

'Did he give you anything to go on, Brendan?' the Chief of Police asked.

'I didn't reckon it was the time, nor place, to stick around and ask,' the sergeant replied. 'It was my own fault, mind. Wanting to get after the feller, I told young Burgherof to get his address instead of saying to hold him until I got back. I'll give the boy credit though. He told that jasper to stay put afore he came after us.'

'I can't see any nigger sticking around at a time like that, unless he was made to,' Everard estimated. 'They don't none of them ever want any truck with the law.'

'Do you have any notion where the crap game he was headed for might be, Brendan?' Madison inquired, also paying no attention to the sheriff.

'No, but maybe the boys who walk this beat do,' O'Toole replied. 'I hope they do, anyways.'

'Why?' the Chief of Police asked.

'Like I said, Burgherof did's I told him 'n' got the feller's address,' the sergeant explained. 'As I know, having walked that district for years, but he don't not having been there much, there's no such address as the one he was given.'

CHAPTER THREE

I WANT *WHOEVER* DID IT!

STROLLING by the end of a barn on a small and yet well appointed ranch about twenty five miles west of Fort Worth, Rita Yarborough, although not conforming to current conventions for feminine attributes and attire, presented a most attractive appearance, calculated to catch the masculine eye.

Five foot six in height, about twenty-five years of age, the girl—she had no rings to establish marital status on her left hand, or any other jewellery—was pretty without being excessively beautiful. Her golden bronzed features were devoid of make up and her reddish-brown hair was cut in a shortish, tousled looking, curly 'wind blown' bob. Contrary to the current trend in fashion—which was already considerably influenced by the dictates of movie stars in distant Hollywood, California—she did not have the now greatly favoured trim and 'boyish' type of physique. In fact, it fell just short of having Junoesque 'hourglass' contours such as had been all the rage a few decades earlier. Instead of seeking a fashionable shape with the aid of a device such as a Poiret-designed 'flattening brassiere', her bosom rose full and firm over a trim midriff. These were emphasised to their best advantage by the snug fit of the masculine dark blue and green tartan shirt she wore, its neck open, top three buttons unfastened and the sleeves rolled up to show arms which were well muscled without losing femininity. As Levi's had not yet commenced production of feminine attire, the trousers she wore were made for a man. Nevertheless, having no need for the support of the floral-patterned brown leather belt with a silver buckle around her waist, they showed off her curvaceously rounded hips and sturdy thighs in a most effective manner. A pair of Indian moccasins upon her otherwise bare feet completed an ensemble which was eye-catching, if not conventional.

If their response was anything to go by, two of the three young men lounging against the wall around the corner of the building were more than just content to study the sight Rita presented as she passed them, apparently without being aware of their presence. Exchanging glances, although their companion did not accompany them, they started to follow her.

The shorter of the pair proved also to be faster. He moved with a long, seemingly effortless stride indicative of hard muscles in his lean frame. Around six foot in height, with a whipcord slender build, he appeared to be in his late twenties. There was something about his deeply tanned handsome features which suggested a wildness of nature and, moderate in length, his straight hair was reddish brown. Bareheaded, he was clad in the attire of a working cowhand. While it was clean, each garment had seen considerable wear. A hunting knife with an ivory handle and eight inch long, clip point blade was hanging in a sheath from the left side of a waist belt of Indian manufacture inscribed with 'medicine' symbols. Instead of the more usual high heeled, sharp toed riding boots, he had on Comanche-made moccasins.

While a good three inches taller than his companion and much more heavily built, despite moving slower there was nothing lethargic or clumsy about the second man. A couple of years younger, possessing tremendously wide shoulders, he trimmed down to a slim, flat bellied waist and his entire physique was suggestive of exceptional fitness, health and strength. Under recently barbered ash blond hair, his almost classically handsome face was pleasant, tanned and clean shaven. Also dressed as a cowhand, including the traditional footwear, his clothing was most costly and even a trifle dandified, but he too wore no hat.

Coming up swiftly and apparently without his presence being detected, the red head threw his right arm around the girl's throat from behind and his left encircled her waist. Having done this, he swung her around so she was facing his larger companion who reached for her with massive hands. If the reaction of the third young man was any guide, he found nothing out of the ordinary about such behaviour. Instead of doing anything positive, if only shouting for help he continued to lean against the wall and watch what was happening.

Should there have been a chance onlooker in the vicinity—although the third member of the masculine trio hardly qualified as that—such behaviour would not have seemed to be in accord with the surroundings. Everything about the area suggested the ranch was prosperous, or that at least its owner had sufficient wealth to create that impression. Made from planks painted white, the two storey wooden main house was well designed to stand up to the vagaries of the region's varying climatic conditions. Like the various out buildings, it was made from the best quality material and maintained in first class condition.

In addition to neatly laid out flower and vegetable gardens, presumably to help feed the occupants, there were pens containing chickens and pigs not too far from the back of the house. Several excellent riding horses and a few just as well suited to working in harness roamed at liberty in two large pole corrals a short distance away. Assorted implements and vehicles which required pulling by working horses were in evidence, but motorized transportation was not ignored. This ranged from a most dilapidated looking Ford Model T—which must have seen better days—via a powerful motor cycle, to two fine sports cars, an expensive limousine and a couple of trucks. Nor was this all the means available for travelling to and from the property. Sufficiently far from the buildings and corrals to avoid the animals being disturbed, was what a later generation would call an 'airstrip'. It had been constructed on level ground and, hardly stirring in the light breeze, a 'windsock' dangled from a tall pole. At one end stood a Douglas DT-2 two-seater biplane. Its red and white colour scheme, civil aviation registration number and lack of armament indicated it had been purchased by somebody other than the United States' Army or Navy.

Judging by appearance, the non-participant was well advised not to have attempted any physical intervention. About the same age as the red head, at the most he was no more than five foot six in height. Youthful and bronzed, his clean shaven face was moderately good looking without coming close to being as eye-catching as that of the blond giant. A low crowned, wide brimmed black Stetson hat dangled by its plaited leather *barbiquejo* chinstrap on his shoulders and exposed shortish curly black hair.[1] He had on a waist length brown leather jacket which hung unfastened. A tightly rolled scarlet silk bandana trailed its long ends down the front of an open necked dark blue shirt with a white 'arrow' motif decorating its pockets. A brown waist belt with floral patterning cut into its two and a quarter inch width and a large silver buckle embossed by the letters 'RC' gave support to fairly new Levi's pants. Their legs, the cuffs turned back a good three inches after the style of cowhands, hung outside fancy stitched Justin boots carrying Kelly 'Petmaker' spurs on their high heels.

Even though the small observer failed to offer any kind of succour, Rita did not behave in any such passive fashion. In fact, if her assailants expected her to respond like the heroines of the popular fiction and movies of the day who—with few exceptions[2]—did nothing other than scream piteously to be rescued or faint when faced with danger, they were quickly disillusioned.

Knocking apart the big hands with her arms before they could grip her, the girl braced herself against the red head. Bringing up and bending her legs, she placed her feet on the chest of the man in front of her. Giving a shove, powered by what were obviously well developed thigh and calf muscles, she sent him staggering backwards a few steps. Having done so, bringing down her legs, she set about freeing herself from her less bulky captor.

Arching forward her torso, Rita jerked it suddenly and sharply to her rear. Caught with some force by her well rounded buttocks, the grunt which burst from the red head suggested he was finding that the sensation was less pleasant than would have been the case in different circumstances. Feeling the arm release her waist and its mate loosen across her throat, she grabbed the latter with both hands. Dropping

---

1. *We have expressed our point of view regarding the current portrayal in Western movies and television programmes of cowhands during the Old West and Prohibition eras as long haired, filthy and heavily bearded in: Item 1, APPENDIX THREE.*

2. *The most prominent of the 'active' actresses in movies up to the period of this narrative was Pearl White, heroine of several 'cliff hanger' type serials. We explained our feelings with regards to the passive roles generally assigned to members of the 'weaker sex' in action-escapism-adventure fiction—not just Westerns—in our Introduction to J.T.'S Ladies.*

to her right knee, while drawing the trapped limb well down over her imposing bosom, she allowed him no time to experience pleasure at brushing against it. Instead, giving a sharp and thrusting motion with her hips against his knees, she completed the ruin of his already disturbed balance. Caused to pass over her shoulders in a half somersault, landing on the hard ground, he might have considered himself fortunate that long experience as a horseman allowed him to reduce the impact of the fall.

Having dealt so competently with the red head, the girl showed what appeared to be a poor assessment of the situation. Instead of keeping an eye upon the blond giant, she turned and started to walk, not run, away. His response proved this to be an error in tactics. Bounding over his recumbent companion with considerably agility considering his bulk, he wrapped his arms around and, interlocking his fingers, squeezed her biceps against her sides. From the way in which she relaxed completely in his encircling grasp, her appearance suggested she was enjoying it. However, he quickly discovered this was far from the case.

Although her upper arms were pinioned, Rita was able to move them below the elbow. Having lulled the blond giant into a sense of false security, she clenched her right fist and ground its knuckles against the back of his right hand. Doing so did not cause him to set her free, but the pain was sufficient to loosen his encircling arms. Having achieved so much, she continued to improve her situation. Forcing her hips against his body and carrying her left leg a long step sideways, she contrived to bend forward at the waist. Reaching rearwards with both hands, she caught hold of his left ankle. Lifting it quickly, she sank until all her weight was resting upon his knee and by forcing upwards on the limb at the same time, she compelled him to topple over. Being released as he started to fall, he too had cause to be grateful for possessing the requisite equestrian skill to lessen the force with which he arrived on the ground.

Once again, having escaped from the grasp of an assailant, the girl did not behave as might have been expected. Instead of taking a hurried departure, or even calling to summon help, she merely stepped a couple of paces away from the two men she had thrown to the ground and dusted her hands together as if considering she had done everything necessary for her self preservation.

'Did I get it right, *Rapido*?' Rita inquired, looking at the third young man in cowhand attire and showing no resentment over his having done nothing to assist her through what had appeared a potentially dangerous situation.

'I'd say so,' estimated the recipient of the question and, although the girl spoke after the fashion of one born and well educated in New England, his accent was that of a native Texan from a similar class of society. 'How do you boys feel about it?'

'You should hang your head in shame, teaching her tricks like those,' claimed the blond giant, also in the tones of a well raised son of the Lone Star State. Coming to his feet and starting to dust off his rear, he swung his gaze to Rita and continued in a seemingly aggrieved fashion, 'And it's all *your* fault—!'

'What is?' the girl was forced to enquire as the sentence had clearly been left uncompleted to provoke the question.

'You know I told you I loved you to distraction and couldn't wait until the day I was good enough to let you marry me,' the blond explained. 'Only, after seeing what you did to poor ole Comanch' and me, I'm starting to have *fourth* thoughts on it.'

'Which I don't blame you for one lil tiny bit,' the red head asserted. He too was obviously a Texan, but apparently from a somewhat lower stratum of society. Also having risen, he was eyeing the cause of his misfortune with more amusement than hostility in spite of his earlier behaviour and the way she had responded to it. 'I tell you, Rita-gal, should you keep on going the way you just did, folks're going to start calling you "Is-A-Man".'

'Anybody who does is *very* quickly going to wish he *hadn't*!' the girl claimed with what could have been severity except that the merry twinkle in her eyes belied the grim timbre of her voice. Having read and heard about the woman in question, whose admixture of white blood had not precluded her from becoming accepted as a Comanche warrior in the late 1870's,[3] she elaborated, 'I've seen pictures of Annie Singing Bear and, much as I admire her for all she accomplished, I've got a far better figure than she had.'

3. *Information about the career of Annie Singing Bear can be found in:* IS-A-MAN, WHITE INDIANS *and* BUFFALO ARE COMING!

'Now was I asked, which I don't calculate I'm going to be—!' the red head began.

'Which isn't going to stop you for one minute from telling us,' Rita declared.

That all depends on what kind of a figure a man's a liking for,' the red haired Texan continued, eyeing the male members of his small audience as if he expected them to take particular notice of his declaration and paying not the slightest attention to the interruption. 'There's them's likes a gal to be close to skinny, which I'll be willing to admit right truthful you're *not*, Rita-gal—!'

'Why thank you for *that*, kind sir,' the girl put in, dropping what would have been a graceful curtsy if she had been dressed properly for making one.

'Shucks, I'm ony part Comanch' but I've been raised right 'n' proper to allus speak the truthful-true like all Injuns,' the red head replied, 'Anyways, there's them's likes their women with more meat—!'

'I've heard tell that cannibals and other barbarians do,' the blond giant offered, his manner helpful.

'I've never *heard* of any of them being *cannibals*, Ranse, but let's leave *your* family out of this,' Rita requested, 'Go ahead, Comanche, don't mind the interruptions.'

'I get so many of them, I never do,' the red head asserted. However, instead of continuing the light-hearted conversation, he gazed along the fairly wide dirt trail which led to the property and the levity left his voice. 'Maj' Tragg's coming and, way he's moving, I'd say something *real* important's bringing him!'

*   *   *   *   *   *   *   *

SITTING hunched at the steering wheel of his Packard coupe, which he was driving at a greater speed than was usual when traversing the less than smooth track connecting his destination with the main road to Fort Worth, Major Benson Tragg had a grim expression on his deeply bronzed face.

In his late forties, six foot tall, the Major's brown hair was turning grey at the temples. Nevertheless, he had the lean and wiry build of one who still followed a strenuous occupation. In fact, although the tailor had failed to cut the jacket so it completely hid the bulge caused by a short barrelled Colt Storekeeper Model Peacemaker revolver, holstered butt forward on the left side of his waist belt, there was no other indication that he belonged to a family which had long been associated with the enforcement of law in Texas[4] His excellently fitting lightweight brown suit, a white shirt, a bolo necktie with the head of a longhorn steer made from Navajo silver and turquoise for its fasterner, and tan coloured, sharp toed, high heeled riding boots, gave him the appearance of being a prosperous rancher who still continued to put in a hard day's work with his cowhands. For all that, he was considered by those in the know to be one of the shrewdest and most incorruptible peace officers in the United States.

Although it was not the first time he had found himself faced by the necessity to deliver the kind of news he bore, Tragg had never found repetition made the task less painful for him. Nor did he believe the news he bore would prove any less distressing because none of the people involved were related to the deceased. Everybody he was expecting to find at his ranch, which served the secondary purpose of supplying restful accommodation for the peace officers under his command between their frequent and most hazardous assignments, had been close friends of Sergeants Jubal Branch and Hans Soehnen. One thing he knew for certain, however, there was a bond between the members of Company 'Z', Texas Rangers, which would ensure all its members would be determined to avenge their murder. Nor, despite his objections to the seeking of personal vengeance as a general rule, did he intend to even try and stop them.

Running his gaze over the girl and three young men as he brought the Packard to a halt, the Major set his face into as close to an impassive mask as he could manage. The grim visage softened, however, as his eyes turned to where the late Jubal Branch's large bluetick coonhound was sprawled on the porch of the ranch house.[5] Raising its head with what appeared to require a considerable effort, it looked at the

---

4. As is demonstrated in the Rockabye County series, covering the organization and duties of a modern day Sheriff's Office in Texas, the Tragg family is still actively connected with the enforcement of law in the State. Some details of two earlier members who also served as peace officers is given in: SET A-FOOT and BEGUINAGE IS DEAD!

5. A detailed description of the bluetick coonhound, Ligtning, is given in: Case One, 'Alvin Fog's Mistake'. YOU'RE A TEXAS RANGER, ALVIN FOG.

vehicle. However, although its tail twitched slightly a couple of times, it made no attempt to rise. Wondering how Lightning—a seemingly inappropriate name to which it lived up whenever sudden action was called for—would get on now its master was dead, he forced himself to put that aspect of the business from his thoughts. On returning his attention to the approaching quartet and studying them, he concluded they had deduced something of considerable importance had brought him to the ranch. Nor did he find it in the least surprising that the smallest of the Texans acted as their spokesman as Tragg climbed from the car to stand in front of them.

'Howdy, Major. You look like there's something bad' wrong!'

'There is, *Rapido*,' Tragg confirmed sombrely. 'Rita, Ranse, Comanche, I reckon we'd best all go into the house.'

The Major was all too aware of the dangers faced by Sergeants Alvin Dustine '*Rapido* Clint' Fog and Mark 'Comanche Blood' Scrapton when working undercover on the kind of clandestine official 'unofficial' assignments for which Company 'Z' was formed.[6] Therefore, to ensure they remained accustomed to answering to their respective sobriquets—selected as having been favourites of their grandfathers when engaged in similar matters[7]—he always insisted the other members of his force used these when addressing them and not their real names.

As the party started to walk forward, without anything further being said, Rita saw how Tragg was gazing at Lightning. A clairvoyance she had never known before struck her and she felt as if an ice cold hand was running along her spine. Letting out a low gasp, she caused the small Texan to look her way. Reaching instinctively to take his right hand in her left, she sensed rather than heard him breathe the words, 'Oh god!' and knew she had guided him into drawing a similar conclusion to her own. They both glanced at the bluetick, but her emotional state was such that she hardly felt his powerful grip

6. *An explanation of the specialized function of Company 'Z', Texas Rangers, is given in:* APPENDIX TWO.
7. *The grandfathers were Captain Dustine Edward Marsden 'Dusty' Fog and the Ysabel Kid, details of whose careers and special qualifications are recorded in various volumes of the* Floating Outfit *series.*

tighten before he realized what he was doing and relaxed it without relinquishing his hold. Although the interplay was noticed by Mark Scrapton and Sergeant Ranse Smith, neither passed any comment. Nor did anybody speak until they were in the comfortably furnished sitting-room of the house.

'Where're Buck and Lorna?' the Major asked, referring to the retired Texas Ranger and his wife who acted respectively as foreman and housekeeper of the ranch.

'They went into Cowtown early to pick up some supplies,' *Rapido* informed. 'What is it, Major?'

'I reckon you'd best sit down, Rita,' Tragg suggested gently, instead of replying to the question.

'Something's happened to Jubal, hasn't it?' the girl inquired, although the words were more in the nature of a statement, but she did not sit down or remove her hand from the small Texan's.

'And to Dutchy,' the Major replied. 'They were gunned down outside the Interstate Vaudeville Theatre last night!'

'*Last night?*' Ranse growled, as *Rapido* placed an arm around Rita's shoulder and, while she made an obvious effort to control her emotions, drew her closer to him. 'Then why the hell didn't y—?'

'I was out in the piney woods coon hunting last night and couldn't be reached, boy,' Tragg explained, showing no resentment over the way in which he had been addressed by a man under his disciplinary control. 'Nor could anybody else who knew you're here.'

'Sorry, sir,' the blond giant apologised, having forgotten in the stress of the moment that the connection between the ranch and Company 'Z' was a closely guarded secret to which only a few non-members were privy.

'Who did it?' the red head demanded and the expression on his Indian dark face gave credence to his earlier reference to being part Comanche.

'We don't know, but it could have been the Chopper,' the Major replied and, after insisting Rita sat down, he told them everything he had heard about the events of the previous evening.

'I know the Chopper's always reckoned to work alone,' the red head commented at the conclusion of the description. 'But do you reckon that black feller they found in the alley could've been in cahoots with him?'

'I wouldn't think so,' Tragg assessed. 'Sure he gave a false address, and name, most likely, but no black ever wants to get mixed up in white folks' troubles; especially if the law's involved. Anyways, the Cowtown police are going to try to find him and we'll leave that up to them.'

'But we're not going to leave it *all* to them, are we, sir?' the small Texan asked, sounding almost gentle, as he sat alongside Rita, allowing her to sob quietly in his arms.

'You can bet your life we're *not*!' the Major assured in tones of grim determination. 'Whether it was the Chopper, or not, I want *whoever* did it!'

'We *all* want that, sir!' *Rapido* claimed and suddenly he no longer looked small. Instead, such was the strength of his personality that—even seated—he gave the impression of being the largest man in the room. 'And none of us are going to rest until we've found him and nailed his hide to the wall.'

Listening to the rumble of concurrence which came from the other two young men and the still tearful girl, Tragg decided he would not care to be in the killer's shoes if they succeeded in their task.

CHAPTER FOUR

THIS WILL HAPPEN ALL OVER TEXAS

'GET it down, ladies and gentlemen! Send it in to beat the book! Double up and beat the book! Watch it! Here they come! Coming out *now*! Eight's the point—And's he's missed it!—Coming out again—!'

Listening to the slightly more refined version of the traditional chanting given by the 'stickman' at the nearby table devoted to the game of 'open craps',[1] Roland Massart glanced around the big main room of the mansion in the best part of Dallas. Everything he saw filled him with a sense of satisfaction. Business was good and, in his capacity of 'floorwalker', he would receive a percentage of the profits as well as his salary for his managerial capacity. The bonus showed signs of being a decent sum. Even though this was the first night of operations in a new location, there was a fair sized crowd present. What was more, in addition to the considerable amount of money changing hands at the various gaming tables, the costly attire and expensive jewellery worn by all the players was testimony to the wealth which had given them access to the latest illicit gambling operation set up in the city by Tobias O'Reilly on behalf of Hogan Turtle.

Aware that operating games of chance, as he was doing, was illegal under the statutes of the Sovereign State of Texas, just as acoholic beverages were being sold in contravention of the Volstead Act, the portly and pleasant faced floorwalker—his 'black tie' attire as well tailored as that worn by any of the players, but lacking the discernible bulge beneath the left arm present in the majority of the other male employees present—felt little concern. Throughout all the years he had worked in

---

1. *The definitive work on 'open craps' and other gambling games played with dice, plus information about the operation of such a game in a casino is:* SCARNE ON DICE, *by John Scarne, with Clayton Rawson.*

the gambling 'houses' run by Hogan Turtle's multi-faceted criminal organization, there had never been any attempt made by local peace officers or Federal Prohibition agents to enforce the laws being broken in whichever premises were currently in use. While his group had only commenced their illicit activities in the mansion that evening, these had merely been transferred from another location. The move had been made with well tested security so that it was not widely known to have taken place. He felt sure there was even less chance of anything untowards happening tonight.

'Come eighter from Decatur! Come, you lil babies, my gal wants a mink coat, not a new pair of shoes!'

Massart's complacent thoughts on the immunity of the 'house' from interference by the forces of law and order were diverted by hearing the exhortation of the player at the open craps table as he shook the dice before throwing in an attempt to make the required 'point' with a score of eight. However, although the words were uttered in a strident tone, such as might have been heard when a group of Negroes were playing rather than the elegantly clad Caucasian and Mexican participants present this evening, he merely glanced and smiled tolerantly. What was more, despite the somewhat unusual appearance of the speaker, the others around the table showed amusement rather than annoyance over his comments and behaviour.

About five foot ten in height, the 'shooter' seeking to make an eight—before he threw a seven for a losing decision—had a build which was slim yet clearly far from puny. It was set off by the excellent fit of the kind of informal dinner jacket—short, made from midnight blue worsted, with a rolling silk collar—known as a 'tuxedo'.[2] His white shirt—although soft as was socially acceptable with 'black tie' attire—black bow tie and matching black silk waistcoat and trousers, with braid side seams, also were equal in quality to those worn by anybody else in the room, even though the white cotton gloves he

2. 'Tuxedo', the American name for what in England is known as a 'dinner' and in France a 'smoking' jacket. It is a dress coat without tails, for use at less formal functions than those requiring the 'white tie' accoutrements of top hat, black tailcoat, white waistcoat and tie. The term arose due to such a garment having been introduced in the United States by a group of millionaires living in the Tuxedo Park district of New York City.

wore were not a mandatory adjunct to such raiment. However, the reason for their unusual appearance being known to everybody present, as was the fact that his hair and features hardly seemed in keeping with the time and place, no complaints or comments were made. His hair was black and crinkly, cut fairly close all round his skull. His face, while pleasant, gave no indication of his true age, and was sooty black except for a rim around the mouth which was white and the lips red. The effect was clearly achieved by using theatrical make up of some kind.

That James Ogilby should elect to come to a high class gambling 'house' with his head looking as it did was understandable to anybody who knew the circumstances which had led him to appearing in public that way.

Using the application of burnt cork on the face, with an appropriate wig to establish the exaggerated character of a Negro, had originated in the minstrel shows which had come into prominence at the turn of the century. While they were losing their popularity to later, different, and in some cases more sophisticated forms of entertainment, performers—particularly comedians—in these other fields frequently worked in 'blackface' even though no longer involved in the minstrel format. Wearing it in addition to loud, or otherwise eccentric, costume now frequently served merely to offer an indication to the audience that something of a comical nature was forthcoming.

Even before what was known as the 'Great War', Ogilby appearing under the name, 'Haysoff Spades'—from the expression, 'Black as the ace of spades'—had had a reputation as a 'song and dance' man who worked in blackface and was one of the top performers in his field. At that time, however, he had had no need to wear his theatrical make up in public. Caught in Europe at the commencement of hostilities, although the United States had not yet declared war against Germany and her allies, like many of his countrymen he had taken service in the British Armed Forces. Ever alert for suitable recruits, Military Intelligence had taken notice of his linguistic and other abilities. Extracted with his complete agreement from the infantry regiment in which he had enrolled at the instigation of Frederick Manton, an English fellow performer who also joined, he had proved a competent and efficient secret agent.

On being transferred to the American Army when his country entered the conflict, Ogilby had remained a member of the Secret Service. It was in this capacity, whilst operating behind enemy lines, that he had learned of a new 'secret weapon' upon which German scientists were working. Using all his skill, he had discovered this was a form of what would become known as 'bacterialogical warfare' intended to spread a very serious communicable disease amongst the civilian population as well as the armed forces of their enemies. His efforts to prevent the completion of the scheme had been entirely successful. However, while on his mission, he had been infected by a less virulent brand of the substance they were creating. This had proved to create a type of *icthyosis*, otherwise known as 'psuedo-leprosy', a scale-like infection which left all his skin bleached with hideous white patches identical to those caused by the real and dreaded disease they simulated.

In spite of the *icthyosis* having conclusively been proven to be non-infective or communicable, the result was unsightly to say the least particularly when it was taken into consideration with the illness it so closely resembled. What was more, regardless of a belief expressed to an earlier sufferer,[3] it had proved incurable. As he had intended to resume his interrupted career of being a professional entertainer in civilian life, the appearance his skin now presented could have ruined his career. In part, this had been saved by his having already established himself as a performer in blackface. Of an equal importance, his sterling service as a secret agent had not been forgotten by his own and the other Allied Governments. A special dispensation was ratified by Congress, to which Great —as it was *then*—Britain and France were co-signatories, allowing him to wear his theatrical make up at all times when travelling outside the United States and entering domains over which they exerted jurisdictional control. Accordingly, he had been photographed in blackface for his passport and, along with the authority for this being included in the document, it was stated further verification of his identification could be obtained by checking his fingerprints against those displayed therein.

3. *See:* Case Three, 'The Blanched Soldier', THE CASE-BOOK OF SHERLOCK HOLMES, *by Sir Arthur Conan Doyle.*

Taking up his career where he had left it off, although the full details were not made public for obvious reasons, enough had become known of Ogilby's activities as a secret agent for him—aided by his still considerable talents, although some said these had declined somewhat during the past two or three years—to allow a return to his previous prominence. He had not yet taken any of the offers he received to tour outside the country, which would have required the use of the special passport. Instead, he had seemed content to travel extensively around the United States.

Despite having missed the second Monday performance because of a stomach disorder, 'Haysoff Spades' had just concluded a successful two weeks appearance in Fort Worth. Continuing his tour on the Interstate Vaudeville circuit, which operated the Alhambra as well as the theatre which bore its name, he had moved to nearby Dallas and, after his opening night show, had come to the mansion with a small party of wealthy local businessmen to indulge in his hobby of gambling for high stakes.

'*Money*!' the entertainer whooped, having sent the two dice with a snap of his wrist so they flew through the air and, striking the padded side wall of the 'single dealer' craps table, rebounded to alight with their upper surfaces each showing a score of four.

'And Haysoff Spades has made it, the hard way!' intoned the stickmen, using the crooked cane held to retrieve the dice. While doing so, he glanced to make sure the 'dealer'—for whom, in his capacity as croupier of the game, he was assistant—was in no need of his help with either collecting the stakes from losing bets or paying the winners. Satisfied this was not necessary, he drew and pushed the cubes until they were in front of the entertainer, continuing, 'Let's hope you're as hot tonight, Sir, as you were at the theatre. We always like to see our players *win*!'

'Just so long's they don't do it too often, huh?' Ogilby suggested, picking up the dice and still giving the exaggerated impersonation of a typical poorly educated Negro's accent, which he employed as much off the stage as during a performance. 'Like you say, I'm hot tonight and I'm going to take you like General Houston took Santa An—!'

What might have been a less than tactful simile, in view of there being a number of wealthy and influential Mexicans present to whom such a reference could be offensive, was brought to an end before it could be completed!

There was a shattering crash and, for all its sturdy construction, the locked and barred side door giving access to the gardens of the mansion was literally burst off its hinges. Clearly this was as a result of having been charged by the left shoulder of the massive young man who entered followed by several more. Although he was in civilian clothes, there was a silver 'star in a circle' badge fastened to the left breast pocket of his longish and loosely fitting open black jacket. All those behind him wore the uniforms of officers in the Dallas Police Department.

Despite there being obvious indications that all the newcomers were peace officers, some of the 'house's' employees started to reach for the revolvers beneath their tuxedos. Giving them no time to bring out the weapons, Sergeant Ranse Smith of the Texas Rangers came to a halt and responded to the threat with a most commendable rapidity considering the way in which he had gained admittance to the room.

By swivelling his hips as he stopped, with feet spread apart to almost the full extent of his enormously wide shoulders, the blond giant showed he was armed in an unconventional fashion. It was, nevertheless, one for which his massive frame—aided by the loosely fitting jacket apparently at odds with his normally close to dandified selection of attire—was ideally suited. Carried in an open fronted spring retention holster on a three inches wide russet coloured belt around his waist,[4] he had a Burgess folding riot gun designed to offer its user comparative ease of concealment.

Grasping the wrist of the butt with his right hand, Ranse shoved the Burgess free from the retaining springs of the holster. Swinging it swiftly upwards, he caused the folded barrel to pivot around on a hinge until it snapped home and automatically locked with the receiver. Such was the excellence of the design that it was possible to have the tubular magazine beneath the barrel filled to its six shot capacity and ready for use even when the weapon was folded for carrying.

---

4. *Although the Burgess Gun Company supplied a holster of more conventional design to be used in conjunction with the 'take-down' riot gun, Sergeant Ranse Smith had the split front spring retention rig made to his own specifications as he considered it would enable him to make a faster withdrawal.*

Deftly catching the foregrip in his left hand as it rose into an operating position, the blond giant continued to tilt the barrel upwards. While doing this, his right hand was manipulating the longitudinally sliding pistol grip and trigger guard assembly. This served the same purpose as the 'trombone' type of foregrip fitted to similar weapons manufactured by other companies.[5] Having done so in a split second, he squeezed the trigger and discharged the shell fed into the chamber from the magazine.

Swiftly as all the movements had been carried out, there was a deep bang and nine buckshot balls shattered the crystal chandelier hanging from the centre of the ceiling. Before the pieces could reach the open area of the floor over which they had been suspended as an attractive whole, a flick of Ranse's big right hand sent the mechanism through its reloading cycle. The empty case sailed out through the briefly opened ejection slot to be replaced by the next available round.

Faced by such an exhibition of speed and dexterity, made all the more impressive by the size and obvious potential of the weapon brought so swiftly into use, the blond giant's actions caused every attempt at drawing revolvers to cease before they could clear leather. Even without the demonstration they had just witnessed, the employees of the house knew no man became a Texas Ranger—much less a sergeant at what was obviously an unusually early age—unless he possessed considerable proficiency in using firearms. Therefore, sharing a mutual desire to preserve their health, none of them had any intention of provoking such an undoubtedly competent member of that organization with gestures of hostility.

'Stand still, *everybody*!' Ranse commanded in a bellow which sounded above the screams and shouts of alarm from female and male players on finding flight was impossible due to more members of the Dallas Police Department appearing in every other doorway. 'I'm Sergeant Alvin Dustine Fog of the Texas Rangers and this is a *raid*!'

'A *raid*?' Massart repeated, placing a somewhat different emphasis on the second word. His tone of puzzlement was genuine.

This was the first time any such thing had taken place while

---

5. *A more detailed description of the Burgess folding riot gun is given in:* Part One, *'Persona Non Grata'*, MORE JUSTICE FROM COMPANY 'Z'.

the floorwalker was in his present employment. Although gambling was illegal in Texas, knowing it would take place anyway, the various law enforcement agencies adopted what they considered to be a sensible attitude towards it. So long as it was run honestly and without the operators making trouble, they tended to turn a blind eye to its existence. Knowing this, Hogan Turtle gave strict instructions with regards to the way in which his 'houses' were conducted, and these were enforced as to do otherwise would incur penalties far more painful than merely being fired.

Nevertheless, being equally aware that the situation could be changed if—for example—anti-gambling crusaders exerted sufficient political pressure, Turtle also insisted measures were taken to avoid the consequences on those occasions when the laws against gambling were to be enforced. There had always been corrupt peace officers, although never anywhere nearly so many as the 'liberal' elements of a later generation's media would imply as part of their campaign to smear the forces of law and order. In every town large enough to make the precaution necessary, at least one member of its law enforcement agency would be bribed to give warning of any moves detrimental to the organizations' various nefarious operations. While the informants in Dallas had always earned their pay in the past, Massart had not received even so much as a hint that action was to be taken against the 'house' under his control.

'A *raid*,' Ranse confirmed, then lowered his voice so that it did not reach beyond the man he was addressing. 'And, after you get yourself bailed out tomorrow, you pass word to Hogan Turtle *this* will happen all over Texas until we get the Chopper for gunning down Jubal Branch and Dutchy Soehnen.'

'You can't get away with anything like *that*!' the floorwalker asserted, but he was not allowed to continue with his intended warning reference to the wealthy and influential people who were present.

'I've got news for you, we've already started to do it—and *more*, as you'll find out soon enough,' the blond giant declared. Then, without waiting for Massart to reply, he looked around and raised his voice. 'All right, gents, take the names and addresses of *everybody* who's here!'

'Yo!' responded the captain in command of the detachment

from the Dallas Police Department, using the traditional cavalry assent to an order.

'Damn it!' boomed a corpulent and expensively dressed player, over the startled and alarmed comments which arose from the others on realizing what was meant by Ranse's words. 'You *can't* do *that!*'

'It's the *law*, Senator Brayne,' the big blond pointed out, resting the barrel of the Burgess on his right shoulder. '*You* and everybody else who've been playing are going against Articles 618 and both sub-sections of 624 of the Texas Penal Code: which cover; "Betting At Dice Games; Miscellaneous Betting and Same, If At Gaming Tables Or Bank." All three bring a fine, but the last can have ten to thirty days jail additional.'

'*Jail?*' the politician almost yelped, the word being repeated around the room with various types of concern. Making an attempt to resume the pompous and self important arrogance of his demeanour, he continued, 'And what might your name be?'

'Sergeant Alvin Dustine Fog,' Ranse lied, as he had been instructed by his commanding officer.

'*Fog!*' Brayne repeated, losing some of his bombast. He was all too aware of the power and influence that could be wielded throughout Texas by men of that name and their kin of the Hardin and Blaze families. 'Are you—?'

'Sheriff Jackson Fog of Rio Hondo County's my *father*,' the big blond claimed. He could see the politician was impressed; perhaps even more than would have been the case if he had used his own name and mentioned his not unimportant family connections.

'By whose authority are you taking this action—*Sergeant Fog?*' asked the Senator.

'We're under orders from Captain Benson Tragg of the Texas Rangers, sir,' Ranse replied, his manner polite yet unremittingly cold. 'And he's got the authority of the Governor for sending us.'

As the blond giant had intimated to Massart, even though '*Keeping Premises For Gambling Purposes*' was a felony liable to incur a penalty of a jail sentence of two to four years, there was much more to the raid than just dealing with a contravention of *Article 625, 'Offenses Against Public Policy And Economy'* section of the Texas Penal Code.

52

In spite of having killed two peace officers—Sergeant Hans Soehnen having lived only long enough to tell the patrolman of the Fort Worth Police Department by his hospital bed of the meeting with Hubert Kretzmer—the Chopper had followed his usual habit of informing the local newspaper that he was responsible. Nor, as he had included certain code words which had never been made public to ensure he received the credit, was there any possibility of somebody either trying to lay the blame upon him or steal his thunder.

While they now knew who to seek, Major Tragg and his men had also realized that their task was anything but a sinecure. Neither the pickpocket nor any member of Hogan Turtle's organization could—or would, if they knew anything,—shed any further light on the matter. All attempts to locate the Negro in the alley had failed. Not even learning that the intended victim was an accountant of some importance throughout the State had as yet produced more than a list of possible suspects who had reason to want him dead.

Faced with a succession of dead ends, even though the identity of whoever had hired the Chopper to kill the accountant might supply a lead, Company 'Z' had been disinclined to wait until—or if—this came to light. Realizing only unconventional methods could induce members of the underworld to disclose what they knew about him, and being sure that some of them must possess knowledge not previously imparted despite the sizeable bounty on his scalp, Major Tragg had formulated a scheme which he believed might bring about a spirit of greater willingness to co-operate. He had been helped in putting this into effect by the liking and respect in which Jubal Branch in particular was held by a great many peace officers of all kinds throughout Texas. Furthermore, the full power of the influential familes of Alvin Fog and Ranse Smith were brought to bear. Learning the Hardin, Fog and Blaze clan and the oil rich Counter family were taking such an interest,[6] members of law enforcement agencies of all kinds who lacked the bond of friendship considered it politic to fall in with the proposals they had

6. *Information about three members of the family to which Sergeant Ranse Smith was related, Mark and Deputy Sheriff Bradford 'Brad' Counter and James Allenvale 'Bunduki' Gunn, can be found respectively in the* Floating Outfit, Rockabye County *and* Bunduki *series.*

53

received. Even those whose income was boosted by bribery felt it advisable, under the circumstances, to forego their illicit activities for the time being. The latter was the reason why no advance warning of the raid had been passed to Massart by the local peace officers on Hogan Turtle's payroll.

While other members of Company 'Z' were engaged elsewhere on similar assignments, Ranse, having learned the location of the new 'house' from one of his wealthy kinsmen, had been instructed to work in conjunction with the Dallas Police Department on the raid. The message he had given to be passed on to Turtle was, it was intended, only one which would be delivered the following day. Other major criminals were also to feel the effects and the pressure was to be continued until somebody supplied the information needed to find the Chopper.

CHAPTER FIVE

IT *IS* HAPPENING ALL OVER TEXAS

'*SALUDOS, senores,*' greeted Salvatoro Nieto, in heavily accented and apparently cheerful English, as he rode out of the darkness into the glow from the headlights of a big Mack Brothers truck. He brought his horse to a halt and signalled for the rest of his party to do the same. While addressing the four armed white men standing by the side of the vehicle, his eyes were constantly scanning the woodland which flanked the narrow trail. 'Never have I had such a good market for my *tequila*. This Prohibition law of yours will make us all rich, no?'

Despite his seemingly jovial attitude and words, the big and burly Mexican kept his right hand thumb-hooked in his fancily engraved *buscadero* gunbelt close to the silver inlaid Tiffany grips of the Colt Cavalry Model Peacemaker in its tied down fast draw holster. Ten of his countrymen—each wearing cheaper, even dirtier versions of his *vaquero's charro* attire and leading two heavily laden pack mules—slouched on their saddles cradling loaded and cocked Winchester Model of 1876 carbines across their knees.

Of the men by the truck, one held a Thompson submachine gun, two had sawn-off shotguns and the last and best dressed of them, carried a Colt Government Model of 1911 automatic pistol tucked into the waistband of his trousers and left in view by his coat being open. However, regardless of the apparently amiable greeting, he had not fastened the jacket. Nor did his companions offer to place their weapons inside the cab of the vehicle.

Although the mules were carrying a large consignment of *tequila*, there was no justification for the close to suspicious way in which the two parties were studying one another. At other times, the Mexicans might have been willing to try and rob the *gringos* of the money brought to pay for the liquor, just

55

as the men by the Mack would have sought to obtain it free. However, Nieto had spoken the truth about the excellence of his market and knew he would have difficulty in bettering it. The same applied to Dimitri 'Joe The Greek' Horopolis, for whom the quartet worked, with regards to the source of supply offered by Nieto. Therefore, as there was no sign of the Volstead Act being repealed in the foreseeable future, neither group wished to kill a goose which consistently laid golden eggs.

Under normal circumstances, the mules would not have required leading individually. Being well trained for pack work, they could have been left loose to follow a mare with a bell fastened to its neck.[1] However, when engaged upon smuggling liquor across the Rio Grande during the hours of darkness, there were disadvantages to employing this system. Not only could greater control be maintained over the animals when led, but in the event of an attempt to hijack the consignment, or the appearance of revenue officers on either side of the international border, they could be more easily defended in a compact group than was possible if they were allowed to move at liberty. Doing so also offered a reason to have several men along, without making it obvious that they had no faith in the trustworthiness of the *gringos* with whom they were doing business.

'Howdy, Sal,' responded Victor Demosthenes, without showing any signs of relaxing vigilance or buttoning his coat. 'Did you have any trouble coming over the Rio Grande?'

'I *never* have any trouble coming over the *Rio Bravo*,' Nieto replied, using the Mexican name for the river which acted as the border between his country and Texas. Satisfied all was well, he swung from his saddle. Dropping the reins, knowing the horse would remain just as still as if he had tied it to one of the nearby trees, he held out his dirty and be-jewelled left hand, continuing, 'I trust Joe is in good health and as prosperous as ever?'

'He sends his best wishes,' Demosthenes claimed with as little truth as there had been sincerity in the enquiry, taking a thick wad of money from his right breast pocket. 'And *this*.'

'*Gracias, amigo*,' the burly Mexican thanked, thumbing

1. *A detailed description of how loose pack mules were handled is given in*: OLE DEVIL AND THE MULE TRAIN.

the wad of one hundred dollar bills he was handed. Satisfied the full amount for the payment was there, knowing its deliverer would not dare take any of it, he reverted to his native tongue and told his men to start handing over the consignment. Then, returning to English, he went on, 'Give mine back to him and say I'll be dropping by to help him drink some *Americano* whiskey one day soon. Now there's a drink I surely like.'

'Give the greas—*boys* a hand, fellers,' the Greek commanded, after waiting until all ten Mexicans had placed the rawhide loops attached to the rings of the carbines over the typically large horns of their saddles. Taking what he knew to have been a hint, he brought a flask from his hip pocket and held it forward. 'Here you go, Sal, try a slug of it now.'

'*Gracias, gring—amigo*,' Nieto assented, having deliberately changed the second word to show he had noticed the offensive name the Greek had begun to use when speaking of the Mexicans.

On receiving the order from Demosthenes, laying the Thompson and shotguns in the cab of the truck, the other three white men went to where the Mexicans were starting to unload the first of the mules. It was obvious, villainous and unprepossessing though their appearance undoubtedly was, that the latter were skilled at their task. Quickly unfastening the lashings and opening out the tarpaulin cover, they passed the wooden boxes to their *gringo* helpers to take and load into the back of the vehicle. However, in spite of the wary way in which they had studied one another on meeting, knowing there was no need to fear a substitution for the *tequila* under the prevailing conditions, neither the Americans nor their leader offered to check that the contents were as ordered.

'What's happening up here, *amigo*?' Nieto inquired, lowering the flask from which he had taken a long and noisy drink.

'Not much hereabouts,' the Greek replied, making no attempt to retrieve his property. 'But I heard that the Chopper gunned down a couple of Texas Rangers in Cowtown last Monday.'

'Good for him, whoever he might be,' the burly Mexican praised. 'I wish he'd come over the *Rio Bravo* and gun down some of our *Rurales*, we've got more of the bastards than we nee—!'

Letting out a snort and tossing its head, Nieto's horse stared at the woodland to the right of the trail and brought the comment to a halt!

'What's u—?' Demosthenes demanded, having heard its owner claim the animal was as good as a watchdog when it came to detecting unseen observers. He reached towards his automatic.

'*Hijo de puta!*' Nieto blasphemed, also grabbing for his gun.

'Peace officers here!' a voice boomed out of the trees to the right, before either weapon could clear leather. Then, while the words continued, the area was illuminated by bright lights from amongst the trees on both sides. 'Stand still, all of you!'

The announcement was repeated in Spanish from the opposite direction!

A moment later moving swiftly and carrying weapons of various kinds, men wearing uniforms and badges of office strode into view. As none of them were holding the sources of brilliant illumination, it seemed likely there were more in the woodland to right and left. All but one were members of the United States' Border Patrol.

The one exception was dressed little differently from the Mexicans, although he was cleaner and neater. Just over medium height, almost as broad as he was tall, his olive skinned and heavily moustached features had such a villainous aspect he might have been one of the Mexicans for he clearly had similar ethnic origins. Nevertheless, he held a Winchester Model of 1897 riot gun and, on the left breast of his black *bolero* jacket was the badge of a Texas Ranger.

Seeing there were peace officers converging from both sides, Nieto and Demosthenes were wise enough to refrain from drawing their weapons!

Not all of their men showed a similar grasp of the situation!

Turning, a Mexican sprang towards the horse which was leading the mule being unloaded. Snatching the carbine from its saddlehorn, he swivelled around!

Knowing the man to be a *bandido* of the worst type and as viciously inclined as a cornered rat, Sergeant Carlos Franco of Company 'Z' did not hesitate before responding. Held at waist level and aimed by instinctive alignment, his riot gun boomed out.[2] Caught by seven of the nine .32 calibre buck-shot balls, a scream burst from the aggressive smuggler and he was thrown off his feet before he could complete his hostile intentions. Operating the 'trombone' slide beneath the twenty inch barrel, evicting the empty case and replenishing the chamber from the five-capacity tubular magazine, the *Chicano* peace officer turned his weapon so it covered the stricken man's companions.[3]

Startled by the detonation of the shot and scream from the Mexican, the horses and mules started to rear and plunge. Seeing what he thought to be a chance, one of the white men dropped the box of *tequila* he was carrying and darted towards the cab of the truck. Throwing up a spurt of dirt just in front of his descending right foot, a bullet from a revolver brought him to a halt still several steps clear of his destination. It was fired by the tall, lean, youthful peace officer—who bore a resemblance in build and features to a young actor, Gary Cooper, already growing popular in movies—placed in command of the Border Patrol group assigned to assist Franco.

Taking the hint, the rest of the men refrained from such obviously futile attempts at hostilities. Nor did any of them try to interfere when some of the uniformed officers holstered handguns and advanced to grab hold of horses. In spite of this prompt action, however, four of the animals and their pack mules were able to dash away. The departure through the woodland was to the accompaniment of splintering wood and shattering glass as various of the loads were burst open.

'Who the hell sold us, Jor—*Mr*. Jordan?' Demosthenes growled, considering it advisable to make the alteration and supply the honorific.

'A gypsy read it in my palm,' replied the senior Border Patrol officer, his voice a lazy Texas drawl, being too prudent

---

2. *Although Sergeant Carlos Franco carried a Winchester Model of 1894 carbine when participating in the raid on Minnie Lassiter's Premier Chicken Ranch near El Paso, Texas—described in* RAPIDO CLINT—*like most peace officers, he varied his offensive armament to what he considered would be the needs of each individual assignment, which might call for something more potent than his basically defensive handgun.*

3. *'Chicano', a person of Hispanic origin born, or permanently residing in the United States.*

to say the information had been supplied by an informer to the Texas Ranger.

'And when Joe the Greek gets you out of the *calabozo* on bail,' Franco supplemented, his English showing just a trace of his Hispanic 'roots', getting down to the main purpose of the ambush—as Sergeant Ranse Smith was doing in Dallas at almost the same time—'You tell him that gypsy's going to keep on reading palms until we've nailed the Chopper's hide to the wall!'

*　　*　　*　　*　　　*　　*　　*　　*

WORK was progressing smoothly at the fair sized former warehouse which had been secretly converted to a well equipped and laid out brewery in the business district of Austin. In fact, looking through the window of the raised office at the left of the main entrance to where beer was flowing into the two large storage vats, the tall, good looking and fastidiously dressed owner was congratulating the white haired, bulky middle-aged German *brau meister* on the rate of production. Leaning on either side of the door, the two armed bodyguards of Talbot 'Dapper Dan' Sharmain—who, like Dimitri Horopolis, had acquired a sufficiently strong criminal force to remain independent of Hogan Turtle's much larger organization—masticated lumps of gum like cows contentedly chewing cud in a meadow. Satisfied that the establishment was not known to either the local police or Prohibition agents based in the State Capitol, neither was alert. On the ground floor, the work force was too busily enagaged in their various duties to bother about what was going on elsewhere within or outside the building.

Therefore, what happened took everybody on the premises completely by surprise!

With a thunderous crash, the big double doors of the main entrance burst inwards!

The destruction was caused by one of the large F.W.D. 'Liberty' four-wheel drive trucks sold off as surplus to requirements by the United States' Army after the Great War. Sturdy as it was when first manufactured, it had been rendered even more suited to its present purpose by having had two thick steel plates in the form of a triangle welded securely in front of its radiator. These had shattered through the reinforced main entrance without damaging the engine.

'What the hell?' Sharmain gasped.

'*Gott in himmel*!' the *brau meister* ejaculated in the same breath.

'It's a *raid*!' announced the bodyguard longest in the gang boss's employment just as simultaneously, having a flair for stating the obvious.

Despite the brakes having been applied on the entrance being effected, the velocity required to gain admittance in such a way caused the big vehicle to keep moving far enough to let a black limousine enter close behind it. The latter was filled with well armed Prohibition agents in civilian clothing. However, also without uniform, the men standing on the running boards at each side, grasping weapons with the hands not engaged in holding them there, wore the insignia of Texas Rangers. As the car swerved and skidded to a halt on the left of the truck, they sprang clear and the men inside started to emerge with an equal rapidity.

Having only recently attained his well paid position, and wanting to prove he was more efficient than his companion, the second bodyguard had drawn his revolver and plunged through the door of the office without speaking or even waiting to ascertain who the newcomers might be. Discovering they were peace officers and mindful that he was wanted for murder in New Mexico, a point he had omitted to mention when applying for the job, he reacted instinctively. However, the shot he fired downwards narrowly missed the man at whom it was directed.

This proved a fatal mistake!

Coming to a halt and showing no sign of being disconcerted by having had lead pass close to his head, the burlier Texas Ranger swung up his Smith & Wesson Army Model of 1917 revolver at arms' length in both hands to aim and fire three times in rapid succession. Hit in the torso by the second and third .45 calibre bullets, the imprudent criminal was spun against the guard rail at the top of the wooden stairs and, breaking through, came crashing to the floor. Having less to fear from being arrested, his companion showed a greater and wiser discretion. Dropping the weapon he had drawn, he raised his hands over his head and preceded his employer and the *brau meister* from the office.

Satisfied there would be no further attempts at resistance, ordering the workers to stand clear, four Prohibition agents raised the Thompson submachine guns they were holding.

Each emptied the fifty round drum magazine into the vats, causing beer to spurt through the holes.

'Come on down, *Mr.* Sharmain,' called the senior agent, after the fusilade had ended. His voice held a blatantly synthetic note of pleasure as he continued, 'We didn't know *you'd* be here, so it's something of a bonus for our night's work.'

'You look sad, *mon ami*,' remarked Sergeant Alexandre "Frenchie" Giradot. Tall, slim, wiry and swarthily handsome, he was as dapper in appearance as Sharmain; albeit, lacking the other's sources of income and less expensively attired. He claimed his ancestors had been Parisian *apache* and his accent had a Gallic timbre.[4] Nodding towards the vehicle which had created access to the brewery, he continued, 'But the idea for strengthening the truck you got from Elliot works very well.'

'Sure it does and I hope it'll serve him as well when he gets the chance to use one like it,'[5] replied Sergeant Aloysius "Paddy" Bratton in his Irish brogue. Slightly taller and much more bulky in build, he wore the kind of loud clothes for which he had acquired a taste while working as a carnival roustabout in his youth. Gazing at the devastation caused by the Thompsons, he went on in a tone of sadness, 'But will you just be looking at all that fine beer going to waste and isn't it knowing I've cause to be just how tasty it was, darlin'. Sure and was things different, I'd not have wanted the Murphy to be paying back an old debt by telling me just where "Dapper Dan"d' got his brewery hid out.'

'I sympathise with you, *mon ami*,' the slimmer sergeant claimed, ignoring what was an admission of the Volstead Act having been broken by his companion and returning his Colt

4. 'Apache' *used in this context does not mean a member of the Indian nation of that name. Pronounced 'A-pash' and not 'A-patchy', it is the name given by the French to a class of small time criminals who once infested Paris. They are best known outside that country for the so called* 'danse apache' *wherein the man throws and drags his female partner around the floor.*

5. *The hope materialized later when Elliot Ness used it in the operations of the special Prohibition Detail he led. Formed from carefully selected agents of the United States' Department of Justice, they acquired the sobriquet 'The Untouchables' because they could neither be frightened nor bribed to prevent them performing their duties. They played a major part in the eventual downfall of Alphonse 'Scar-Face Al' Capone, supreme leader of the Chicago underworld. See:* THE UNTOUCHABLES, *by Eliot Ness (with Oscar Fraley).*

Goverment Model automatic pistol to its shoulder holster. 'Let's go and warn *M'sieur* Sharmain this kind of thing's going to keep on happening until we get the Chopper.'

*   *   *   *   *   *   *   *

'YES, Talbot, I know and *how* I *know*!' Hogan Turtle said into the mouthpiece of the telephone, his somewhat nasal and high pitched drawl sounding almost petulant although far more patient than he was feeling. 'But it's no good you, Joe the Greek and all the others who've been calling me, saying it *can't* be happening. The *fact* is, it *is* happening all over Texas and I'm being hit just as hard as *anybody* else.'

Sprawling rather than just sitting in a comfortably padded leather swivel chair specially designed to accept his massive figure, behind a well polished large oak antique desk, there was nothing visible to indicate the speaker was the most powerful criminal in the Lone Star State. Surmounted by thick and curly brown hair, which rumour—never mentioned in his hearing, as his resentment was known to be most painful—claimed needed regular tinting to conceal grey streaks, his face was reddened by good living and, except in rare moments of rage, seemed bland to the point of innocence. The white flannel suit, matching silk shirt and flowing dark blue silk cravat, embellished with a diamond stickpin of considerable dimensions, were reminiscent of a wealthy Old South plantation owner. However, lethargic and somnolent as he gave the outer impression of being, he had inherited and even improved upon the cunning, intelligent, completely ruthless attributes which enabled his ancestors to build up and maintain a criminal empire second to none in Texas.

Although only a week had elapsed since Company 'Z' began to implement the plan set out by Major Benson Tragg, already all of the major and minor gang leaders were starting to feel its effects!

Flown sometimes with as many as three passengers crowded into the Douglas DT-2 biplane piloted by Ranse Smith, members of the Company were constantly on the move throughout Texas. Making the best possible use of information acquired from all their multifarious sources, some of it even being donated free by professional stool pigeons out of respect for the memory of Jubal Branch, they had struck constantly at various illicit enterprises in conjunction with peace officers from their own and other law enforcement agencies.

Among other things, aided by the 'bomber boys'—as investigators in the Enforcement Branch of the Inland Revenue Service's Alcohol & Tobacco Tax Division were frequently called—Sergeant Colin Breda caused so much disruption to the vehicles trying to make deliveries, and destroyed so many long established stills, that the 'moonshining' activities for which Jack County had long been renowned were practically brought to a halt.[6] Informers in the port of Brownsville had allowed Alexandre Giradot to send a Coast Guard cutter which intercepted and captured a a small cargo ship from the West Indies carrying a consignment of liquor for Turtle. Supported by United States' marshals, the crime being 'Federal' due to its perpetration occurring on an Indian reservation in the Panhandle district, Sergeant David Swift-Eagle—a Kiowa—had ruined a previously lucrative cattle stealing trade as a result of details acquired from members of his tribe.[7] Learning where more high stakes gambling 'houses' could be located, the blond giant had been too busy acting as pilot, and had left dealing with them to Aloysius Bratton.

One result of all these activities, supplemented by more from other law enforcement agencies without needing the co-operation of Company 'Z', had been a spate of telephone calls and meetings between the leaders of different gangs. Being so prominent amongst them, all had at some time made contact with and sought advice from Turtle. Cautious by nature, he had refused to accept the onus of being the first to make the decision which they all knew must eventually be reached. It was the first conversation he had had with Sharmain. However, in spite of guessing the delay was caused by the other wishing to show independence, he was giving no suggestion of the annoyance his suppositions had aroused.

'Yeah, I've heard you've been getting your share of hassle,' the Austin gang leader admitted, as if wanting to give the impression he was conferring a favour. 'How much longer do

6. *Information regarding the proclivity of people in Jack County, Texas, to operate illicit liquor stills is given in:* THE LAW OF THE GUN *and Part Three, 'The Trouble With Wearing Boots',* THE FLOATING OUTFIT.

7. *Although people in other States refer to that particular crime as 'rustling', Texans prefer to call it by a blunter and more accurately descriptive name, see:* THE COW THIEVES.

you reckon it's going to keep on?'

'Until Benson Tragg gets what he wants,' Turtle estimated sombrely. 'And, accepting that and bearing in mind the people he's got backing him, we *all* know there's only one way to stop it.'

'We do,' Sharmain agreed, then paused to show he was waiting for the suggestion to come from the man to whom he was speaking.

'I don't know who the Chopper is,' Turtle asserted.

'Nor do I.'

'But we both—and all the others—know how to get in touch with him.'

'You mean we should pass the word for him to get the hell out of the country until this blows over?' Sharmain inquired, although he felt sure such a course would not satisfy Major Tragg.

'Something like that, Talbot,' Turtle replied, having drawn an identical conclusion. 'Something like that.'

CHAPTER SIX

I'D KILL MY OWN MOTHER

'HAVE any of you folks ever been in a Polack bingo parlour?' asked the comedian on the small stage of the Turtleback Cottage in Brownsville. 'You can always tell if you do go in one. The feller calling the numbers starts off, "One. Two. Three. Four"—And I'm going to keep on counting until you laugh!' He paused until the audience responded enthusiastically to his ethnic humour, then went on, 'All right, so I'm not *real* funny. For the kind of money Hogan pays, you expect maybe Haysoff Spades?'

'Have you noticed how they all look at *me* before they laugh at something like he just said?' Hogan Turtle inquired, with an air of self satisfied complacency, beaming and waving a languid right hand in acknowledgement of the bow directed his way by the entertainer.

'We *noticed*,' Dimitri "Joe the Greek" Horopolis admitted sourly, being less interested in the behaviour of the well dressed people in the night club than the matter which had brought him there. Big, heavy set, with crinkly short white hair and a teak brown face, he looked a hard man and had proved himself to be just that whenever the need arose. For all that and despite clearly feeling ill at ease in such formal attire, he had donned a tuxedo and black bow tie because he had been informed his host expected such attire and, especially with the unsatisfactory conditions which continued to prevail throughout the whole of Texas, he had no desire to antagonize so potentially dangerous a competitor by disregarding what had unmistakably been made a qualification for being admitted. 'Only seeing it don't help us figure out what to do about what's going on.'

There was a low rumble of concurrence from five of the other six, each—apart from the abstainer—the leader of a criminal organization in a section of Texas, who were seated with the speakers!

66

Glancing from one to another of the group, Turtle was pleased he had taken the precaution of insisting neither they nor any of the bodyguards—limited to three apiece—he allowed them to bring were armed. Insisting the same be done by their representatives to himself and his trio, he had had them all searched and whatever weapons they carried removed on arrival. Either it had not occurred to any of his visitors, or whoever thought of it had also decided against mentioning the matter, but nobody had pointed out they were in a place he owned and that its employees were not included in the searching. Having been placed in a waterproof bag, all the weapons removed from them had been concealed beneath the mass of cubes in the large ice box and Turtle had described them with his heavy-handed sense of humour as 'frappe hog-legs'.

Having grown increasingly concerned over the amount of calls over the telephone being made by his somewhat less powerful contemporaries from various parts of Texas, and being aware that the lines connecting them could be 'tapped' by law enforcement agencies, the leader of the largest organization had called them together to discuss face to face the worsening of the situation which had arisen after the killing of Sergeants Jubal Branch and Hans Soehnen. Earlier optimistic hopes that the peace officers would soon slacken their activities had failed to materialize. In fact, the harassment had grown worse. There was no field of crime which had not suffered disruption and serious loss of revenue from the onslaught. Therefore, every one of the gang leaders present—and those who had not been invited, or declined to come—were feeling the pinch to a far greater extent than when Talbot 'Dapper Dan' Sharmain made his first telephone call of protest to Hogan Turtle.

'God damn it!' growled Royston Benedict, whose organization controlled much of the criminal activity in the Texas Panhandle county. Shortish, thickset, dark of complexion, even more than Horopolis, he seemed unsuited to the semi formal attire he too had been compelled to wear. 'For what you get *paid*, you god damned shysters ought to be able to do something about stopping the bastards.'

'There are *limits* to how much we of the Bar can *help* criminals to get away with,' replied the man to whom the comment was directed, not having troubled to conceal the distaste he felt over hearing members of his profession referred to as "god damned shysters". He had a well deserved reputation for being the most unscrupulous defense attorney in Texas, fully conversant with *every* means by which the course of justice could be perverted and always willing to employ them for the benefit of those clients able to meet his high fees. Nevertheless, he always kept up a pretence of being completely honest and incorruptible. 'The law is undoubtedly an ass in many respects, but there are *limits* to how asinine it can be—!'

'I've a notion all that god damned fancy lip flapping mean's how you can't do *nothing* for us,' Benedict interrupted dryly.

'It *means*,' the lawyer corrected with the offended dignity of one who knew he was safe from reprisals under the circumstances. 'That, unless the authorities should go outside the proscribed bounds in doing so—which I assure you I have checked they have *not* so far—there is *nothing* we can *legally* do to prevent them from interfering when dealing with what we *all* know are the committing of various crimes.'

Six foot tall, broad of shoulder, in his mid-fifties, Counsellor Reece Mervyn was the best dressed of the gathering and, with the exception of Turtle and Sharmain, most at ease in such surroundings. He had the appearance of a former athlete whose good living had made him run somewhat to seed. There was a tinge of grey in the thick brown hair set in a series of precise waves. While otherwise good looking in an obvious way, it was apparent his nose had resisted setting after being badly broken. Everybody present knew this injury had not been caused by an accident in sport, but had come about as a result of his proclivity for feminine company other than that of his wife.[1]

'Like Roy said, fancy lip-flapping like that don't help,' Horopolis grumbled. 'God damn it, can't any of those politicians we've been sloughing cash to for years do *nothing* to stop 'em?'

'Unfortunately, they have always been in a *small* minority,' Mervyn answered, the question once again having been

---

1. *How and why the injury was inflicted is told in*: THE JUSTICE OF COMPANY 'Z'.

clearly meant for him. 'And, like all politicians, especially of their kind, they know when it wouldn't be wise for them to go against the tide.'

'Well *something's* got to be done and *pronto!*' Benedict stated.

'And we *all* know what that *something* is,' Turtle claimed, running his gaze in a pointed fashion around the table.

'Er—if my *legal* services are no longer required—?' Mervyn put in, concluding the reason of the gathering was about to be raised and, having no desire to be present while whatever illegality might be decided upon was discussed, starting to ease back his chair.

'Very well, Reece,' Turtle assented. Knowing the lawyer invariably kept up the pretence of honesty, requiring every client to pretend to be an innocent victim of circumstances, he was aware of the true motive behind the intended departure. Deciding against exercising his sense of humour by pretending to insist Mervyn remained, he was on the point of authorizing the absence. Then, seeing the direction in which the Counsellor was gazing, he continued in a manner which was clearly prohibitive, 'If you have any notions about *her*, I'd *advise* you to forget them.'

'Don't tell me that you've put your brand on her, Hogan?' Sharmain inquired, also having had his eye on the cause of the comment.

Clad in an even more abbreviated version of the attire worn by a 'French maid' on the stage, particularly in farces or musical plays supposedly based in that country, the girl carrying a tray with various smoking materials, about whom the remarks were being passed, was worthy of the attention she was receiving from practically every male customer. The decollete of her black satin dress was bordering on the indecorous and its hem—above shapely legs in sheer black silk stockings—extended barely two inches below the well rounded curves of her buttocks. Although they were all picked for their looks, she stood out from the other similarly attired female employees moving about the room. Not one of them, conforming as they did to the modern trend for a slim figure, could match the rich curves she was displaying. Attractive and with rather more fiery red hair than might currently be considered fashionable, as she passed between the tables carrying her tray of wares, the skimpy nature of the garment established beyond any doubt that her Junoesque

69

contours were produced solely by nature.

'Not at all, Talbot,' Turtle denied. 'Beau Wiggins tried to yesterday, just after she'd arrived to take the job and changed into her costume.'

'*Tried?*' Sharmain repeated, knowing the man in question to be his host's chief bodyguard and had a less than savoury reputation where treatment accorded to female employees was concerned.

'*Tried,*' Turtle confirmed. 'It seems that, when he walked up behind her and slipped his hands under her skirt to—er, well you know *what* he meant to do—she turned 'round, rammed her fingers into his eyes and kicked him where he'd *know* he'd been kicked.'

'And she's still *walking around?*' Benedict inquired incredulously, equally aware of Wiggins' habits.

'Beau didn't feel up to doing anything about it straight away,' Turtle explained. 'Which was fortunate.'

'She sure was,' Horopolis grinned, being equally well informed about the bodyguard.

'Not just for *her*, Dimitri,' the host of the gathering corrected, one of his traits being never to employ a sobriquet unless intending something bad would befall the person he was addressing. 'In fact, as soon as he was able to understand, I told Beau he mustn't touch her.'

'Getting kind hearted, Hogan?' another of the lesser gang leaders suggested with a sly grin at the rest of his contemporaries.

'Not so *you* would notice it, Wilbur,' Turtle replied and there was a trace of warning in his voice. 'I gave her the job as a favour to young Big Andy Counter, who it seems has designs on whatever virtue she has left, and, with the heat that's on these days, the last thing I need is to have more of it coming my way because she wound up in hospital after Beau had worked her over.'

'Times have *changed*,' Benedict commented dryly, although he realized how much pressure a member of the oil rich Counter family could bring to bear on the local peace officers if they felt it was necessary.[2]

---

2. *Andrew Mark 'Big Andy' Counter is respectively the son and father of Mark and Bradford 'Brad' Counter, q.v.*

'They *have*,' Turtle confirmed. However, although he did not add a warning of, 'But *I* haven't', it was implied in his tone and attitude. 'And there's only *one* way we can get them back to *normal*.'

'That's why we've got together,' Sharmain conceded, turning his gaze reluctantly back to the table from a sight he had found much more diverting than the grim faces of the men around it.

Having halted not too far away to serve a customer who was lounging alone at the end of the bar, even though nominally standing still, the rear view which the fiery haired cigarette girl was presenting was made even more sensually attractive by the rotating motion she was contriving to impart to her shapely buttocks.

Even though the customer was of a striking appearance, it was unlikely at that moment if any other man in the room was taking the slightest notice of him. Clearly young, he was tall and slim. Having his shining coal black hair parted straight down the centre, his handsome brown face and moustache added to the Hispanic flavour of his attire. He had on a snugly fitting black *bolero* jacket much decorated by gold and silver braid as were the outer seams of his tight legged, albeit flaring bottomed, grey trousers. His frilly bosomed white shirt was clearly silk and each 'wing' of his black bow tie was embellished by what appeared to be a diamond. Not unexpectedly, for one dressed in such a way, his well polished black boots were sharp toed and high heeled.

Considering subsequent developments, it might—depending upon one's point of view—have proved advantageous if more attention had been paid by some of the men present to what happened while the cigarette girl was serving her current customer, rather than enjoying the view she was offering!

*   *   *   *   *   *   *   *

PAUSING at the entrance to the main dining-room of the Turtleback Cottage, Sergeant Alvin Dustine '*Rapido* Clint' Fog was dressed in the style required before one was granted admission to one of the most expensive 'night spots' in the seaport of Brownsville!

Having glanced in the full length mirror alongside the alcove of the 'hat check' girl in charge of the cloakroom, the young Texas Ranger had been pleased by the appearance

71

he saw reflected. Studying the excellent fit of his tuxedo and its accoutrements, he had wondered whether his illustrious grandfather had also given the impression of being better dressed than was usual—no matter what the quality of attire being worn—when adopting the personality of their mutual *alter ego, Rapido* Clint. He considered, with satisfaction, that he looked much more impressive than usual in the semi formal garments he was wearing. Certainly the men positioned on either side of the main entrance, obviously keeping watch to prevent unwanted arrivals, had seen nothing about him to which they could object. What was more, as had proved the case on other occasions, if he had been searched, he was confident that something seemingly innocuous he was carrying in the right side pocket of his trousers would not be recognized for the most effective weapon it could become in hands as skilful as his own.[3]

Glancing around the room, Rapido received in passing a nod from one of those already present which signified a prearranged precaution had been taken. Satisfied on that most important point, he strolled forward exuding nonchalance and with his right hand in his trouser's pocket. Apparently by accident, he made his way towards where Hogan Turtle and the other gang leaders were seated at a table some distance away from everybody else. However, before he reached the open space separating them from possible eavesdroppers, he was brought to a halt.

'The bar's over that way, mister,' Beauregard Wiggins stated, rising from where he sat at a table with the senior bodyguards of his employer's guests. Towering over the young Texan he was addressing, his eyes were still inflamed from having the knuckles of the cigarette girl thrust and ground into them when he tried to molest her the previous afternoon. 'There's *nothing* for you over that way.'

'I'd reckon *I'm* the best judge of that, *hombre*,' *Rapido* replied, his manner deliberately cocksure and arrogant.

'The hell you are, short stuff!' Wiggins denied, reacting as the sergeant had planned, and giving a gesture intended to bring over two of the night club's bouncers.

'You figure on making me change my mind all by your lonesome?' *Rapido* challenged derisively. 'Or do you reckon you'll

3. *One such occasion is described in*: RAPIDO CLINT.

72

be needing those two jaspers you've just wig-wagged to come on over?'

'*I'll* be enough!' Wiggins stated in a snarl, conscious of the other senior bodyguards watching him and aware that his reputation for toughness had been weakened by his being unable to take revenge for the treatment he had suffered at the hands of the cigarette girl.

Saying the words, the big man reached out to grip his much smaller intended victim by the shoulders!

As Wiggins did so, it seemed a change came over the other!

Suddenly, such was the strength of his personality, *Rapido* no longer appeared small to his would be assailant!

Instead, the small Texan gave the impression to the burly bodyguard of having taken on size and heft which made him loom larger than anybody else in the room!

The sensation caused Wiggins to freeze into immobility!

Making the most of the situation he had hoped might be created, as it often had in the past at times of similar stress, *Rapido* brought his right hand from the pocket. It was not empty, but grasped the object which he had counted upon having been dismissed as innocuous if he had been searched on entering the night club. About six inches in length, it resembled a piece cut from the oak handle of a broom. Although his hand concealed them, there were several grooves carved around the middle to offer a firmer grasp and each end was rounded. Harmless though it appeared, it was a most effective—albeit basically primitive—weapon which he had been taught to wield very effectively.

Driven forward in a sharp and thrusting motion, the rounded end of the *yawara* stick protruding before the small Texan's thumb and forefinger rammed with considerable force into Wiggins' *solar plexus*. Letting out a strangled croaking profanity, he reeled back with his hands going to the point of impact. Unfortunately for him, his retreat was neither fast nor far enough to avoid what happened next. Whipping up his right arm, *Rapido* directed the opposite end of the weapon in a backhand swing to the centre of the bodyguard's face. Sent onwards by the powerful blow, blood spraying from his nose—which subsequently proved to be badly splintered rather than just broken—Wiggins twirled and ran headfirst into the wall with a force which rendered him unconscious.

73

Looking from one to the other of the converging bouncers, but paying no discernible attention to the commotion aroused by his actions throughout the rest of the room, the small Texan pointed elsewhere and said in a mocking tone one word which came out as, *'Nooo!'*

Swinging their gaze in the direction being indicated, the bouncers received a surprise!

Startled exclamations burst from the other senior bodyguards as they too looked towards the bar!

Although his attire was so tight fitting it seemed impossible for him to have been able to bring such a large firearm undetected past the experienced watchers at the front entrance, the slim Hispanic looking young man by the bar was pointing one towards the table occupied by the gang leaders. Without knowing it was a British made Webley-Fosbery 'automatic' revolver, but realizing the danger it posed to their employer, the bouncers came to a halt. Drawing a similar conclusion and all too conscious of being unarmed themselves, the senior bodyguards also decided it was advisable to take no hostile action.

'Sorry to disturb all you good folks,' *Rapido* called, when satisfied the situation was in hand. 'Go on with what you're doing. There'll be no more fuss.' Having waited until his suggestion was being acted upon, he returned the *yawara* stick to his trousers pocket and crossed to the table for which he had been making when interrupted by Wiggins. 'Howdy, you-all, Mr. Turtle, gents. The name's "*Rapido* Clint". My *bueno amigo* Comanch' over by the bar and I've just recently got back from fighting for General Lee Christmas in a revolution down to one of those "banana republics".[4] We're needing work and reckon there's something we can do for you-all.'

---

4. *'Banana republic': colloquial name for Central American countries such as Guatemala, Honduras, Salvador, Nicaragua, or Costa Rica, whose economy was dependent upon a single type of crop, generally bananas. Information regarding the career of 'General' Lee Christmas, an American soldier of fortune active thereabouts, is given in:* Chapter XVIII, 'One Man Army Corps', TRIGGERNOMETRY, *by Eugene Cunningham. We also based our series* REBEL OF THE IRON ROAD—*which was first commenced in* VICTOR *boys paper on October the 9th, 1965—upon incidents from his eventful life.*

Concluding the introduction, the small Texan was ready to take whatever action might be called for as a result of the name he had given to make himself acquainted. He had used it the previous year while engaged upon a case which took him to England and he had been exposed as being a sergeant of the Texas Rangers by a message he believed had originated from Turtle. He also realized the gang leader was aware of the true identity of the original 'Rapido Clint'. However, despite having an explanation for both which he hoped would be acceptable, he was alert for any indication of trouble.

'And what might that be, Mr. Clint?' Turtle inquired, waving away those of his employees who were approaching.

'Getting the Chopper for you,' Rapido supplied. 'Because you gents have gotten together here tonight to talk about how to have it done.'

'Who the hell told you tha—?' Royston Benedict commenced, anticipating a similar question from the other gang leaders.

'How about it, Mr. Turtle?' the small Texan inquired, before the query could be completed. 'Happen you take us on, you're going to get a bonus. So do we talk turkey?'

'What would the bonus be?' the massive gang leader countered, but was not entirely able to conceal his amusement over the way in which Benedict was being treated.

'A son-of-a-bitch from the Texas Rangers called Alvin Fog went over to England pretending to be me, and a gal whose big high mucky-muck owlhoot daddy he helped kill got word to me's how she'd admire to have him made wolf bait,' the small Texan explained, watching for and failing to see any suggestion that his story was not believed by the man for whom it was intended.[5] 'But, happen you make the price right and take us on, I'm willing to forget doing that and stirring up more fuss like you've got on your hands right now.'

'That's most considerate of you, Mr. Clint. Have a seat, please,' Turtle said, the invitation being given without so much as a glance for confirmation from the other gang

5. *Alvin Dustine 'Cap' Fog claims he is now of the opinion that the betrayal to which he referred did not originate from Hogan Turtle as he assumed it had at the time. However, he declines to say who he believes was responsible.*

leaders. Instead, after the chair left vacant by the departure of Counsellor Reece Mervin had been occupied by the newcomer, he pointed to where Sergeant Mark "Comanche Blood" Scrapton still leaned by the bar, although now with the revolver dangling towards the floor. 'How did your friend manage to bring that gun in here?'

'He comes from a long line of Comanche medicine men on his great grand-daddy's side,' *Rapido* replied, instead of telling how the weapon had been smuggled in by Rita Yarborough —who had obtained a position as cigarette girl, with the willing assistance of Andrew Mark "Big Andy" Counter,—under the goods on her tray and delivered on the pretence of making a sale to his companion. Then, making it clear he felt nothing more need be added to the subject, he continued, 'Well, gents. Do we have us a deal?'

'First of all,' Turtle said, almost mildly it seemed, before any of the others could express a point of view. 'Are you a descendant of the "*Rapdio* Clint" my grandfather knew?'

'Nope,' *Rapido* lied, albeit with a convincing simulation of veracity. 'But, going by what I've heard of him, I wish I had been.'

'I had an idea it might just be a "summer name",' Turtle declared, using the old range country term for an alias.

'Why sure,' the small Texan agreed. 'I just took it because I liked all I'd heard about him.'

'We won't ask your real name,' the massive gang leader promised.

'I wouldn't want *anybody* to,' *Rapido* stated, this time speaking the unvarnished truth and putting a timbre of warning into his voice. Then, adopting the aura of one determined to get down to business without further delay, he continued, 'Well, gents, do you want Comanch' and me to get the Chopper for you?'

'We do,' Turtle assented, after having glanced at and received nods of confirmation from his fellow gang leaders; all of whom had shared his unspoken disinclination to use one of their own men for the task. 'But I thought you professional kil—gentlemen of your occupation—never went up against one another?'

'I'd bill my own mother if the price was right,' the small Texan declared. 'And I reckon the price'll be *right* for

76

Comanch' and me to take out the Chopper.'

'It *will* be,' Turtle asserted. 'The only trouble is, if what I've found out is correct, you may have to go to England to get him.'

CHAPTER SEVEN

I WAS WORRIED FOR
YOUR SAKE

'ARE you all right, Lady Herban?' asked a masculine
voice.

'Rather better than that slut you provided is, I'd say,' a
feminine speaker replied, her voice implying satisfaction.
'She'll be feeling *far* worse than I do.'

'You certainly roughed her up good and proper, Your
Ladyship.' the man went on, but his tone held no suggestion
of sympathy for the recipient of the 'roughing up good and
proper'; rather the opposite, in fact.

'I did rather, didn't I?' the woman admitted. Then, her
tone suggesting she was indifferent over the possibility of an
answer in the affirmative, she inquired, 'You didn't mind me
doing it, did you?'

'Not at all,' the man answered. 'In fact, Nickerson's been
getting idle recently and needed to be taught a lesson. But I'll
admit, even though you told me about those unarmed combat
lessons you've been taking, I was worried for *your* sake when
you asked if you could have a go at it with one of them. That's
one reason why I picked on her and told her to take it easy on
you. She's done them before with the other girls and, being
idle like I told you, I reckoned I could count on her not to be
too rough.'

'You didn't need to tell her to "take it easy" on *my* account,
Churgers,' the woman protested, in a way which indicated
she considered the other a social inferior. 'As you saw, I know
how to take care of myself. By the way, considering what I did
to her, I don't suppose there's any danger of her complaining
to the police?'

'You've got nothing to worry about on that score. She may
be stupid as well as bone idle, but knowing what'd happen to
her if she did, she's got more sense than try anything like
that.'

'I'm pleased to hear it. Somehow, I don't think my *darling* husband would be any too pleased if he should get to kn—Not that he would give a *hoot*, of course, Churgers. We go our *separate* ways and—!'

'I understand, Lady Mary,' the man claimed, as the woman's amendment to what she had clearly realized—almost too late—would have been a most indiscreet remark was brought to an equally indecisive end. His tone indicated his understanding of all its ramifications, and that he was seeking to reassure her. 'And you don't have noth—*anything* to worry about from Nickerson.'

'Or *anybody* else, I hope,' the woman said and there was a note of warning in her voice.

Without either speaker realizing it, their conversation was being overheard by the attractive girl they were discussing!

Having finished drying herself, after taking a shower which had done little to relieve her suffering, Molly Nickerson had crossed to where her underclothing lay on a chair at the dressing-table. The words came to her through the wall which divided two of the small rooms provided for the benefit of entertainers appearing at the Pinhole Club on Leicester Place, not far from Leicester Square, in London. Despite the words being a trifle muffled, she could identify the speakers by their voices.

Although they had met for the first time that evening and only exchanged a few words, there was a *very* good reason why the beautiful and shapely girl was able to recognize the upper class accent of the aristocratically named woman next door. Furthermore, having been employed by him ever since she was brought into what—due to a disinclination to accept any kind of gainful occupation which entailed work—had become her main occupation, even the unusually solicitous tone used when the first question was put would not have prevented her from knowing it was William Maxwell 'Billy' Churgwin speaking. Regardless of his efforts to conceal it with a more cultured timbre for the benefit of the wealthy clientele drawn to the club, there was no mistaking his nasal Cockney intonation.

A growing sense of resentment and annoyance assailed Molly, caused by the disclosures she heard whilst eavesdropping. It was aggravated further by the sight of her face reflected in the mirror of the dressing-table. She had known

79

while taking the shower that her right eye was closed to no more than a puffy slit. Now she could see there was a blackened discolouration around it which, in conjunction with her badly swollen top lip, would not help her regular business. Nor, because of what had happened to her at the hands of Lady Mary Herban, was she in any condition to think of going and attending to it. What was more, even if she felt like arriving at her usual 'pitch' with every muscle and fibre of her shapely body giving off a dull, throbbing ache, there was no way she could conceal the facial injuries sufficiently for her to attract the kind of customers who paid best.

Being as as lazy as Churgwin had claimed, Molly was normally not vindictive by nature. In fact, even when engaged in the kind of activity by which she had—albeit with reluctance, due to the strenuous activity it involved, —recently started to supplement her earnings as a prostitute in the wealthiest part of the West End, the other participants belonging to her profession considered her to have a pleasant disposition. However, what she had overheard aroused her to anger and a desire to be avenged upon the cause of her misfortunes.

Having seen the reaction of the other customers when two 'ladies of the evening' were separated after having come to blows in the main dining-room, Churgwin had decided—in his capacity as owner—such a thing offered an opportunity to provide an unsual form of entertainment which he felt certain would be much appreciated by his wealthy clientele. Therefore, after the pair had been allowed to resume hostilities and settle their difference of opinion, he had announced that in future the Pinhole Club would hold a 'Cat Fight Night', featuring similar events, at regular intervals. As 'apartment house' and mud wrestling would be a few decades later in the United States,[1] the 'sport' had caught on and ensured a full house every time it was offered.

Finding 'combatants' had not been difficult for a man who controlled the majority of the prostitutes working the West End. They were supplied from members of his 'stable' and supplemented by girls in the lower echelons of the theatrical world eager to earn payment for making appearances. While they were required to give realistic and vigorous perfor-

1. *A description of 'apartment house' wrestling is given in*: THE SHERIFF OF ROCKABYE COUNTY.

mances, Churgwin, wanting to avoid repercussions from the law, had warned them to keep their aggressive tendencies under control while performing and avoid inflicting pain that would cause tempers to be lost. He had also taken precautions to reduce the chances of even an accidental serious injury.

Molly was a compulsive gambler, and despite the not inconsiderable remainder of her earnings after Churgwin had deducted his 'cut', she was sufficiently in need of extra money to acquire it by volunteering to take part on 'Cat Fight Nights'. Until her recently ended 'bout', she had found it a satisfactorily lucrative—although more strenuous than she liked—way of increasing her income. Like the other girls involved, she had felt no animosity towards her 'opponent' and none of the previous events had gone beyond tussling with as little pain inflicted as possible. Even the added titillation of having clothing torn off, which distracted the male customers in particular from noticing the lack of serious efforts at harming one another, was brought about as painlessly as possible by having their garments suitably weakened at various points.

Such conditons had not prevailed that evening!

On arriving at the Club, Molly had been told that her 'opponent'—a girl with whom she had worked twice previously and knew to be experienced in all aspects of the 'sport'—could not come. Having a substantial gambling debt for which a bookmaker was demanding payment, she had raised no objections when she was asked to take part in a bout with Lady Mary Herban who wanted to participate. Knowing how the wealthy customers were always seeking some new form of experience, or thrill, she had not been surprised at such a request. On the other hand, needing the 'appearance fee' and feeling confident she could deal with any pampered member of the upper class, she had felt sure that she would have nothing to fear from accepting the aristocratic beauty as a subsitute for her absent opponent.

Once the bout started, the girl had quickly found it was far different from those in which she had previously participated. The way she had been sent crashing to the well padded floor with a wrestling throw, was dragged up by the hair and was sent down again, warned she was not involved in the usual kind of lively and yet friendly tussling. In fact, it was a serious fight which the other woman was clearly intent on winning.

What was more, her earlier belief that she would have nothing to fear from a sensation seeking 'posh bird from Up West' had quickly been dispelled.

Not only had Lady Mary proved far stronger than Molly expected, but she also appeared to possess a knowledge of fist fighting as well as wrestling, which had put Molly in serious difficulty before she realized the full extent of the danger. By the time she knew what she was up against, although she fought back vigorously and, in part, repaid some of the suffering being inflicted upon her, she was too weakened to stave off the inevitable defeat. It had not come quickly and, before she was rendered *hors de combat*, both had had their attire reduced to just badly torn stockings and French knickers. Furthermore, this time when—she was carried out at the conclusion of the fight as she had been on those previous occasions, when she took her turn at 'losing'—she really had been rendered unconscious by a knock out blow.

Brought around in the smaller of the dressing-rooms by a doctor from the audience, the girl had been told she was not seriously hurt. However, although sore and aching, she had refused the offer of a sedative. Instead, left to her own devices, she had taken a shower and was about to dress when the conversation between Churgwin and Lady Mary came to her ears. From what she had heard, not only had Churgwin known of the skill in unarmed combat acquired by her first serious opponent, but he had also been willing to let the fight take place in the hope that Molly would be 'taught a lesson'.

Regardless of her normally slothful and amiable nature, Molly was furious at the discovery. Looking at her reflection in the mirror, she swore that she would be avenged upon both Churgwin and the 'posh bird from Up West'.

However, the problem was, how to take the desired revenge? Molly felt sure letting Lady Mary's husband know of the incident would serve her purpose in that direction in spite of the fact that Lady Mary pretended he would not be infuriated or even interested in what had taken place, especially if he knew how scantily they both had been clad at the end of the fight. Nevertheless, one thing was obvious. Before she could do anything about the woman, her employer must be out of the way. There was, she concluded after a moment's thought, probably only one man who could effect his removal. Certainly none of her criminal associates would even make the attempt, no matter what inducement she offered. He was too 'big' for any of them to be willing to tackle.

The man whose name came to the girl's mind not only could, but would, willingly do what she required!

What was more, Molly believed she had all the inducement necessary to persuade Mr. J.G. Reeder to take on the task!

Getting dressed quickly, her resolve becoming stronger with the added suffering inflicted upon her shapely and aching body by the donning of her far from excessively thick garments—the clothes destroyed in the fight having been supplied for that purpose by the Club—the girl left the dressing-room. Nobody was in sight, so she went and knocked on the door of the manager's office. Receiving no response, she opened it and looked inside. Satisfied it was unoccupied, she closed the door behind her and hurried to the desk. A check on the directory supplied her with the number she required and, lifting the receiver of the telephone, she dialled it. Listening for the slightest indication of anybody being about to come in, or even walking along the passage outside, she waited with baited breath for somebody at the other end to answer.

* * * * * * * *

'THAT was a most impressive display this morning, Colonel,' commented what appeared to be the youngest of the four men seated around the table in the dining-room of Daffodil House. 'Of course, it will need a considerably better aeroplane before it reaches its full potential.'

'The trouble with you military chaps, John—with no disrespect to you and our honoured guest, of course,' put in the one who gave the impression of being the second youngest and who bore a strong family resemblance to both the previous and the next speaker. 'Is that you will insist on getting ready to fight your *next* war with equipment based upon what could have been useful in the last. Don't you agree, Jimmy?'

'Yes, I am inclined to -um- agree with you, Jason,' asserted the host of the dinner party who was, apparently, the oldest of the quartet. 'As I believe the late and -um- unlamented Crazy John Flack is said to have pointed out with regards to the Encyclopedia Of Crime he wrote while -um- incarcerated in Broadmoor, because of the strides forward science is continually making, its doubtless plethora of information would only be of use for a few years at the most.[2] And the same applies to the development of -um- military devices.'

To the other residents of Brockley Road, the occupant of Daffodil House was a source of pride in one respect and an irritant in many others. For one thing, although he had a lengthy occupancy which extended for a great many years—generally a condition calculated to grant acceptance in such a middle class, middle management portion of suburbia—he had what most of his neighbours considered to be less than desirable traits. For one thing, even in an area where casually dropping in for a cup of tea and a chat—known to be a trait of the lower classes—was not regarded as socially acceptable, he was accounted stand-offish in the extreme. With only two exceptions, he had never consorted on friendly terms with anybody in the vicinity.

Considering the difference in age involved, the first association had hardly been calculated to meet with the approval of the other residents. However, Miss Margaret Belman had taken employment elsewhere and, as a subsequent announcement in the *Times* proclaimed, had married somebody else.[3] Later, although he apparently shared a no longer practiced interest in raising chickens, and had helped his next door neighbour out of a serious predicament, even John Southers had never been granted access to his home.[4] Every attempt by others to become more closely acquainted had ended in failure. When requested to attend a function, no matter what kind, he invariably declined politely on the grounds that he had a previous and unavoidable engagement.

Like all their class, the residents felt an antipathy and resentment towards anybody who differed from the norm and who could not be classified as being either above or below their respective personal status. They preferred everybody to

2. *The exact words are recorded as being, 'I've put a fortune in the hands of any clever man—providing, of course, he is a man of resolution and the books fall into his hands at an early date. In these days of scientific discovery, what is new today is commonplace tomorrow.' See*: TERROR KEEP, *by Edgar Wallace.*

3. *How the association between Miss Margaret Belman and Mr. J.G. Reeder commenced, and progressed is told in*: THE MIND OF MR. J.G. REEDER *and* TERROR KEEP, *by Edgar Wallace.*

4. *What the predicament was is told in*: Part Three, 'The Case Of Joe Attymar', RED ACES, *by Edgar Wallace.*

be in a niche similar to their own and to which they could relate. Mr. J.G. Reeder of Daffodil House most definitely did not come into that position. The uncertainty he created was most annoying, all the more so because various things implied he almost certainly could claim—if he wished—a social standing superior to their own.

One could categorize Mr. Smith, bank manager, Mr. Brown, senior clerk for a long established stock broker, or Mr. Jones, owner of a chemist's shop in a suitable district: but where did one place a detective, particularly when his exact standing in that field had never been established. Over a great number of years, Mr. Reeder had been described in newspapers—even the exalted variety to which the neighbourhood subscribed and which was considered infallible on most issues—variously as a private detective, a consultant for the Bank of England, a member of Scotland Yard and an official in the service of the Director Of Public Prosecutions; but which of these occupations was the real one had never been definitely established. Not only had Mr. Reeder himself proved unapproachable for supplying the requisite information, but his domestic employees—generally a source for the satisfying of curiosity—were equally uncommunicative. His housekeeper was not the kind to exchange confidences, even with those in a similar position to her own. Nor, as they did not live on the premises and disclaimed all knowledge of his affairs, were his maid and gardener any more helpful when questioned.

Mr. Reeder offended local susceptibilities in another way. Everybody else in the neighbourhood followed long established conventions regarding their attire, especially those who—as he did—had employment which took them into what was generally referred to as 'the City' and meant that area of London wherein its main business and financial interests were based.

Even when inclement weather caused Mr. Reeder to add either a mackintosh or an overcoat—each equally old fashioned and the latter *embellished* by a long woollen scarf which was regarded with even greater revulsion—his clothing was invariably as archaic as his physical appearance. Almost six foot in height, with a lean frame, his sandy side-whiskers, rather outstanding ears, mournful cast of features and fairly prominent nose—upon which, secured to the lapel of his jacket by a silk cord, steel rimmed *pince-nez* spectacles perched so far down it was impossible for him to see through them without adjustment—combined to imply he was no longer in the first flush of youth. His attire was of a style which had been practically *de rigueur* for the bailiff of a County Court, or a coroner's officer, in an earlier decade. He sported the kind of high and flat crowned black bowler hat which had ceased to be fashionable several years ago. Nor was his black frock coat, buttoned tightly about him as if to deliberately emphasise his slender frame, any more up-to-date in its cut. Furthermore, a ready-made black silk cravat of the broad 'chest protector' pattern—buckled under a white 'Gladstonian' shirt collar—narrow legged trousers and black, square-toed boots added to the general impression of advanced middle age. His sole concession to modern trends was a tightly rolled umbrella which he always clutched in his right hand when he was to be seen beyond the boundaries of his property.

There was still another factor about Mr. Reeder which aroused resentment. It went beyond his unconventional appearance, or whether a detective—no matter what his exact status might be—could be considered an acceptable member of their community. Some claimed his presence in the area would act as a deterrent to thieves and other undesirable elements. A second school of thought were of the belief that his being there tended to lower the tone of the neighbourhood.

No matter which point of view was held, all were in agreement on one subject!

A noisy neighbour of the normal kind could be the subject of complaint!

However, how did one deal with a person who—while never rowdy himself—had had a man shot to death on his doorstep,[5] or was himself subjected to an assassination bid by gun fire from a passing car?[6]

On the subject being raised by a deputation of residents in the street, not even Mr. Green—in his capacity as senior clerk to a noted barrister—could supply an answer. Lacking any

---

5. *Told in*: Part Two, 'The Shadow Man', MR. J.G. REEDER RETURNS, by Edgar Wallace.
6. *Told in*: 'CAP' FOG, TEXAS RANGER, MEET MR. J.G. REEDER.

legal precedent for objections and, perhaps, unwilling to risk arousing the animosity of one who might be able to instigate reprisals of an unpleasant nature, they had elected to take the easy way out and leave their perhaps undesirable, albeit apparently illustrious in some circles, fellow resident to his own devices.

Despite the decision, or rather because of it, the neighbours took an overt interest in the doings of Mr. Reeder. They avidly devoured every reference to him in the newspapers and on the radio, pretending to enjoy his successes and revelling in reports of his occasional failures. Furthermore, every visitor he received was subjected to a surreptitious scrutiny.

Therefore, that evening, more than one set of curtains had been parted a trifle so that the person behind them could satisfy his or her curiosity when two cars had drawn up in front of Daffodil House. Not that any of them could identify the callers, even though all had been visitors on more than one occasion in the past. Two, looking to be respectively in their late-forties and mid-thirties, bore a physical resemblance to Mr. Reeder and were commonly believed to be his sons. If this was the case, neither had inherited his sartorial tastes. Like the third man—who was shorter, somewhat older, with a distinctly military bearing similar to that of the younger—they wore excellently cut semi-formal evening wear of the latest style.

While Mr. Reeder and his guests had been aware of the furtive scrutiny to which they were subjected, none of them cared greatly about it.

Having eaten an excellent dinner, the party were discussing the events of the day. After their host had told of his activities, Colonel Brian Besgrove-Woodstole, D.S.O., M.C. and Bar, had described a demonstration of a proposed addition to the equipment of the Royal Air Force which he and Major John Gray had witnessed that afternoon. Based upon a development of American aircraft designer, John M. Larsen, it was a two-seater aeroplane carrying no less than twenty-eight Thompson submachine guns with one hundred round drums mounted—twelve pointed slightly forward, six directly downwards and ten inclined slightly to the rear—in its belly and intended as a ground attack weapon.

The comments from Jason Grant and Mr. Reeder had changed the direction of the conversation!

'They never did find that blasted Encyclopedia of his, if it ever existed, did they?' Colonel Besgrove-Woodstole inquired.

'It -um- existed all right,' Mr. Reeder replied. 'In fact, he let the Governor see one of the -um- sixty-three—I believe it was—volumes he had written by hand.'

'Then why didn't the Governor confiscate them?' the Colonel demanded.

'He tried,' the elderly looking detective answered. 'Unfortunately, by the time he had read the first and realized the -um- potential of them, they had all been spirited away and have never been seen since.'

'They weren't anywhere to be found around Charles Wagon's place when we finally finished him off,' Major John Gray supplemented, the dinner party being to celebrate his recent promotion to that rank. 'And his daughter claimed he'd had them destroyed when we questioned her.'

'Do you believe her?' Besgrove-Woodstole wanted to know.

'Far be it for me to doubt the word of a -um- lady, though that is hardly how I would describe Miss Olga Flack,' Mr. Reeder said, the question having been directed to him. 'But if she should tell me that Monday is the day before -um- Tuesday, I would immediately check upon the calender to verify it.'

'Nobody in the underworld believes they were,' Jason Grant declared. 'In fact, from all I've heard, it's the ambition of every criminal to lay his hands on the—!'

'Excuse me, Mr. Reeder,' said the large and grim looking woman whose knock and entrance had caused the interruption. 'But there's a telephone call from a girl. She won't give her name, but I think it's one you should take.'

'Very well, Mrs. Grible,' the detective responded, showing no hesitation before accepting the summation given by his housekeeper. Shoving back his chair and rising, he continued, 'Excuse me please, gentlemen. I shouldn't think this will -um- take long.'

CHAPTER EIGHT

YOU'RE JUST WHAT *SHE* WANTS

'MR. REEDER?' Molly Nickerson said, when a masculine voice replaced that of the gravel toned woman who had answered the telephone call she was making.

'It is,' replied the man at the other end of the line. 'May I -um- enquire to whom—?'

'No, you *can't*!' the girl interrupted. 'But I've got something to say you'll want to hear.'

'Carry on, my dear,' Mr. J.G. Reeder authorized, knowing the procedure required by such a call and refraining from pressing the matter of identity.

'Not on the blower,' Molly refused, darting a worried glance at the door of the office. While she had heard nothing to disturb her, she was disinclined to spend any longer in conversation with the detective than was absolutely necessary. 'I'll tell it to you opposite the Essex Head on Essex Street—Do you know where it is?'[1]

'I do,' Mr. Reeder confirmed, his speech quicker than usual as past experience led him to conclude—correctly—that the caller had a sound reason for not wanting to make an extended use of the telephone.

'Can you be there by half past twelve?'

'Yes. But how will I know you?'

'I'll know *you*!'

'Is there any danger for you?' Mr. Reeder asked, knowing Mrs. Grible would have followed their established procedure by trying to have the source of the call traced and seeking to gain time for this to be done.

---

1. *By a remarkable* coincidence, *the Essex Head public house on Essex Street, London, WC2, had its name changed to the 'Edgar Wallace' some years after this narrative and we had the privilege of attending the pre-opening reception.*

'Only if I get caught on the blower,' Molly assessed. 'Will you come?'

'I will,' the detective promised. 'But it might be safer for you if you tell me from whence you are speaking.'

'I'll tell you that when I see you,' the girl countered and hung up the receiver with shaking fingers.

It was not until Molly had removed her hand that the enormity of what she had so impulsively done struck home. She had been born and raised of a law abiding family, with no criminal connections, in the respectable London district of Hanwell. However, since her disinclination for honest toil had led her into prostitution—in addition to having sought to remove all traces of her inborn accent from her voice—she had come to know much about the unwritten code of the under-world. Therefore, she was aware one rule more than any other was considered inviolate—even if frequently broken—by habitual criminals. It was that nobody informed upon any other person. Having seen what happened to a 'nose' who was caught out in his transgression, she had no desire to fall victim to such a fate.

Wondering if the revenge she sought to attain against Lady Mary Herban and William Maxwell 'Billy' Churgwin was worth the risks involved, the girl hurried to the door. Opening it and peering out with what she believed was sensible caution, yet which would have aroused suspicions if she had been seen, she satisfied herself it was safe for her to leave. A glance at her wristwatch informed her that she could reach the rendezvous which she had suggested to Mr. Reeder easily in the time she had allowed. However, she was disinclined to remain in the Pinhole Club. Hurrying to the dressing-room, she collected her evening cloak and handbag. Donning the former, she was grateful for it having a hood which would not only hide the damage inflicted by the upper class woman in their fight, but could also be drawn forward far enough to conceal her features as she waited for the detective near the Essex Head public house.

Without realizing it, being unacquainted with most aspects of the way in which the Pinhole Club was run, Molly had made a terrible mistake when using the telephone in the office of the manager!

If the girl had confided in Mr. Reeder with regards to the location from which she was making the call, even though it would have been too late to prevent her committing the error, he could have warned her of the danger she had created for herself!

Nevertheless, as it was, Molly did not remain oblivious to her peril for long!

Hurrying downstairs, the girl suddenly found herself confronted by three formally dressed men forming an arrowhead formation which prevented her passing between them!

Although the lighting was far from brilliant, Molly recognized the foremost of the trio as the male victim of her intended betrayal!

Big and burly, dressed in immaculate 'white tie and tails', 'Billy' Churgwin had black hair plastered flat with bay rum and parted down the centre. His face was tanned, his nose suggested he had on at least one occasion participated in fistic activities. While his expression could soften and become subservient when consorting with the very wealthy customers of the Club, it was showing no such emotion at that moment. Rather he was looking as menacing as he always did when something had occurred to arouse his ire.

Deducing from past experience that her employer was angry, Molly was made even more uneasy at the sight of the two massive men who were following him. While they sported dinner jackets and black bow ties, by no stretch of the imagination would anybody have taken them for customers unless being of a most unworldly nature. Molly was certainly not unworldly and she knew they were two of Churgwin's 'minders'. She concluded that somebody was in trouble.

With a sense of chilling shock, the girl realised the person they were after was herself!

'Going somewhere, Molly?' Churgwin inquired, sounding almost mild.

'Home, Billy,' the girl replied, trying without too much success to prevent her consternation from showing. 'I don't feel up to going on my pitch after what that posh bird from Up West did to me.'

'So you're going *home*, huh?' queried the owner of the Club, who was also the controller of most of the criminal activities in the 'West End' and surrounding districts of London.

'Yes.'

'*Straight* home?'

'Y—*Yes*!'

'Not by way of the *Essex Head* then?'

'H—How did you k—*know*?' Molly gasped, her face going white except for the badly discoloured area around the closed eye.

'I do know and that's enough for you,' Churgwin snarled, without disclosing that he had a man permanently monitoring and recording all worthwhile calls passing in and out of the premises. 'So you're going to nose on me to that old bastard Reeder, are you?'

'N—*Nose*?' the girl croaked, attempting to give the impression that she had no idea what the term implied.

'*Nose*,' the gang leader repeated, then gestured with his right hand. 'Let's go back upstairs, shall we?'

'Go ba—!' Molly commenced, then opened her mouth to scream.

Before any such sound could leave the girl, showing the skill he had acquired as a boxer even though it had failed to prevent his nose being broken, Churgwin drove forward his left fist in a close to classic punch. Giving vent to a strangled squawk instead of the shriek she had intended as the knuckles sank into her midriff, Molly folded at the waist. Catching her by the shoulders, he twisted and slammed her head first against the wall. Supporting her as she was rendered unconscious for the second time that night, he scooped her into his arms. Then, glancing behind to make sure they were not being observed, he carried her towards the floor from which she had descended. Taking her into the office of the manager, he tossed her to the floor with no more care than if he had been handling a sack of rubbish.

'What're you going to do with her, boss?' the taller of the minders inquired, his badly slurred voice suggesting he too had spent time in a boxing ring although not as successfully as his employer.

'This's'd be a good chance to get old Reeder,' the second estimated, speaking in a similar fashion to his companion. 'He'll come to Essex Street like she told him, then we can duff him up good 'n' proper.'

'You don't reckon he'll go there alone, do you?' Churgwin challenged. 'No, we'll leave him to the bloke I've got coming from America. He should be arriving any day now and I've heard he's the best there is in Yankee-land'

'Polly Agathy's downstairs with a "can" she's going to con, boss. Why not send her to tell him the tale?' the first minder remarked, his manner helpful. 'You could lumber Lou Birsktone for one of his "naughties" by having her reckoning that's what she'd asked him to come and hear.'

'We're not dealing with some thick flatfoot on the beat, nor even a busy out of "the Yard",' Churgwin pointed out derisively, making it clear that his disinclination to accept these suggestions was not because the female confidence trickster in the dining-room was already working on an intended victim. He had considered and discarded, on the grounds he had just stated, a similar idea for using Pauline 'Polly' Agathy—the carrying out of whose activities in the West End was to a great extent dependent upon his good offices—to supply information which could bring about the arrest and removal of a rival gang leader. 'Polly might have conned that "can" Educated Evans out of his winnings,[2] but Reeder'd go through her like a dose of salts if she tried to tell the tale to him.'

'Then what're you going to do about him, boss?' the second burly man wanted to know.

'*Nothing*,' Churgwin replied, his manner brooking no argument on the subject. 'Let the old bastard go to Essex Street. He won't find her there and he'll even be too late to get a drink at the Essex Head. Maybe if he hangs about long enough waiting for her to show up, he'll catch his death of cold and snuff it.'

'That'd be handy,' rumbled the taller minder, then jerked a thumb towards the motionless girl on the floor. 'What's going to happen to *her*, boss?'

'Don't you worry about *that*!' the gang leader commanded. Then, bending down to pat Molly on her bruised cheek, he went on enigmatically, 'You're just what *she* wants, my girl!'

* * * *   * * * *

'WAS it a wild goose chase, Jimmy?' asked Jason Grant, as he sat over coffee with Mr. J.G. Reeder and Major John Gray after, as was always the custom in such cases, they had finished their breakfast without making any mention of the events of the previous night.

'I'd be inclined to -um- say *not*,' the elderly looking detective assessed, then looked at the fourth occupant of the room. 'What do you think, Mrs. Grible?

To anybody unacquainted with the true situation, the consultation with the woman hovering in the background who had

---

2. *Told in*: Part One, 'A Change Of Plan', GOOD EVANS, *by Edgar Wallace*.

produced the excellent breakfast might have seemed surprising!

Almost six foot tall and weighing in the region of two hundred pounds, none of which was flabby fat, Mrs. Jane Amelia Grible was hardly likely to arouse the speculations of even the most suspicious minded or fault seeking neighbour in regards to her exact relationship with her employer. Framed by dark brown hair invariably seen in a tight and unflattering bun, her face surmounted three chins. She had a somewhat masculine nose between a tight mouth that was *never* brightened by even the slightest touch of lipstick, and her chilling blue eyes made her far from beautiful by any standards. Her attire was always of a sombre black, with little adornment and nothing even remotely approaching frivolous. Her clothes were tailored in a style calculated to avoid creating even the slightest suggestion that she was trying to arouse the instincts of *any* man sexually. Therefore, despite her having been Mr. Reeder's housekeeper for a number of years, *nobody* even for a moment considered there might be some closer relationship involved.[3]

'She sounded right to me, sir,' the housekeeper stated, her voice deep and gravelly, but giving not the slightest suggestion as to which part of England she came from.

Aware of the inherent danger in responding to a request which had come from the anonymous female caller, Mr. Reeder was far too experienced to take it at face value. Donning simple disguises, with the aid of old clothes from the extensive wardrobe maintained at Daffodil House for such occasions, his three guests had armed themselves with handguns out of the armoury concealed in the sturdy wooden plinth supporting a particularly revolting bust of Napoleon which stood to the right of the front door.[4] Having made these preparations, they had taken their cars and preceded him to

3. *Information regarding the exact status of Mrs. Jane Amelia Grible is given in*: APPENDIX ONE.
4. *Edgar Wallace did not learn of the existence of the armoury whilst working on the various volumes of biography about Mr. J.G. Reeder. Therefore, he inadvertently claimed an air pistol and not, as was the case, a Webley & Scott Mark 1 .177 air rifle was used to frighten away two criminals lurking outside Daffodil House one night: see; Part Two, 'Kennedy The Con Man', RED ACES, by Edgar Wallace.*

Essex Street. By the time he arrived, they were positioned so they could cover and support him should the need arise. However, although they had waited for over two hours, the woman responsible for their presence had not put in an appearance. Nor had anything else happened to enliven, or otherwise break the monotony of their vigil. Colonel Besgrove-Woodstole had said he would go directly to his own home when they decided there was no point in waiting any longer, but the other two had returned with their host to Daffodil House. On their arrival, by common consent, they had elected to withhold any discussion of the matter until after breakfast that morning.

'They didn't manage to trace the call?' Jason Grant suggested rather than asked, knowing it was standard procedure to attempt to do so whenever people contacted the detective in such a fashion.

'I'm afraid -um- not,' Mr. Reeder admitted, his tone seeming to imply he was remiss in some way for the failure and was apologetic over what he must next confess. 'Nor, regrettably, was there any sound in the -um- background, I believe is the appropriate theatrical term, to help hazard a -um- guess as to her location while speaking with me.'

'What did you make of her voice, Jimmy?' John Gray inquired, aware the detective had an exceptionally good ear for such matters.

'She was a Londoner, although not born within the -um- traditionally accepted sound of Bow bells. Hanwell, rather than Hoxton, I would estimate,' Mr. Reeder replied and received a nod of support from Mrs. Grible. 'From working -um- class origins, with a family income and background approaching middle class. She had contrived to -um- irradicate all trace of her original accent, but it showed in the stress of the moment as she was speaking. And, at the risk of being -um- uncharitable, I would hazard a guess that she was a "lady of the -um- evening" —I believe is the term—if not actually a more actively participating criminal.'

'That's *likely*,' Jason Grant supported. 'Even if an ordinary shop assistant, or office worker wanted to tell you something, she'd hardly be likely to feel it necessary to arrange a meeting that way.'

'The thing is,' John Gray remarked. 'Did she really have something to tell you, Jimmy, or was it just a trick to try to lead you into an ambush?'

'I would be inclined to suppose she was -um- genuine,' Mr. Reeder assessed. 'Do you concur, Mrs. Grible?'

'I do, sir,' the housekeeper declared, without hesitation and exuding conviction.

'And, as she failed to put in the promised -um- appearance,' the detective continued, noticing without surprise that his guests showed a similar willingness to accept as worthwhile the support he had received from Mrs. Grible. 'I assume she changed her -um- mind, which I have been informed is the prerogative of a lady—!'

'Or?' John Gray inquired, despite being able to guess the alternative.

'Or she was *prevented* from coming,' Mr. Reeder obliged and there was an underlying timbre of grimness to his apparently mild voice. 'And I'm -um- afraid we all *know* what *that* means.'

'She's not been admitted to any hospital, sir,' Mrs. Grible claimed, proving she for one was aware of the ramifications if the woman had been detected in the act of making the telephone call and had set into motion the means to try and discover if this was the case. 'And so far no Division's reported to the Yard that what could be her body has been found.'

'Then let's hope *neither* happens,' Jason Grant said and everybody else present nodded in agreement.

'Assuming she *is* a "lady of the evening",' Mr. Reeder remarked, turning his gaze to the big woman. 'Would you be so good as to institute your specialized -um- enquiries as to whether any of them have gone inexplicably -um- missing, please, Mrs. Grible?'

'Certainly, sir,' the housekeeper promised and, although neither of the guests found the suggestion in any way out of the ordinary, the other residents in the vicinity of Daffodil House would have been amazed—and probably horrified—if they had been aware of how much knowledge and sources of information she had with regards to prostitutes and other female denizens of the underworld.

'And that, I'm -um- afraid, is all we can do about our mysterious caller for the time being,' the detective claimed in tones of sombre finality. 'That and await -um- developments.'

'Is there anything interesting in the newspaper, Jason?' John Gray asked, accepting without question the decision of his host that the matter under discussion was closed for the time being and indicating the unopened copy of the *Megaphone* lying near the other guest.

'Nothing of importance in the headlines, anyway,' Jason Grant declared, having picked up and opened the newspaper. Then his attention was caught by the picture of a man wearing a straw boater and with a blackened face standing waving from the gangway leading off a docked liner. 'Hum, I see that entertainer chap who calls himself "Haysoff Spades" is coming to appear at the Palladium, then go on a tour of the other major music halls. Do you know him, Johnny?'

'No,' the Major denied. 'He'd been transferred to American Military Intelligence before I was seconded from the Rifle Brigade, but he was certainly quite a chap from all I heard.'

'He's an excellent entertainer, too, by all accounts,' Jason Grant commented. 'We'll have to take the girls to see him on opening night if we can get tickets, Johnny.'

'That's a good idea,' John Gray assented, then looked at their host. 'Will you join the party, Jimmy?'

'I'll -um- decline, with apologies to your good lady wives, of course,' the detective said. 'Like Margaret and Jason, my taste for -um- entertainment is more on the lines of a Drury Lane -um- melodrama.'[5]

*   *   *   *   *   *   *   *

'GOOD afternoon, Mr. Gaylor,' Mr. J.G. Reeder greeted, answering the gentle buzz from the telephone on the desk in his sanctum at the office of the Director Of Public Prosecutions. 'I *hope* you haven't called to say you have -um- found the unfortunate young woman who called me last night?'

Although there had been no trouble on the way to, from, or at the appointed rendezvous the previous night, the elderly looking detective had been alert for the possibility of a delayed attempt to capitalize upon it. Therefore, he had taken the precaution of travelling from Brockley Road to Number One, Richmond Terrace and reaching his office in a way which would prevent any intended assailant from intercepting him. Knowing he would be informed if his mysterious caller should be discovered in either of the conditions envisaged by

5. *One occasion when Mr. J.G. Reeder indulged in his favourite form of entertainment is decribed in:* Part Five, 'Sheer Melodrama', THE MIND OF MR. J.G. REEDER, *by Edgar Wallace.*

Mrs. Grible, or if anything further should develop, he had given his full attention to the matter with which he had already been dealing. Lunch had come and gone, without any messages from his housekeeper or elsewhere until that moment.

'I'm afraid not,' replied the voice of Chief Inspector Frank Gaylor of Scotland Yard and a good friend. 'But I thought you'd be interested to hear about what's happened to Olga Flack.'

'I'm *always* interested in any and *every* -um- thing that happens to that particular young lady,' the detective admitted, with good cause.

Daughter of the deranged master criminal 'Mad' John Flack, the woman in question had inherited much of his intelligence and malevolent nature. Arrested for her involvement in the scheme which had resulted in her father's death,[6] she was serving a fifteen year sentence at Holloway prison. Although she had never given the slightest indication of it verbally, Mr. Reeder had sensed during the trial—and on the two occasions he had seen her since her incarceration—that she possessed a hatred for him equal to, perhaps even exceeding, that of her insane father. However, while he and Mrs. Grible—whose contacts with the female side of the underworld were even more extensive—had arranged for a watch to be kept upon her, she had shown no sign of being other than a model prisoner with no desire for revenge upon the cause of her misfortunes.

'You've lost an interest in that case,' Gaylor stated. 'She collapsed in Holloway this morning, showing all the symptoms of acute appendicitis. As they haven't any way of handling an operation of that kind in the nick, she was sent out to hospital. On the way, the ambulance crashed and caught fire. *Nobody* got out of it.'

'*Nobody?*' Mr. Reeder repeated. 'I trust you will forgive me for -um- asking, but I have this terrible perversion—!'

'Your "criminal mind",' the man at Scotland Yard supplied, as the detective paused.

'As you -um- say, my criminal mind,' Mr. Reeder confirmed. 'A most regrettable -um- affliction which I hope you will—!'

6. *Told in:* 'CAP' FOG, TEXAS RANGER, MEET MR. J.G. REEDER.

'There were a driver and a male attendant in front and a wardress in the back with her,' Gaylor interrupted. 'Four bodies were found in the wreckage and, although they're all charred beyond any hope of recognition, the pathologist says one of them is the right age, build and sex for her.'

'That *sounds* sufficiently -um- conclusive to presuppose we have finally seen the last of her,' the detective admitted. 'And, regrettably as it might strike some people, I find myself unable to feel the slightest sorrow over the -um- possibility.'

'Or me,' Gaylor agreed, with more feeling even though he had suffered less at the hands of the Flack family. 'And we should have heard the last of Crazy John's Encyclopedia of Crime now she's gone.'

'*Perhaps*,' Mr. Reeder replied. 'But it is my opinion, sharing the criminal mind, that there will always be those who harbour illusions and fairy tales and will therefore continue to hope to find that veritable cornucopia of illegality.'[7]

---

7. *One occasion when Mr. J.G. Reeder made use of the trait of criminals to 'harbour illusions and fairy tales' is described in:* Part Two, 'The Treasure Hunt', THE MIND OF MR. J.G. REEDER, *by Edgar Wallace.*

CHAPTER NINE

HE'S ONLY THE -UM- HOME GROWN VARIETY

'GOOD afternoon, Sergeant *Fog*,' Mr. J.G. Reeder greeted, with such warmth and apparent sincerity he might really have believed this to be the name of the man—ostensibly having just arrived on the boat train from Southampton in Hampshire—he had come to meet at the Southern Railway's passenger station at Waterloo. Shaking hands, he continued, 'Welcome to our -um- country and London.'

'Why thank you 'most to death, sir,' Sergeant Ranse Smith declared, also looking towards the press photographers who were lining cameras. Despite it being the first time he had visited the British Isles, he went on, 'And I'm rightly honoured to be *back again*.'

The meeting in so exposed and public a place, attended by reporters brought there by what a later generation would term a 'leak' deliberately passed to their respective newspapers, was a continuation of the attempt to bring the Chopper to justice!

Having been accepted for the task of removing the problems caused by their 'fellow hired killer', Sergeants Alvin Dustine '*Rapido* Clint' Fog and Mark 'Comanche Blood' Scrapton had sought to gain the confidence of Hogan Turtle by explaining how 'Comanche Blood' had been able to produce the Webley-Fosbery 'automatic' revolver in the Turtleback Cottage night club. Far from being annoyed over the deception played so capably by Rita Yarborough, the gang leader had praised her for the competence of her performance and stated that he considered her treatment of Beauregard Wiggins completely justified. Nevertheless, *Rapido* had decided it would not be politic to say he had struck the second blow—as a result of which the senior bodyguard was still hospitalized—harder than was absolutely necessary as a result of having heard of the attempted molestation upon a person for whom he had a mutually shared fondness and affection.

Such had been the amiability displayed by Turtle that, aware of how he and his contemporaries were eager to bring their very serious difficulties with the law enforcement agencies to a lower level if not a complete end, the young 'undercover' peace officers had become convinced that he was satisfied with the story he was told about the Texas Ranger supposedly having visited England posing as Alvin's *alter ego*, *Rapido* Clint. Certainly he had not shown the slightest hesitation before supplying them with all the information he had acquired and which might be of assistance to them in their assignment on behalf of himself and the other gang leaders.

While young, the two peace officers were too experienced at undercover work to ask many questions. In spite of that, Turtle had proved forthcoming in his desire to help them locate the man he wanted killing. Saying that the 'word' had reached him from an undisclosed source in New York, he had claimed that the Chopper had early anticipated the full extent of the animosity caused in law enforcement circles by the murder of Sergeants Jubal Branch and Hans Soehnen. Therefore, it seemed that he had considered a complete change of scenery was called for until things quietened down. Although he had never before left the United States, as far as it was known, he had accepted a contract for a killing which was passed to him via the leading crooked lawyer in London, England.

Unfortunately, the gang leader had been unable to learn the names of either the go-between for whoever was hiring the Chopper, or the intended victim. Nevertheless, Turtle had been positive the information was correct. Seeking additional verification, he had sent a message through the channels which could normally reach the killer. It had offered what he claimed was a lucrative contract, which he considered it advisable to have handled without involving any of his own 'enforcers'. Although no reason was given, the reply asserted that the Chopper would not be available for some time to come and would enquire at an unspecified future date whether the contract still needed to be fulfilled.

Contacting and discussing the matter with Major Benson Tragg, *Rapido* and Comanche had found he was in agreement with their supposition that Chopper had indeed accepted the offer from London. There was no way of guessing from which port in the United States he would sail. Nor was Turtle able to supply the information, which had been requested by the two 'hired killers' on the grounds that it would help them to carry out their task more quickly if they could catch their victim before he was able to leave the country. However, in spite of notifying the appropriate authorities in every major shipping city along the Eastern seaboard of the suspected departure, the commanding officer of Company 'Z' had decided not to wait until the results of all departing vessels being searched—whatever these might be—were reported.

Major Tragg had realized it was imperative for his men to travel to England at least as swiftly as the Chopper. Despite it having been decided that Rita should be included in the party, making the fullest use of his influential connections in 'high' places, he had arranged for them to be taken from Brownsville by the United States' Navy. While a destroyer would have been swifter, such vessels lacked the necessary fuel capacity to cross the Atlantic Ocean at full speed, so they were tansported aboard the latest cruiser. Having the requisite range, this was at least as fast as any passenger ship and had the added advantage of offering accommodation for the girl which would not have been so readily available in a destroyer.

In addition to notifying Scotland Yard that the professional killer might be coming from the United States, the Major had informed Mr. J.G. Reeder even more thoroughly. It was the elderly looking detective, possessing equally influential contacts in just as high places, who arranged for the party from Company 'Z' to be landed in the Royal Navy's dockyard at Gosport—not far from Southampton—instead of needing to come through a civilian port. They therefore avoided the usual formalities of passport examination and inspection by His Britannic Majesty's Customs and Exise officials. They had even been granted permission from a more powerful authority to bring their personal weapons with them.

For his part, the gentle seeming detective had had other things to occupy the attention of himself and his organization over the past few days besides making the arrangements for the arrival of the contingent from Company 'Z', Texas Rangers.

One matter had been trying to discover the identity of the anonymous female whose telephone call had taken Mr. Reeder on the abortive trip to Essex Street. From her sources,

Mrs. Jane Amelia Grible had learned that a prostitute, Molly Nickerson, had not been seen since the most recent 'Cat Fight Night' at the Pinhole Club. While the housekeeper was not acquainted with her personally, finding out where she had been born and raised—added to the discovery that she had had a reason to feel animosity towards William Churgwin, as a result of what he had allowed to happen to her—had suggested she might be the caller. While she had no previous record of having been an informer, 'ladies of the evening' like herself frequently learned of illegal acts. Feeling she had been treated badly, she might have decided to report some such discovery she had made about one or more of her employer's 'naughties' as a means of taking revenge.

Questioned about her absence, the gang leader had claimed she was sent abroad to take a holiday which was paid for by the woman at whose hands she had suffered an unexpected and severe beating in a bout on 'Cat Fight Night'. Lady Mary Herban when asked for verification, had asserted she was motivated by a desire to avoid unfavourable publicity, rather than generosity, as her victim had threatened to give the story of the fight to the newspapers. Further inquiries had established that a woman with the appropriate passport and answering to Molly's description had crossed the Channel by the New Haven-Dieppe ferry boat and given her intended destination as Paris. However, on checking at the instigation of Mr. Reeder, detectives from the *Surete* had announced that she had left the hotel at which she had taken a room without supplying any forwarding address and she had not been reported as seen since.

As far as Mr. Reeder was concerned, there had been an unexpected outcome from the report of Olga Flack's death having appeared in the newspapers. Although there had been no reference to it before from any source, he was notified by three usually reliable 'noses' that—shortly after having been incarcerated at Holloway Prison For Women—she had offered to present the 'Encyclopedia of Crime' written by her father to whoever killed the man she held most responsible for his demise.

That there should have previously been such reticence with regards to a matter of such importance to him came as no surprise to the gentle detective. Professional informers who would normally be willing to report the activities of even major criminals had always been afraid to do so where members of the Flack family were concerned. Its mentally deranged head had had a well deserved reputation for being able to inflict a most painfully lingering death upon anybody who aroused his ire and this mantle of menace had descended upon his daughter. However, now convinced there was no longer anything to fear with the last of the evil brood being dead, tongues were ready to wag. Although no names or other confirmatory evidence had been supplied by the informers, Mr. Reeder suspected three recent abortive attempts to kill him were carried out with the intention of earning possession of the collection of books.

Putting to use the faculties of what he frequently referred to as his 'criminal mind', which meant no more than he had a facility for following the frequently devious thought processes of those who broke the law, Mr. Reeder had formed a theory with regards to the disappearance of Molly Nickerson. However, before he was able to put it to the test, he had become distracted by the news of the offer made by Olga Flack. This in turn had been supplanted by the even more pressing information that the Chopper was coming to England with the intention of carrying on his murderous trade.

Considering the latest development to be of such importance it must take precedence over the other two, Mr. Reeder had sought to discover who had hired the American professional killer or—failing this—the identity of the intended victim. However, despite suspecting he could name the dishonest lawyer, he had felt sure there was nothing to be learned in that direction.

Wallace Oswald 'Wally' Marks, Solicitor and Commissioner of Oaths to give him his formal title—also known as a 'Getter-Out-Of-Trouble' and 'Putter-Up-Of-Jobs' to a large portion of what the popular press referred to as the 'London underworld'—was too well versed in all aspects of the British legal system to be tricked, persuaded, or otherwise induced to divulge the required information[1] Nevertheless, while calling to see him had been no more than a formality, the gentle

---

1. *Information regarding the later career and ultimate end of Wallace Oswald 'Wally' Marks is given in*: Chapter 16, 'The Passing of A Master Mind', UNDERWORLD NIGHTS, *by Charles Raven.*

detective had come away even more convinced in the validity of the news received from the commanding officer of Company 'Z', Texas Rangers.

Once again, the 'criminal mind' of Mr. J.G. Reeder had produced a theory upon which he was willing to act!

Suspecting he might be the proposed victim who the Chopper was coming to kill, regardless of there being numerous others with an equal desire to be avenged upon him, the gentle detective further surmised the possible motive. Nor did he believe the death of Olga Flack would prevent an attempt being made to earn the 'Encyclopedia'. She did not have the books with her in Holloway, so they were sure to be in safe keeping and, unless he was mistaken with regards to her warped mentality, arrangements would have been made to ensure her wishes would be carried out even if she should die before her purpose was attained. Despite knowing how little loyalty existed between members of the criminal fraternity as a general rule, especially in the event of the demise of one party, he was disinclined to rely upon the custodian deciding to make a healthy profit by disposing of the 'Encyclopedia' for monetary gain rather than as payment for vengeance extracted on behalf of a now dead woman.

Instead, Mr. Reeder had elected to try to lure a would be killer into making an attempt upon his life!

The coming of the Texas Rangers had offered what he considered could prove to be an ideal opportunity!

Communicating his wishes by radio to Major Tragg, the detective had secured co-operation for his scheme and his suggestions were passed to the young peace officers aboard the rapidly approaching cruiser!

On coming ashore at Gosport, in accordance with the arrangements made by their commanding officer and Mr. Reeder, Ranse Smith had parted company from Rita, *Rapido* and Comanche. While they were to make their way to London in transport provided by the detective, with Major John Gray acting as chauffeur, guide and mentor, the blond giant—his hair dyed black—had travelled on the boat train from Southampton as if his arrival had been in the conventional fashion, to be met at Waterloo Station by Mr. Reeder and in the presence of several newspaper reporters and photographers.

The pair made quite a contrast standing side by side!

The detective was clad in his usual fashion, the tightly

furled umbrella dangling by its crooked handle from his bent left arm, but his appearance was nowhere so much of an attraction for the newspapermen compared with the attire of his much younger companion.

Topped by a white Stetson with a leather band carrying silver *conchas* around its crown, Ranse had on an excellently tailored brown lightweight two piece suit of the latest Western style. His large bolo necktie was made from Navajo silver and turquoise in the shape of his home State and his white shirt was silk. On the wide and floral patterned brown belt around his waist was a gold plated buckle inscribed with the initials, 'A.D.F.' and his cowhand boots were fancily stitched. He had his badge of office suspended from the left breast pocket in plain view, placed there at the request of the photographers. However, so proficiently had the jacket been cut that—even when fastened, which it was not at that moment—it gave little indication of there being a Webley-Fosbery 'automatic' revolver in an open fronted, spring retention shoulder holster against his left ribs.[2]

Posing for the photographers, Ranse was impressed by the evidence of his host's obvious potential as a means of supplying 'copy' for newspapers. Even though the well known American entertainer, James 'Haysoff Spades' Ogilby, was also on the boat train—having arrived more prosaically and conventionally by the latest passenger liner to reach Southampton—he and Mr. Reeder were receiving considerable attention.

In spite of his thoughts, knowing why he and his companion had met in such a fashion, the blond giant was far from oblivious of his surroundings. Without needing conscious guidance, he was instinctively running his gaze over the men standing in front of them.

Since becoming a member of Company 'Z', Ranse's activities had caused him to face a similar situation involving members of the press on more than one occasion. However, even though two of these had occurred since the commencement of the scheme to gain information about the Chopper,

2. *Sergeant Ranse Smith had presented the second Webley-Fosbery 'automatic' revolver he owned to Sergeant Mark 'Comanche Blood' Scrapton when the latter had expressed interest in its specialized qualities for use as a close quarters defensive weapon.*

he had never grown accustomed to looking dispassionately into the impersonal glass lenses of cameras in the hands of press photographers. In fact, he invariably felt uneasy when doing so.

Thoughts of his dislike were driven from the blond giant's head by another of vastly greater importance!

One of the cameras was not showing the moulded convex glass of a lens where it should be!

Instead, there was only a black hole with what appeared to be a hollow tube inside the vacancy!

Nor did Ranse need to wonder about the meaning of what he was seeing!

'Look out!' the blond giant ejaculated and his right hand went swiftly towards the left side of his open jacket.

At the same moment, Mr. Reeder demonstrated he was equally alert to the danger and just as perceptive!

What happened next was further proof of the prescience shown by the gentle detective!

Concluding the bait he was offering might be taken and an attempt made upon his life, Mr. Reeder had implemented preparations to cope with it. One of these, knowing there might be shooting, had been to try to avoid endangering the lives of innocent bystanders. Before allowing himself and the big young Texan to be photographed by the assembled cameramen, as he had concluded this might be the moment selected for the assassination bid, he had made sure they were standing not too far in front of a trolley piled high with wooden boxes. In that way, he was satisfied there could not be anybody immediately behind them whose life might be placed in jeopardy should the eventuality he envisaged occur.

The precaution was fully justified!

Even as the blond giant spoke and Mr. Reeder sprang aside, moving with a rapidity surprising for one of his less than youthful appearance, there was a crash and flame erupted briefly from where the lens should have been on the camera which was held by a tall man in the centre of the photographers. The bullet expelled from the concealed heavy calibre revolver missed its intended mark, but only by a *very* slender margin. In fact, it struck and knocked the umbrella from the still bent left arm of the detective as he was moving away from his companion.

Seeing he had failed to make the hit he hoped for, the bogus photographer bounded backwards. Turning and starting to run, he flung the body of the camera from the Smith & Wesson Model of 1917 revolver—chambered for the British Service .455 Eley cartridge—which he had hidden inside it.

Twisting the Webley-Fosbery out of the retention springs of the shoulder holster, Ranse brought it from beneath his jacket with what appeared to the amazed onlookers to be close to blinding speed. However, as he was doing so, he discovered there was a very great and disturbing difference between the men in front of him and the kind of people to whom he was accustomed. Finding themselves in a similar situation, having a long history of gun fighting to guide their response, any crowd in Texas would have immediately and hurriedly taken the precaution of putting themselves out of the line of fire.

Lacking the requisite knowledge, the reporters and photographers let out yells of consternation, but refrained from performing such a basically self preservative course of action!

'God damn it all to hell!' the blond giant growled bitterly, as he saw the would be killer escaping through the intervening reporters and photographers who were preventing him from taking effective measures to halt the flight.

Letting out the profanity, Ranse set off in pursuit. He was followed by Mr. Reeder, who had drawn a Colt Government Model of 1911 automatic pistol from the holster tucked into the waistband of his old fashioned trousers, and was still moving in a remarkably sprightly fashion. As the crowd saw the massive figure of the blond giant approaching so precipitately, the far from small revolver seeming almost tiny in his big right hand, they began to clear hurriedly from his path. Two of them, fortunately reporters and not photographers, moved a trifle too slowly and were flung aside as he burst between them with no more apparent impediment than if they were infants rather than grown men.

Swiftly as the Texan and the detective had acted, by the time they emerged into the open, the matter of the escaping would be assassin was taken from their hands in no uncertain fashion!

Mr. Reeder had taken the precaution of having Jason Grant, Major John Gray and several detectives from Scotland Yard under the command of Chief Inspector Frank Gaylor, all suitably disguised to avoid attracting attention, and armed, mingling amongst the crowd at the station. However, although they were aware that the attempted killing had taken place, they too were restricted in their course of action by the people milling about them. Therefore, running with the revolver still in his hand, the would be killer was able to make his way unopposed through the main entrance. On doing so, he presented the foremost of his pursuers with an unrestricted view of him.

'Halt or I fire!' Major John Grant commanded at the top of his voice, skidding to a stop on spread apart legs and raising both hands to shoulder level and at arms' length he pointed his Webley "Pistol No. 1, Mark VI", a six shot revolver in spite of its name.

Although the man heard the order and made a turning halt, it was clearly not with the intention of surrendering. Instead, he began to raise his weapon into alignment. Conscious of the number of innocent people to his rear, the Major responded immediately. Sighting swiftly and with all his considerable skill, having drawn back the hammer to assist his aim, he fired in a way which he hoped would serve his purpose of protecting the public while also bringing about the capture of the intended killer. Such was his ability that, perhaps aided by a modicum of luck, the .455 calibre bullet he discharged struck the point at which it was aimed.

A shriek of pain burst from the man as the sizeable chunk of flying lead cut through his right leg. Throwing aside his weapon unfired, he spun around and started to go down. Before he landed on the ground, the drawn curtains of a black Daimler sedan towards which he had been running were eased apart slightly more than the small gap already in them. Emerging without there being any sign of the person holding it, a small automatic pistol spat four times. Each bullet tore into the torso of the already stricken man, but fortunately lacked the power to pass straight through. With the cocking slide operating to eject the fourth spent cartridge case, the pistol was withdrawn and the vehicle—which had obviously been waiting with its engine idling—was set into motion. It sped away from the station at a rapidly increasing speed and two police cars, awaiting such an event, failed to prevent it from gaining The Cut. It quickly made for Blackfriars Road with them in hot pursuit.

'This's the British model,' Ranse assessed, after he and the other peace officers had collected around the sprawled out body, gathering up and examining the discarded Smith & Wesson revolver. Tapping the words, '.455 Eley' inscribed on the barrel, which told him all he wanted to know, he went on, 'So, unless he's picked one up since he got here, I'd say this isn't the Chopper.'

'I'm inclined to -um- agree,' Mr. Reeder seconded, studying the face as his intended killer's already lifeless body was turned over by a detective. 'In fact, while I'm afraid I can't recall him to my -um- recollection, I should imagine he's only one of the -um- home grown variety.'

'Which means,' Jason Grant remarked pensively. 'Either somebody couldn't be bothered waiting for the Chopper to arrive, or there are more than one of them after Mad John's "Encyclopedia".'

'I fear it may prove to be the latter -um- alternative,' Mr. Reeder claimed with a sigh, and shook his head apparently in pained resignation. 'That is *one* of the penalties of being so -um- popular.'

CHAPTER TEN

I'D KILL YOU WHERE YOU STAND

'MR. MARKS?' queried the vaguely defined figure standing in the shadow of a shop doorway on a poorly illuminated section of Argyll Street between the Palladium Theatre and Oxford Circus.

'It is,' admitted the solicitor, glancing around to make sure there was nobody else in the immediate vicinity. The two 'minders' loaned to him by William Maxwell 'Billy' Churgwin, although close enough to reach him quickly should there be any need, were obeying his orders to keep out of sight. Having satisfied himself on both counts, he continued in his professionally unctuous manner, 'And may I ask who you are?'

'They call me "the Chopper",' the indistinct shape introduced, in a masculine American voice of a kind which a later generation would define as 'Mid-Atlantic' and which supplied no clue as to his regional origins. 'That's *all* you need to know.'

Despite having an extensive and *very* profitable association with most of London's major criminals, Wallace Oswald 'Wally' Marks felt as if an icy cold hand was running over him as he heard the name. It was the first time he had been brought into contact with a professional killer even close to the calibre of this man. He had followed instructions given to him over the telephone and had come to meet the killer shortly before midnight. Under different conditions, he would not have thought of obeying such a summons. However, the highly positioned gang leader in New York who had put him into contact with the Chopper had warned him that any conversation he might have with the professional killer would be in strict and anomymous secrecy. He had also been warned that he would be most ill advised to refuse to pander to the whims of the 'hired gun' and, when he considered the

111

nature and reputation of the man he was addressing, he had decided to obey the instruction about the rendezvous.

While holding a position in the legal profession almost identical to that of Counsellor Reece Mervyn in Texas, the dishonest solicitor was nowhere nearly so impressive a figure. Prematurely grey, with a sallow and pouchy cast of features even his mother might have been forgiven for not loving, he was tall although his rounded shoulders tended to make him appear smaller. He had a broad brimmed black slouch hat drawn forward over his face. The long black ulster he wore concealed an expensive dark purple three piece suit which, as was invariably the case with his everyday attire, was liberally smothered by cigarette ash. When he spoke, his breath gave off the sickly aroma of the cheapest Empire port—of the kind derisively known as 'jungle juice'—which he drank in copious quanties without it in any way impairing his faculties. In one respect, the Chopper might have considered it fortunate that they were not in his office. He always offered every client a glass of his favourite tipple and was reported to dislike being refused.

'As you wish, boy,' Marks assented, employing the usual form of address for his clients.

'*Boy?*' the American repeated, his tone menacing and indicating he was not enamoured of the designation.

'As you wish, *sir*,' the solicitor amended, surprised by the obvious resentment for a term which had been accepted without objections by such prominent luminaries of the London underworld as Billy Churgwin and Louis Arnold 'Lou' Birkstone. 'And may I ask why you asked to meet with me in such a fashion instead of coming to my chamb—?'

'Is *somebody* trying to pull a double-cross on me?' the Chopper interrupted, his manner indicating more than mere indignation.

'A *double-cross?*' Marks repeated, in a genuinely puzzled manner.

'That's what I said!' the American confirmed coldly. 'God damn it, the first thing I see when I hit this city of yours is somebody trying to gun down the feller I've been brought over to take out.'

'*You* were at Waterloo this afternoon?'

'If that's the name of the railroad depot I got down at.'

'I thought that might be what you wanted to see me about,'

112

Marks admitted, having heard about and conducted an investigation into the attempted murder and its aftermath of Mr. J.G. Reeder.

'Then *you* knew it was going to happen?' the Chopper challenged grimly.

'Certainly *not*!' the solicitor denied hurriedly, for once, with complete justification for his aura of innocence. 'But, with what's at stake, it doesn't surprise me that somebody else wants to have Reeder killed.'

'And just what *is* at stake?' the American asked.

'There's what you'd call a bounty been put on his head,' Marks explained evasively. 'And, with so many wanting him dead anyway, it's an added inducement for them to try to get him killed. I can assure you that Mr. Churg—your client—wasn't responsible. He's willing to leave it entirely up to you.'

'That's *real* smart of him,' the Chopper claimed dryly. 'Because I wouldn't be any too *pleased* if I found I'd been brought all this way and some smart-assed Limey son-of-a-bitch figured on cutting me out now I'm here.'

'I assure you that *isn't* the case,' the solicitor declared. 'In fact, when I mentioned I was meeting with you—but not *where* or *when*—he told me to ask if there was *anything*, money, female company, whatever you wanted and, to make sure you got it.'

'Have you found those two fellers I asked you to fix down for me?' the American inquired.

'Yes,' Marks confirmed and reached into the right side pocket of his ulster to extract an envelope. 'They're in here with your advance payment. It's half in sterling and half in dollars, as you requested.' .

'Thanks,' the shadowy figure said, but remained where he was, compelling the solicitor to move forward so that the offering could be accepted.

'And perhaps there's something *more* you'd like me to arrange for you?' Marks hinted, stepping back and wishing he was able to see anything that supplied a clue as to the identity of the hired killer. He was not averse to turning informer if the profits were sufficiently attractive.

'No, there's *nothing* else I need,' the American stated. 'Tell whoever's given me the contract that I'll get word when I'm ready to make my hit, so's he can get himself a real good alibi.'

'I will,' Marks promised, realizing with a sensation of

annoyance that the other man obviously considered their conversation was at an end and was dismissing him. Being used to receiving more deference from even prominent members of the British underworld, he found the attitude annoying. Therefore, wanting to avoid the impression that he was willing to accept such cavalier treatment, he went on, 'I heard that a Texas Ranger has arrived looking for you?'

'He could be,' the Chopper admitted in a disinterested fashion. 'It's been done before and I'm still around. Anyways, there's nothing more to say now so we might as well both be on our way.'

'Don't you ever worry when you meet somebody like this that they might have an electric torch in their pocket and shine it to see your face?' Marks inquired, still wanting to leave with the impression that the conclusion of the meeting was his decision.

'Not so's you'd notice it,' the American answered dryly, guessing that something of the kind had occurred to the solicitor. 'Because, if you *had* and *did*, I'd kill you where you stand'

* * * * * * * *

'YOU certainly introduced yourself to the British public in fine style, Ranse,' Rita Yarborough praised, waving a hand towards a pile of newspapers which she and the other occupants of the dining-room at Daffodil House had read before hearing a first hand description of the events at Waterloo Station. 'I can't think of *anything* you missed doing, apart from maybe spinning that big "six shooter" of yours around a few times on your trigger finger before you leathered it.'

'Shucks, that's what comes of being brainy as well as all beautiful and shapely,' Sergeant Ranse Smith replied, adopting a spurious air of becoming modesty. 'Which I'm *all* of them, 'though I must 'fess up that I didn't think of doing *that*.'

'Bit I liked best, *amigo*,' drawled Sergeant Mark 'Comanche Blood' Scrapton, lounging at ease on a comfortable armchair and conveying much the same impression of latent deadly menace exuded by a mountain lion draped over a branch while resting, 'was that lil ole "sob sister" in the *Daily Express* saying you was "handsome, virile and redolent of the wide open spaces from which you came".'[1]

---

1. *'Sob sister', colloquial term for a female journalist specializing in articles of a cloyingly romantic nature.*

'Well I *am*, aren't I?' the blond giant enquired.

'That's what *Ranse* likes about him, Mr. Reeder,' Sergeant Alvin Dustine "*Rapido* Clint" Fog drawled. 'He's so *modest*.'

'I had noticed that most desirable -um- trait,' the elderly looking detective admitted, apparently in as sober a fashion as the comment had been put. 'It does him -um- *credit*.'

'Not *everybody* else does, though,' the girl claimed, losing all trace of levity from her voice. Picking up a newspaper with the tips of her right thumb and forefinger, as if it was something unclean, she went on, 'If you'd got a dog, Mr. Reeder, I could tell you a real *good* use for a tabloid like *this*.'

'I have heard one can -um- teach one's dog to pay attention to one's commands by tapping its nose gently with a -um- rolled up newspaper,' the detective answered, in his most mild—therefore *very* sardonic—tone. 'I presume *that* is what you have in -um- mind, young lady?'

'Well no, not *exactly*,' Rita corrected, tossing what she clearly considered to be a most undesirable object into the wastepaper basket. 'What I had "in -um- mind" was to spread it on the floor so the dog could shi—be house-trained on it.'

While Mr. J.G. Reeder had known the arrival of a Texas Ranger would attract attention, especially in view of his own involvement, the response had been far greater than he anticipated due to the thwarted assassination.

In addition to the formalities required by the incident, the detective and the blond—currently 'black' haired—giant had given interviews to the assembled reporters. Although a statement about the shooting had been taken from Mr. Reeder, the reporters and photographers had given far more attention to Ranse. They had asked him to repeat the drawing of his 'six shooter', as they insisted upon calling his Webley-Fosbery 'automatic' revolver. Receiving a nod of authorization from his companion, he had put aside his reluctance and obliged. While he did not consider himself particularly fast by the standards which still prevailed in Texas, acknowledging willingly—if not openly at that moment—that Alvin Fog for one was much more proficient in such matters, the onlookers had been very impressed by what they considered to be the exceptional speed with which he produced the big weapon from its place of concealment.

With the demonstration completed and the revolver returned to its holster, the blond giant had replied, when

115

questioned, that he was a 'tolerable good' shot; which was true enough. He had been amused by some of the other questions put to him. Admitting that he had indeed ridden horses since he was large enough to sit a saddle, he had gone on to point out that most of his duties which involved travelling were performed in a car or on a motor cycle, and that he was also a qualified pilot. One unexpected result of the latter disclosure was an invitation from 28 Squadron of the Royal Air Force's Fighter Command for him to be a guest at their Station near Brockley, Kent, and give an opinion of their latest aircraft. Being interested in all aspects of aviation, he had stated his intention of accepting if the situation permitted.

However, despite having had similar experiences in Texas with members of what a later generation would refer to as the 'media', Ranse was grateful when Mr. Reeder announced they must take their departure as there were reports needing to be made at Scotland Yard and he was sure his visitor felt in need of resting after having completed such a long journey.

Regardless of what the detective had told the newspapermen, he had not taken Ranse to Scotland Yard or even his own office. Instead, making sure they were not followed, they had gone directly to Brockley Road. Waiting until after night had fallen and coming by the rear way of reaching Daffodil House, as a precaution against being seen should the building be under observation, Major John Gray had delivered the rest of the contingent from Company 'Z'. After the necessary introductions had been performed, as had happened on the night of the abortive visit to Essex Street, it had been decided to leave all discussion of the day's events until the following morning. Nor, despite certain reports having arrived during the evening, had the decision been rescinded.

On assembling in the dining-room for breakfast, a study of the morning's newspapers had satisfied the party that there could now be few people throughout the British Isles who did not know 'Sergeant Alvin Dustine Fog'—related to one of the country's oldest noble families as a result of his paternal grandfather having married into it[2]—had come from America to help the famous detective hunt down a notorious professional killer.

2. *For information regarding the connection between Alvin Dustine 'Cap' Fog and the aristocratic British family, see: Item 5, APPENDIX TWO.*

Every newspaper and the British Broadcasting Corporation had given their version of the incident. The latter had requested an interview with the blond giant later that day and it had been confirmed he would oblige.

With one exception, the reports in the newspapers were favourable to the young Texan!

Impelled by the envy filled paranoiac hatred their kind were already developing towards the United States, the 'liberal' management of the *Daily Working Man* in spite of the fact that none of their representatives were present at the shooting and every other reporter having stated that 'Sergeant Fog' had only drawn his gun—with lightning speed was the most used description—and not used it, demanded in an editorial why an American 'gunman' was permitted to open fire upon a fleeing British citizen without being detained by the authorities, prior to being deported, for having committed such a heinous act. There was no mention of the fact that the victim was a notorious criminal whose speciality was killing for hire who had already attempted to ply his trade. They deplored the police—inevitably described as 'repressive implements of the privileged monied classes'—being allowed to carry firearms to 'the detriment of the public'. Nor did they mention that, when shot, the criminal had already turned upon his pursuers and was ready to open fire at them regardless of there being a large number of innocent people in the vicinity who might have been struck down by any of his bullets which missed their intended targets.

'Those crummy liber-radical soft shells all sound alike, no matter what country they hail from,' Comanche commented, for once speaking like the college graduate he was rather than the less well educated cowhand he generally pretended to be. 'Way they flap their lips, reckon there weren't any peace officers at all in that Russia they're all so fond of putting up as the most beautiful place in the whole world to live in.'

'What I can't understand,' Ranse declared, aware that his companions shared his annoyance over the comments in the 'liberal' newspaper. 'Is why, seeing as they're so all fired dissatisfied with living in their own country and being so shouting-out-aloud fond of it, they don't haul their butts to take up a home in Russia.'

'Quite,' Mr. Reeder said, agreeing with the points of view expressed by the girl and the two Texans. 'However, despite the -um- adverse comments in that most *inestimable* newspaper, I feel we have gone a *long* way towards achieving our primary purpose.'

'Then it's up to us next,' *Rapido* declared, looking pointedly from Rita to Comanche. Then, swinging his gaze to their host, he went on in a voice charged with seriousness, 'But from now until we get the Chopper, you go *real* careful, Mr. Reeder. There's only one thing we know for *sure* about him and that is he's damned good at his game.'

'I'll never let it out of my -um- thoughts,' the detective promised. 'What do we know about his -um- *modus operandi*, I believe is the foreign expression I am seeking?'

'Not a whole heap, and far from as much's we'd like to,' the smallest of the sergeants admitted, being acknowledged by the others as the spokesman for their party. 'Major Tragg's sent you a list of all his known killings, but just about all we've come up with from our studying of it is he mostly works in some kind of disguise and almost always makes his hit after sundown.'

'And he has never made a -um- "hit" anywhere other than in a large city,' Mr. Reeder remarked rather than questioned.

'Not so far as we know,' *Rapido* answered, suspecting—correctly he discovered later—that the Englishman had already made a thorough study of all the available information about the Chopper. 'At least, if he has, he's never spread the word to the big shot owlhoots thereabouts before, or told the local newspapers it was him who'd done the killing when he'd made the hit, like he does everywhere else we know he's been.'

'Could be he stays away from smaller towns because he knows a stranger'd be conspicuous in them and more likely to attract attention than in a big city,' Ranse offered.

'I must admit that is a -um- possibility,' Mr. Reeder conceded, almost pensively. 'However, let us *hope* he proves less -um- successful over here than he has in your country.'

'How about that yahoo who tried to make wolf bait of you at the railroad depot?' Comanche inquired, having reverted to the way of speaking he mostly employed when working undercover. 'Have you-all read his brand yet?'

'If you mean, do we -um- know him,' the detective replied, peering benignly at the maker of the equiry over what his guests realized was a totally unnecessary *pince nez*. 'The answer is in the -um- affirmative. Those detestable chaps from Scotland Yard informed me that he is -um- Herbert McPriest, a *most* unsavoury -um- personage from the North of England.'

'And *you* didn't recognize him straight away?' Rita challenged.

'Regrettably, my dear young -um- lady,' Mr. Reeder replied, his manner redolent of apology for having to make such a confession. 'I am *far* from being as -um- omniscient as people give me credit for. While I *suspected* his identity, but *nothing* more, I preferred to await verification from Chief Inspector Gaylor before making any -um- pronouncement.'

'Do you know who he was working for?' *Rapido* inquired, as amused as were his companions by the seemingly apologetic and close to dithering attitude of their host.

'Regrettably, I am again at the -um- mercy of my completely invalid reputation for -um- omniscience,' the detective confessed. 'However, I would be willing to ascertain—doubtlessly in -um- error—that it was either Mr. Louis Birkstone or Mr. William Maxwell Churgwin. Whichever of them in -um- fact, who has not hired the Chopper for what my -um- criminal mind leads me to assume, mayhap with undue lack of -um- modesty, is to bring about my -um- untimely demise.'

'Excuse me, sir,' Mrs. Jane Amelia Grible said, coming into the dining-room before any more could be said. 'Mr. Golden is on the telephone for you.'

'Thank you,' Mr. Reeder replied and, muttering an apology, he crossed to pick up the receiver of the extension on the small table by the door.

'It wasn't *bad* news, I hope,' Rita said, having seen how the detective had stiffened whilst listening to the person making the call.

'*Hardly*,' Mr. Reeder replied and, for once, he looked very much younger and virile than was the impression he generally conveyed. It was obvious he was not only delighted, but impressed by whatever he had just heard. 'His Majesty has graciously requested that he and the rest of the Royal Family pay a visit to our head—chicken farm in Brockley.'

'Do you know something,' the girl inquired, a twinkle in her eyes belying the sober way in which she spoke. 'You said a whole sentence without going "-um-" even *once*.'

'Goodness -um- gracious, did I?' the detective asked and there was no doubt about the merriment behind his seemingly pained expression. 'I really must -um- watch out. Why I might forget to carry my -um- umbrella next!'

* * * * * * * *

That there was to be a visit by the Royal Family to the property owned by Mr. J.G. Reeder was known to more than just the people most concerned!

News of the event had reached the last person whom the detective would have wished to become privy to it!

Less than four hours after Mr. Reeder was informed of the honour to be paid to his organization, this person contacted Billy Churgwin by telephone at the Pinhole Club, where he was making arrangements for another 'Cat Fight Night' that weekend. In spite of the mechanical distortion caused by the difficulties in which the conversation was taking place, Churgwin could tell the caller was finding the news to be of as great an interest as it was to himself; albeit for a vastly different reason.

'It gives me the chance of ruining *them* for all time,' the all too familiar feminine voice asserted to the gang leader.

'That's all very well,' Churgwin replied, wondering why his caller invariably referred to Mr. J.G. Reeder in the plural. 'But what about that Yankee bloke I've brought over here to get rid of the old bastard?'

'Let him do what he came for, *if* he can.' the speaker authorized, albeit in a manner clearly indicating she had grave doubts over the abilities of the hired killer. 'But, whether he does or not, I intend to go ahead with what I have in mind for Mr. Jeremiah Golden Reeder and all his family. It will pay them back for what they did to my dear departed father.'

CHAPTER ELEVEN

I ABHOR THE DESECRATION OF -UM- GRAVES

'MR. MARKS will see you now,' announced the smaller of the two female occupants in the shabby waiting room, its grubby wallpaper hardly enhanced by a garnishing of dusty framed caricatures depicting judges and counsel of bygone days. Her demeanour was that of one who considered herself to be conveying a favour by even addressing the visitors, and her middle class accent was redolent of thinly concealed disdain as she went towards the door from which she had just emerged, speaking over her shoulder, 'Walk this way.'

'I don't know how it is over here, *amigo*' Sergeant Ranse Smith commented *sotto voce* to Mr. J.G. Reeder, studying the sensual undulations of the woman's rear view. In order to continue the masquerade of being Sergeant Alvin Dustine Fog, he was dressed in much the same fashion as he had been at Waterloo Station the previous afternoon. 'But we'd get arrested for sure in Texas if we even *tried* to walk *that* way.'

Having a natural appreciation of the opposite sex, the blond giant concluded he could not remember ever having seen two such vastly contrasting women in one place as those who had greeted—with all too obvious suspicion and little discernible courtesy—the elderly looking detective and himself on their arrival at the 'chambers' of Wallace Oswald 'Wally' Marks, Solicitor and Commissioner of Oaths.

The office was situated in a less than salubrious area where the 'City' area of London joined the East End and, having once visited the scrumptiously luxurious offices of Counsellor Reece Mervyn in Austin, the premises came as quite a surprise to the Texan. Reached by climbing two flights of filthy stairs covered with threadbare linoleum, they gave not the slightest indication—apart, perhaps, from the appearance of one of the women in the waiting-room—that their occupant was a highly successful, albeit completely unscrupulous, member of the Bar who made far more money from his clients than was earned by his honest and law abiding contemporaries.

Petite, attractive, with platinum blonde hair cut in a frizzy pile, the shorter woman was expensively be-jewelled and dressed in the height of latest fashion. Her attire showed off her curvaceously trim figure *very* well, although feminine opinion—perhaps inspired by jealousy—might have considered her rather older than was regarded as 'proper' to be garbed in such a revealing fashion. Seen at close quarters, it was obvious the colour of her curly locks was retained by judicious use of peroxide and make-up could not entirely hide the slight coarsening time had given to her skin.

Unless possessing tastes of an unconventional nature, there was nothing about the other woman to attract male attention. In fact, Ranse concluded she was just about the most homely and formidably masculine female he had ever come across. She was close to matching him in height and, being built on very massive lines, conceivably weighed as much if not more. Her face, far from improved by a fuzz of almost moustache-like proportions on her top lip, was rugged to the point of appearing repellent. Nor did the heavy tweed coat and skirt, a man's white shirt with a stiff collar and tie and thick woollen stockings ending in blunt toed, flat heeled brown shoes do anything except emphasise the shapeless bulk of her figure.

Hiding his amusement over the comment made by his companion, Mr. Reeder followed the solicitor's senior private and confidential secretary across the waiting-room. Arriving at the door she had thrown open, still displaying indications of her distaste for finding it necessary to perform such a task, he ignored the pointed glance she directed at the hat and umbrella he was clutching in his hands as if afraid they might by snatched from him. Retaining his hold on them, he went past her with Ranse following on his heels.

'Thank you, Miss -um- Cornelius,' the detective remarked in passing, 'What a *splendid* place you work in. I'm *sure* you must be the -um- envy of all your friends.'

Having the door slammed behind them, without comment and receiving only a glare redolent of dislike close to loathing, Mr. Reeder and Ranse found themselves in the presence of the man they had come to see!

Sitting resplendent in a cigarette ash covered dark green

suit, in a saddle-back chair which was losing its stuffing, the solicitor was behind a massive desk of the kind which the blond giant had once heard described as, 'You'd have to be very poor, or very rich, to own it'. Obviously an antique, apparently it had never received the slightest care or attention to maintain its original condition. It was piled high with papers, files, a telephone, an open cigarette box, an ashtray so filled to overflowing with stubs it—like his deeply nicotine stained right first and second fingers—implied he was a chain smoker, and a partially depleted mate to the empty Empire port bottles seemingly tossed willy nilly about the floor.

'Good afternoon, Mr. Reeder,' Marks greeted sourly, putting down the glass filled with port which he had been sipping when his visitors were admitted by Miss Sylvia Cornelius. 'I can't give you *long*—!'

'Long enough one -um- hopes for us to conclude the business which brings us here,' the detective stated rather than suggested.

'Then I hope that won't take *too* long,' the solicitor declared and waved a grimy white hand. 'You'd better have a seat.'

'Thank you,' Mr. Reeder assented, dusting the chair he selected with deliberately offensive vigour before sitting on it.

'Drink?' Marks grunted, watching the blond giant occupy an equally musty looking ancient chair without the embellishment he knew had been carried out by his other unwelcome visitor to annoy him.

'Thank you, *no*,' the detective refused, aware that to do so rated as an insult where the solicitor was concerned.

'And to what do I owe the *pleasure* of this visit?' Marks growled, pushing aside his glass with a gesture redolent of unspoken animosity.

Studying the less than prepossessing features of the crooked solicitor, Ranse concluded he was *very* wary in the presence of a foe for whom he had considerable mistrust and no liking. The assumption verified the less than flattering comments made by the detective on the journey from the Director of Public Prosecutions' offices. Certainly there was no suggestion of friendly relations based on mutual respect for a worthy opponent in their association. On the other hand, the blond giant considered the reaction on the part of one so well versed in all aspects of evading the meshes of the British legal system was a tribute to the capability of the man he was accompanying.

'I have come to see you in your capacity as legal -um- counsel for Miss Olga Flack,' Mr. Reeder explained.

'As the lady is now deceased,' Marks pointed out. 'I can hardly be her legal counsel any more.'

'Of course -um- not,' the detective conceded, seemingly distressed by the error he had committed. 'However, I am under the impression, doubtless -um- erroneous, that you are the executor of her -um- estate, I believe is the accepted legal -um- term.'

'It *is* and I *am*!' the solicitor confirmed definitely and, watching him carefully, the big Texan saw he was becoming even more noticeably alert and warily hostile. 'So what do you want to know?'

'Are you *absolutely* certain she is now -um- *definitely* deceased' Mr. Reeder inquired with apparent mildness, but his air of seeming to be deeply distressed over having to raise such a point failed to impress or deceive either of his small audience.

'How do you mean?' Marks asked, reaching for and fingering absently at the almost empty glass of port. 'The coroner's jury found she was burned to death when the ambulance she was in crashed and caught fire.'

'They pronounced that the -um- bodies of *two* women inside the ambulance were burned to -um- death when it caught fire,' the detective corrected, if so strong a word could be applied to his apparently aplogetic deneamour. 'Which, in my humble -um- layman's opinion, is an entirely different -um- proposition.'

'Are you saying it *wasn't* Olg—Miss Flack—in the ambulance?' Marks challenged, knowing the older of his visitors was never more dangerous than when seeming most hesitant and ill at ease. 'Damn it all, I *saw* her body before it was buried!'

'I too was allowed to view the -um- remains,' Mr. Reeder reminded. 'But, although I too had had the dubious -um- honour of her acquaintance, all I saw was a body burned so -um- badly that identification was, at best, a matter of -um- conjecture.'

'*So?*'

'So I am afflicted, as you may well have -um- heard, with a criminal mind. This peculiar perversion, with which your

124

good -um- self is probably *not* endowed, leads me to speculate upon the possibility of there having been a -um- deception perpetrated?

'*Deception?*' Marks queried, staring at the elderly looking detective in a way which reminded Ranse of a rabbit confronted by a poisonous snake. 'In what way?'

'This is purely -um- speculation at the moment, I trust you will bear in -um- mind,' Mr. Reeder explained, his manner seeming to plead for forgiveness and understanding. 'However, it has come to my -um- attention that a "lady of the evening", Molly Nickerson to wit, went absent from her "pitch"—if that is the appropriate -um- terminology—?'

'That's what they call it,' the solicitor supplied, before he could stop himself, as the other paused and gave the impression of seeking such confirmation.

'Thank you,' the detective intoned, seeming genuinely grateful for the assistance. 'As I was -um- saying, this "lady of the evening" disappeared from her pitch the night before Miss Flack met with, if the *facts* are taken at their -um- face value, what proved to be a fatal accident.'

'So?' Marks was unable to prevent himself asking.

'So Miss Nickerson, who -um- incidentally was the same age, height and -um- build as your client—,' Mr. Reeder obliged, pausing and raising an apologetically prohibitive hand as he saw a comment was coming from the solicitor. 'Your -um- *presumably* deceased client—was alleged to have been sent upon a well earned holiday to -um- Paris. However, by a *remarkable* stroke of good -um- fortune, Inspector Dreyfus of the *Surete* was able to obtain a picture taken by the -um- photographer hired by the hotel in which the woman purporting to be Miss Nickerson stayed overnight—And I have acquired -um- witnesses who claim it was -um- *not* Miss Nickerson.'

'Come on now,' Marks said, trying to sound derisive and unconcerned, but not quite succeeding. 'You know what tarts are like, Mr. Reeder. They'll *always* tell you what they think you want to know.'

'Not -um- *always*,' the detective corrected. 'Furthermore, the makers of the -um- identification were not "ladies of the evening." They were Miss Nickerson's eminently respectable parents, assorted law abiding neighbours and the local -um- vicar. *All* were most definite in their -um- assertions that the woman in the picture was *not* her.'

'What's that got to do with Miss Flack?' the solicitor demanded, after having topped up the glass with port from the bottle and emptied the contents down his throat in a single gulp.

'Miss Nickerson had her appendix removed when she was a -um- baby,' Mr Reeder answered, his manner seemingly eager to please by doing so.

'And?' Marks prompted, although he was all too aware of what was portended by the medical information.

'Much as I deplore the desecration of -um- graves,' the detective went on. 'In view of my -um- suppositions, I am going to apply for an order of -um- exhumation and, if the body should prove to be lacking its appendix, I fear this will raise grave -um- doubts as to whom it really is.' Thrusting back his chair and setting his hat at something close to a jaunty angle on his head, as the blond giant also rose, he went on, 'Well, Sergeant Fog—whom I was sufficiently remiss to have forgotten to -um- introduce—and I have taken up enough of your valuable time. I thought that, as Miss -um- Flack's legal counsel—or *executor*, as the case may be—you should be informed of my -um- intentions and, having done so, we will be on our way.'

Giving the solicitor no opportunity to speak, Mr. Reeder walked with Ranse from his office.

'I think you should take your employer another -um- bottle of port, Miss Cornelius,' the detective suggested, as he and his companion were crossing the waiting-room, looking to where the women were seated together at one of the desks. 'Toodle-oo!'

Although the blond giant did not know it, the last word uttered before leaving the 'chambers' was Mr. Reeder's supreme piece of flippancy!

Snatching from the open box the cigarette he had been craving all through the increasingly disturbing interview, Marks lit it with a hand which shook unsteadily. He was vigorously puffing at it when the blonde came in. Giving a snarling demand to be left alone, he dismissed her without offering to satisfy her curiosity. Granted the privacy he required, he took out and mopped his face with a large red silk handkerchief. Waiting until his composure was somewhat restored, he picked up the receiver of the telephone and dialled a number. On being answered, he reported what had taken place between himself and his far from welcome visitors.

'That could be what he wants to happen,' the solicitor warned, on being informed of the measures it was intended to implement as a means of circumventing the examination of the body before it could be reclaimed by legal exhumation. 'If so, it'll be a trap.'

'If it is,' replied the well educated feminine voice at the other end of the line. 'It's going to be sprung on *him*!'

    *   *   *   *   *   *   *   *

'That was as fine a piece of "tailing" as I've ever seen,' Ranse Smith praised, as he and Mr. Reeder climbed from the small and ordinary looking Austin car—its engine having been replaced by one of far greater power—on Woolwich Road. 'They didn't have any notion that we were after them.'

'One does one's -um- best,' the detective replied, not displeased by the well deserved praise. 'And it wasn't too -um- difficult once I deduced from the direction our friends were taking that this was where they were in all -um- probability heading.'

Having done all they could to create the situation they wanted, and hoping that Wally Marks would play his part in their plans, Mr. Reeder and Ranse had returned to Daffodil House. The other members of the contingent from Company 'Z' had already left, escorted by Jason Grant in the guise of a successful jewel thief, one he often adopted when wishing to circulate secretly and freely amongst members of the underworld, to put in an appearance around various night clubs that evening.

Knowing they would be spending their time in less salubrious circumstances and conditions, the blond giant and the detective had made their own preparations for the activities they anticipated. Although Mr. Reeder had arranged for support to be made available from Scotland Yard if it should be needed, he and the blond giant had gone alone to carry out the first part of their assignment. However, they had taken precautions against the eventualities envisaged by the detective. Both wore dark shirts and sombre attire. Not only had the Texan exchanged his Stetson for a black one with no decorative band, which might perhaps catch and glint in a chance light, but he was also wearing a fringed buckskin jacket which was more loosely fitting than his usual coats. As a further aid to avoid being seen in the darkness, each had blackened his face with burnt cork.

Taking the Austin, as being much less conspicuous and likely to attract attention than his Frazer Nash Fast Tourer, the detective had driven his companion to the cemetery in which the body claimed to be that of Olga Flack had been buried. Leaving the vehicle where it would pass unnoticed, but was readily available if needed, they had gone on foot to take up a position of concealment from which they could keep a watch on the grave. Both were experienced in that most onerous of law enforcement duties, maintaining a 'stakeout', and had passed the time exchanging *sotto voce* reminiscences of their respective activities.

Nothing had happened until just after half past three in the morning!

Coming in silence across the cemetery, four men carrying shovels had opened up the grave under observation. Removing the body from the coffin and wrapping it in a sheet of tarpaulin, after filling in the excavation and doing what they could to remove traces of their unofficial exhumation, they had carried it to a small delivery van. With that done, still unaware that they had been seen, they had boarded the vehicle and taken their departure.

In what the blond giant willingly conceded was a masterly feat of 'tailing' under the prevailing conditions, the streets being almost devoid of other traffic, the grave robbers had been followed by their still unsuspected watchers. The detective had soon announced he believed they were making for a destination by the River Thames with which he was acquainted and, stopping at a police telephone box, he had put a call through to Scotland Yard before resuming the pursuit. Despite the Texan's misgivings over the delay, they had soon come into renewed view of the van. Shortly after, it had turned from Woolwich Road.

Halting the Austin out of sight of the entrance into which the other vehicle had disappeared, Mr. Reeder had stated they would complete the remainder of their journey on foot. There was no sign of the van when they arrived at the corner around which it had disappeared. However, there was only one direction it could have taken and they assumed that, wishing to avoid attracting unwanted attention, the occupants had switched off its headlights when no longer needed to avoid being stopped by the police on the street.

Going along the narrow alley which gave access to Stivinn's Wharf, Mr. Reeder was pleased to discover the conditions were still much the same as on his previous visit.[1] Although the entrance gates were wide open, he halted just outside instead of entering the property. Motioning for his companion to take up a similar position at the other side, he stepped behind the wall to his right. Looking across, he saw Ranse was reaching beneath the buckskin jacket. Having been told there might be the possibility of serious trouble, with a distinct likelihood of shooting, the blond giant brought from its holster the Burgess folding riot gun he had elected to carry as more suitable than his Webley Fosbery 'automatic' revolver.

Waiting until his companion had opened out the shotgun ready for immediate operation, the detective removed the magnesium flare he carried for convenience inside his umbrella. Slipping his forefinger through the primer ring, he jerked it out to ignite the combustible compound. Tossing the device through the gates, he and Ranse remained behind the wall and shut their eyes against the brilliant glow which erupted from it.

A moment later, the silence of the night was shattered!

From the river at the opposite side of the property, the searchlights of police launches waiting at the instigation of the detective illuminated the van from which the grave robbers were removing their gruesome loot!

Nearer at hand, a voice with a pronounced Glaswegian accent bellowed, 'The old bastard's on to us. Awa' oot with you the noo and shoot anybody's gets in the way!'

---

1. *A description of the events which took place during the previous visit of Mr. J.G. Reeder to Stivinn's Wharf and what it looked like is given in*: Chapter Twenty, 'Your Name Is Alvin Dustine Fog', 'CAP' FOG TEXAS RANGER, MEET MR. J.G. REEDER. *The property also features in*: Chapter Three, 'Bones And The Wharfingers', BONES IN LONDON, *by Edgar Wallace.*

CHAPTER TWELVE

THERE'RE A LOT OF BLACK
FACES ABOUT

ACTING upon the shouted suggestion, three men carrying sawn-off double barrelled shotguns burst out of a dilapidated building—which had once housed a weigh-bridge and its office—at the right just inside the main entrance to Stivvin's Wharf. They were brought at once into the brilliant glow emitted by the magnesium flare. Big and brutal looking, there was suffcient likeness between their rage suffused faces to imply they were closely related. Despite the Glaswegian accent of the speaker, their attire was no different from that of any working man spending a 'night out' in London, regardless of his nationality.

Having glanced towards the bank of the River Thames and discovered it was being illuminated by the searchlights of the police launches, the trio clearly discounted any idea they might have had of selecting it as a possible avenue of escape. However, on starting to run towards the open main entrance, startled imprecations burst from them as they found themselves confronted by Mr. J.G. Reeder and Sergeant Ranse Smith, who had stepped swiftly into view from either side of the gates. Finding their intended departure was also likely to be impeded in that direction, they immediately skidded to a stop.

Recognizing the Hamilton brothers of Glasgow from the photographs of them he had seen in the Criminal Records Office at Scotland Yard, and knowing their reputation and numerous illegal activities, the elderly looking detective felt certain they had *not* halted with the intention of throwing away their weapons and surrendering. Aware that the act of merely carrying a gun in the commission of a crime entailed the addition of up to seven years as a sentence, the general run of habitual law breakers in the British Isles either refrained from being armed or did so merely to frighten a victim. They would discard their arms when threatened by arrest. However, Mr. Reeder knew the trio did not belong to the general run of criminals. In fact, they had been selected by their current employer—on account of their mutually vicious and callous disregard for the sanctity of human life—as the most suitable perpetrators of the task they were to carry out.

Therefore, even if the nefarious William 'Bad Wullie' Hamilton and his brothers failed to recognize their proposed victim because of the burnt cork he had applied to his otherwise easily distinguishable features, they would not have the slightest compunction over opening fire in order to make good their escape.

The correct identification of Mr. Reeder had, in fact, been made by the trio at first sight!

However, while aware of how dangerous an antagonist the apparently meek and ancient detective could be, not one of the brothers appreciated just how competent was the opposition with which they were confronted!

What none of the trio realized was that they were in contention against a kind of law enforcement officer *far* different from any with whom they were acquainted!

On the other hand, the sergeant of the Texas Rangers had no need of his British colleague to warn him about the type of men they were facing!

The way in which Ranse responded to the threat was that of a peace officer trained in the hard school of Texas' gun fighting. Even in that day and age, given the added inducement of the situation inadvertantly caused by the ratification of the ill-advised Volstead Act, this was still likely to prove as effective and deadly as it had in the days of the Old West's *pistolero valientes* such as Dusty Fog, John Wesley Hardin and his maternal grandfather, Mark Counter.

Therefore, without needing any prompting from Mr. Reeder, the blond giant swiftly brought the Burgess folding riot gun into the firing position!

Sighting with an equal rapidity along the twenty inch barrel, aware of just how lethal the sawn-off shotguns would be at such a distance, Ranse squeezed the trigger almost as soon as the brass butt plate settled against his right shoulder and before any other combatant could open fire.

With his well developed instinct as a gun fighter suggesting he had hit his selected target in spite of the speed with which he was moving, the big Texan gave a smooth jerk with his right hand to manipulate the slide action and replenish the chamber of the Burgess. Simultaneously, his left arm was swinging the barrel into a fresh alignment. Before the ejected shell case completed its flight through the air, the weapon crashed again and vomitted another nine .32 calibre buckshot balls. Seven of them ripped into the chest of the second brother, being one more than had hit his already mortally wounded sibling. They proved equally efficacious. Twirling around, he fell in the wake of the first Hamilton to be stricken, who still had not yet arrived on the ground.

Holding his Colt Government Model of 1911 automatic pistol doubled handed, having leaned his umbrella against the wall and drawn the gun after igniting and throwing the flare, Mr. Reeder had as little doubt as his companion over how to cope with the situation!

Nevertheless, ignoring his knowledge of how dangerous a type of criminal they were up against, the detective hoped to take a prisoner who could be questioned. With that in mind, he sent off a bullet as accurately and at the same target as Major John Gray had selected outside Waterloo Station the previous afternoon. Unfortunately, the wound he inflicted proved less of a deterrent against further attempts at hostility.

Hit in the leg, Bad Wullie Hamilton stumbled against the side of the dilapidated building without dropping his sawn-off shotgun. Finding he was not completely incapacitated, although reduced to a condition in which rapid flight would be impossible, he braced himself against the wall. Then, mouthing obscenities it is *unnecessary* to repeat,[1] he tried to use the weapon!

Although Mr. Reeder hesitated, still hoping for a captive, the blond giant did not!

Acting as he had been taught was the only sensible way when faced with a wounded criminal who was still holding a weapon and showed signs of meaning to use it, Ranse once more changed the direction in which the Burgess was pointing and fired for the third time.

---

1. *We have recorded our sentiments with regards to the use of gratuitous and, to our way of thinking,* completely *unnecessary profanity as an alleged attempt to create 'realism', in the third paragraph of our AUTHOR'S NOTE.*

Slammed back by the buckshot which ploughed into his torso, the last of the evil brothers discharged both barrels of his shotgun!

Fortunately for the intended victims, the impact of the six balls caused the twin barrels to be inadvertantly elevated *just enough!*

Mr. Reeder's high crowned old hat was sent spinning from his head by one of the discharged load!

Another ball passed through the wide brim of Ranse's Stetson and snatched it upwards to the rear, but its fancy *barbiquejo* chinstrap kept it dangling on his broad shoulders!

However, the rest of the flying lead passed harmlessly above the intended victims!

'Are you all right, *amigo*?' the blond giant inquired, instinctively operating the mechanism of the Burgess to recharge it and keeping his attention upon the three sprawled out men.

'Yes, thank you,' Mr. Reeder replied, with none of the usual hesitancy in his voice. 'Are you?'

'Carved a hole through my J.B is all,' Ranse drawled. 'I'm right pleased it wasn't my best one.'

'That would have been a *tragedy* of -um- magnitude,' the detective declared, reverting to his normal tone. Warily starting to walk forward, with the blond giant by his side, holding their weapons ready for further use if the need arose, he ran his gaze from one to another of the brothers. None of them were moving and he concluded that, if appearances were any guide, they never would again under their own power. Knowing the full extent of their unsavoury activities, which were believed to have included four particularly brutal and cold blooded murders—although sufficient evidence had never been obtained on any occasion to permit them to be brought to trial—he felt disappointed that none would be able to supply information; but not the slightest remorse over having to help cause their deaths. 'I wonder what kind of story the -um- *Daily Working Man* will fabricate about *this*?'

Much the same sentiments were uttered by Chief Inspector Frank Gaylor of Scotland Yard when he crossed from the other side of Stivinn's Wharf to report that his part in the operation had met with just as complete, albeit less fatal, success. Working in conjunction with Inspector Jonathan

Ambrose 'Johnny' Wade of the Thames River Police,[2] he and their men had dashed ashore just in time to prevent the grave robbers from throwing the purloined body into the water. There had been some attempt at physical resistance, the men engaged for the unpleasant activity being brutal rather than brainy, but they had been taken into custody suffering from nothing worse than concussion and some minor bruising.

The interview he had had with Wallace Oswald 'Wally' Marks had convinced Mr. Reeder that the theory developed by his much vaunted 'criminal mind' was correct. Therefore, he had known that any attempt to have the corpse legally exhumed would be delayed by the crooked solicitor with the intention of causing sufficient time to elapse to prevent the true state of affairs being ascertained. However, acting as the detective wished, the person most vitally concerned with avoiding the truth being established had inadvertantly played into his hands. While the means in which he intended to acquire the requisite information were completely unofficial (nevertheless being carried out with the tacit approval of the Director of Public Prosecutions) he considered they were fully justified if they helped circumvent the person he believed to be behind the robbery of the grave.

Also in the raiding party, in fact having been an active participant in the ensuing fight—despite the apparent impropriety of such behaviour by one of his eminence—was Britain's leading pathologist. He had agreed to come along as a gesture of friendship for Mr. J.G. Reeder, and had just as willingly overlooked the fact that there was no official sanction for his presence; to carry out the tests necessary to establish whether the corpse was indeed that of Olga Flack. Unlike Molly Nickerson, who the detective felt sure had been the actual occupant of the rifled coffin, the daughter of the mentally deranged and now deceased master criminal had not had her appendix removed. Therefore, if that particular internal organ was absent—as could be ascertained by such a skilled pathologist, despite the badly charred condition of the body—it would provide incontestable proof that the working of Mr. Reeder's 'criminal mind' was on the right track.

2. Some details of the career of Inspector—as he was at the time of this narrative—Jonathan Ambrose 'Johnny' Wade, of the Thames River Police, are given in: THE INDIA RUBBER MEN, by Edgar Wallace.

'I'll say one thing, though,' Gaylor remarked, at the end of a most satisfactory report which had included the fact that, 'Sir James has whipped *it* away to do the carving'. Big, burly, with a ruggedly good looking face which was normally cheerful, Gaylor continued to employ what his elderly appearing associate and good friend Mr. Reed occasionally referred to as his 'painful sense of humour'. 'You two look so *pretty* made up like you are, you might even be able to get a date with Sylvia and Nina from Wally Marks' chambers.'

'Knowing *my* luck,' Ranse drawled, aware that the two female private and confidential secretaries of the crooked solicitor shared sexual proclivities which made them completely disinterested in masculine company. 'I'd be willing to bet I get the *ugly* one.'

'I don't know how it is in the -um- "Colonies", old boy,'[3] Mr. Reeder remarked, in his most apparently sober and, therefore, most humorous frame of mind. 'But in the Mother Country, we *always* say like cleaves to like.'

'Nina *could* have her *good* points,' Gaylor asserted, knowing the massive woman supplemented her secretarial duties by acting as an exceptionally proficient bodyguard for her less than savoury employer. Becoming serious, he went on, 'Anyway, from what I heard before I left the Yard, there're a lot of black faces about tonight.'

'How do you mean?' Mr. Reeder queried.

'Of course, you wouldn't have heard. You've been here all night,' Gaylor said. 'Do you know Frederick Manton?'

'Not -um- personally,' the detective admitted. 'Although even *I* am aware he is the star of the musical -um- extravaganza at the—I *believe* it is— Apollo Theatre on the Shaftesbury Avenue.'

'He *was* the star,' Gaylor corrected. 'But somebody shot

---

3. *Like many English people of his and other generations, Mr. J.G. Reeder was inclined to claim, perhaps 'tongue in cheek', that the world is divided into two parts, Great—as it was in those pre-Welfare State days—Britain and its Colonies. For other adherents to the belief, see the comments of Mrs. Winifred Amelia 'Freddie Woods' Fog, neé Besgrove-Woodstole, q.v., Captain Patrick 'the Remittance Kid' Reeder, q.v., and 'Brit', respectively in,* THE WHIP AND THE WAR LANCE; *YOU'RE A TEXAS RANGER, ALVIN FOG;* THE REMITTANCE KID *and* RIO GUNS. *Also our Dedication in:* KILL DUSTY FOG!

him as he came out of the stage door after tonight's—*last night's*, before *somebody* tells me—performance.'

'Good heavens, that seems a rather -um- drastic way of registering *disapproval* of his performance,' Mr. Reeder stated, feeling sure there was something of considerable importance behind the information he had received. 'Or wasn't the -um- perpetrator a theater-goer?'

'He *could* have been,' the Chief Inspector claimed.

'But there is reason to -um- presuppose *otherwise*?' the detective hinted, as he knew he was supposed to do.

Like every great performer, Mr. James Garfield Reeder knew and was always willing to oblige when he was expected to play the 'straight man' in a conversation!

'There *could* be,' Gaylor conceded, in an impressive, albeit mock, judicial fashion. 'The Orator was *lucky* enough to get the case and he told me at the Yard, just before I came to *rescue* you two, that a witness had seen the chap who did it.'

'And the afore-mentioned -um- "chap" was something out of the *ordinary*?' the detective suggested, sounding as if he harboured grave doubts as to whether a person as insignificant as himself could possibly have arrived at a correct solution.

'You *might* say that,' the Chief Inspector confirmed dryly. 'Unless the witness was seeing *things*—which we all know does *occasionally* happen—the man who shot Mr. Manton was *black*.'

* * * * * * * *

'UNLIKE in *your* section of the -um- Colonies,' Mr. Reeder pontificated gravely, yet apparently with such diffidence that he gave the impression he was expecting to be taken to task for some error at any moment. 'If you will accept my most -um- *humble* apologies for having employed such a term in *your* presence, my dear young -um- lady?'

'I would have preferred the "um" *between* the "dear" and the "young",' Rita Yarborough asserted, before continuing in so sombre a voice she might have been formally presenting the elderly looking detective with the 'keys' to the whole United States of America. 'But feel free.'

'We in this country do not have any great number of -um- coloured denizens of the—as the popular -um- newspapers call it—underworld,' Mr. Reeder obliged. 'Furthermore, those who do infringe upon our -um- hospitality by committing acts of -um- criminal violence tend to restrict themselves to nothing more up-to-date than razors of the -um- "cut-throat" variety, which I believe you Colonials refer to as -um- "Harlem scalpels". Mostly they refrain from the usage of firearms.'

The time was half past four in the afternoon following the thwarted attempt at grave robbing!

Having caught up with some sleep and dealt with the in-escapable paperwork and other routine details attendant to the incident, the detective and Ranse Smith were engaged in what amounted to a council of war with the rest of the contingent of Company 'Z'; to which the girl was an unofficial, yet tacitly approved, serving member. To aid their pose of being American criminals on vacation in England, she, the other two sergeants and Jason Grant, still in his guise as the jewel thief, were staying at a small and luxurious hotel in London. However, to avoid the chance of arousing suspicion if they should all be seen together, this meeting was taking place at the chicken farm which served as the headquarters—Daffodil House being their main base in town—of Mr. Jeremiah Golden Reeder's organization in Brockley, Kent.

In spite of the misgivings expressed by the detective and Chief Inspector Gaylor, there had been hardly any mention of the incident at Stivinn's Wharf in the morning newspapers. This was, in part, a result of the lateness of the hour at which it had occurred and also because the area around the location was very thinly populated outside the normal working day. However, by far the most important factor behind the dearth of coverage—which, for obvious reasons, Mr. Reeder and his associates hoped would continue—had been the murder of the prominent West End actor, Frederick Manton. As it had occurred so close to the Capital's main entertainment region, it had attracted newspaper reporters who might otherwise have been at a loose end, thereby picking up word of the activity in the more remote section of the River Thames.

A remark about how fortunate they were to avoid such undesirable and unwanted attentions from the press had caused Mr. Reeder to speak of a most interesting factor in the killing of the entertainer. Meeting Chief Inspector Oliver Rater by chance, while attending a conference at Scotland Yard, and accompanied by Ranse, they had discussed the case. Eager to obtain the advice of the Texan in particular, the

Orator had waxed exceptionally loquacious on the subject most puzzling to him.[4] While unable to offer anything which might lead to the solution of the mysterious slaying, Ranse had expressed the opinion—with which Mr. Reeder and the policeman tended to be in agreement—that the colour of the suspect seen by the witness could most likly prove to be no more than a disguise similar to that which he and the detective had adopted the previous evening, albeit for a different purpose.

'We don't have too many black gunmen around the good old U.S. of A., comes to that,' Sergeant Alvin Dustine 'Rapido Clint' Fog asserted. 'And, from what I've noticed over here both times, one would be a whole heap more conspicuous than he'd be likely to be in 'most any city back to home. Anyways, did you learn anything from those four yahoos who dug up the body?'

'Nothing,' Mr. Reeder said and, although his attention was concentrated on the matter which he and his companions were considering, he was later to remember the remark which preceded the question from the small Texan. 'They're all old -um- lags, but none of them had previously done anything even remotely in the nature of robbing a -um- grave. In fact, as I said to Mr. Gaylor when we parted in the wee hours of this morning, it is the very first occasion when even -um- *I* have come across a case of it.'

'Isn't there *any* way you can get them to tell you who hired them?' Rita inquired.

'If there is, I'm afraid we haven't -um- ascertained it as yet,' the detective confessed, seemingly considering he must have been to blame in some way for the omission. 'All four are so *completely* lacking in -um- intelligence, their idea of playing a guessing game would be for one to leave the room and the rest have to *try* to guess who it was who went.'

'That was a Polack joke the last time I heard it,' the girl complained.

'Good gracious, *was* it?' Mr. Reeder queried, apparently aghast at the discovery. 'Be that as it may, while they are

---

4. *Some details of the career of Chief Inspector Oliver 'the Orator' Rater— whose sobriquet was derived partly from a play of words on his name and because of his reputation for brevity of speech—are given, although the case referred to above is not included, in:* THE ORATOR *by Edgar Wallace.*

somewhat lacking in -um- intelligence, they are equally stubborn in their *complete* disinclination to satisfy our curiosity in *any* -um- way. In fact, faced with what I suppose is to them an understandable -um- reticence, one might wish we could emulate your use of the -um- rubber hose which, I believe is considered a most efficacious instrument for inducing confidences.'

'I can't bring to mind *any* time us good ole boys of Company "Z" *ever* used a rubber hose, or any other kind, on *anybody*,' *Rapido* protested. 'Nor has any other peace officer I'd call a *friend*, comes to that.'

'I know I *never* do,' 'Comanche Blood' affirmed, exuding what seemed an aura of conscious virtue until his next words spoiled the effect. 'Give me staking 'em out on an anthill any old time.'

'I would imagine that is a *most* -um- meritorious system,' Mr. Reeder assessed, adopting his quizically judicious manner. 'Unfortunately, however, it is -um- impractical over here due to the most lamentable -um- dearth of anthills.'

'Not having any would make using them *difficult*,' Rita consoled, aware such comments were frequently passed between men who had developed strong bonds of friendship and mutual respect for one another as a means of helping to stimulate more serious thought.

'How very -um- *true*, my dear,' the detective conceded. 'By the by, our grave robbers have already acquired legal -um- counsel.'

'Not that Wally Marks *hombre* I've been hearing tell so much about?' the Indian dark Texan suggested, the knowledge having been imparted by Jason Grant.

'Nobody so -um- eminent,' Mr. Reeder denied, his manner implying he wished to save the solicitor from being falsely accused. 'However, Mr. Bill Kinnock is to Mr. Marks what the jackal is to the lion. He takes on such lesser clients as are unable to meet Mr. Marks' high fees.'

'But Marks is behind it,' *Rapido* stated rather than inquired.

'He undoubtedly -um- is,' the detective confirmed, with complete conviction. 'and, behind him, as Sir James has established to my entire -um- satisfaction, is a very much *alive* and well Miss Olga Flack.'

'She must've managed to fake the appendicitis so they'd

take her to hospital,'[5] *Rapido* guessed. 'Then some of her boys grabbed her off the ambulance, put the girl in with the three attendants and set in on fire.'

'Yes,' Mr. Reeder agreed, having informed the party of the incident, his manner cold and angry. 'If only Miss Nickerson had told me where she was when she called to arrange a meeting, I could have warned her there is *always* a man downstairs listening to every message in and out of that damned Club—!'

'You'd been too late to save her,' Comanche pointed out.

'Churgwin wouldn't have dared do anything to her, knowing I knew where she was,' Mr. Reeder countered bitterly. 'As it was, he decided he could take the chance of getting rid of her and, knowing a substitute was needed to supply the body they had to have in the ambulance, he decided to use her. It would amuse Flack to think she was being replaced by somebody who might have been trying to warn me of what was being planned.'

'*Nice* people!' Rita breathed, noticing how all the hesitancy had left the detective's voice and he suddenly seemed far younger. In fact, his attitude reminded her of *Rapido*, Comanche and Ranse on the day they had heard about their two *amigos* having been murdered by the Chopper. As she had felt then, she decided she would not care to be in the shoes of the person responsible for the change. 'Where do you think the Flack woman is hiding?'

'Even with my -um- celebrated "criminal mind", I'm afraid I do not have the slightest -um- idea,' Mr. Reeder confessed, making an almost visible effort and returning to his usual manner of speech and demeanour. 'However, as her *alter ego* was last seen alive therein, the -um- Pinhole Club might produce at least a -um- suggestion.'

Neither the girl nor the Texans thought any the worse of the elderly looking man for going back to a posture intended to deceive people in general and unsuspecting criminals in particular with regards to his true potential. It was maintained—even in the presence of those privy to the secret —for the same reason '*Rapido*' and '*Comanche*' were always

---

5. *At the period of this narrative, the operation for acute appendicitis was still considered one requiring major surgery beyond the facilities offered by the medical staff of Holloway Prison.*

called by their aliases, to lessen the chance of it being forgotten and the truth revealed at an inauspicious moment.

'Then,' Comanche growled, looking like one of his Indian warrior ancestors in an especially ugly mood. 'There's some's might say the easiest way to find out'd be go in head down and horns a-hooking to take a look.'

'If it were only that -um- *easy*,' the detective sighed. 'Regrettably, being on the surface so eminently -um- respectable an establishment—albeit offering a somewhat unconventional form of -um- entertainment on the so called "Cat Fight Nights"—with the majority of its clientele drawn from high -um- society, we would be required to produce a most *excellent* reason for making a -um- raid upon it.'

'But, happen you had that *excellent* reason,' *Rapido* drawled. 'You'd be able to go in, huh?'

'Without -um- hesitation,' Mr. Reeder confirmed. 'And without subjecting those who assisted me to the inconvenience of legal repercussions over having done so.'

'Then,' the small Texan declared, suddenly giving the impression of being the largest man in the room. 'It just *might* be you'll get the said *excellent* reason one night *real* soon!'

CHAPTER THIRTEEN

GO GET HER, RITA-GAL!

'WELL, old boy,' Squadron Leader Arnold Blandish said, walking with Major John Gray to where Sergeant Ranse Smith had just landed and was climbing from the cockpit of a Sopwith 7F. 1 Snipe biplane. Although he tried, he was not entirely successful in concealing the relief he felt over the safe return of the fighter aircraft. It belonged to 28 Squadron, Royal Air Force—of which he was commanding officer—and had just been put through a series of daring aerobatics by the American whom he and his pilots had invited to be their guest at their Station near Brockley, Kent. 'How do you like her?'

'She's a mite snug around the hips for somebody my size, but she's real good to handle,' the blond giant assessed, removing the flying helmet and goggles he had been loaned; their use being mandatory even though his flight was unauthorized by 'higher authority' and against *King's Regulations*. 'Only, from the look of your face, you're pleased I've brought her down without breaking anything.'

'Only for *your* sake, old boy,' the Squadron Leader asserted, realizing something of his perturbation must have shown to the keen eyed visitor from 'overseas' and also grinning. 'Although I must admit that when you beat up the field at *very* low level, I couldn't help thinking what a *pity* it would be if *the* Service was to lose *me* before I could become "Himself" himself, Marshal of the Royal Air Force.'

'Actually, *Alvin*, the *Army* doesn't have a " 'Himself" himself, Marshal of the Royal Air Force",' the Major explained, as soberly as if imparting information of the greatest importance, having noticed the emphasis placed upon the word, '*the*' with which their host had tried to indicate the superior status of his 'Service'. 'In fact, we even chucked out the *Royal Flying Corps* as unlikely *ever* to be required in *civilized*

142

warfare.' Then, eyeing the Squadron Leader with the thinly hidden satisfaction of a soldier able to give a reminder that another branch of the Armed Forces was not at that moment in the good graces of 'higher authority', he went on, 'I would imagine "Their Airships"[1] would be a trifle miffed if Alvin had broken that barbaric *device* of yours, Arnold. After all, you crab-fats[2] seem to be making a habit of *mislaying* your infernal flying *contraptions* these days.'

'Not in *the* Command, old boy, *we* haven't lost a fighter in *days*,' Blandish protested. 'Of course, one wouldn't expect a pongo of the licentious soldiery to know the difference between *us* and the boffins in "Wings and Bangs" at Martlesham[3] and it was *them* who lost that Yankee—no offense meant to *you*, Alvin—inventor chappy's kite.'

'No offense taken, *amigo*,' Ranse assured. 'Shucks, like every raised-right *Texan*, I was twelve years old before I learned "god-damned-Yankee" wasn't all *one* word.'

It was three o'clock on Friday afternoon, the fourth day after the arrival in England of the contigent from the Texas Rangers' Company 'Z'.

There had been a few developments in the matter which had brought the blond giant and his companions from the United States, but none of them appeared to help in the search for the Chopper.

On Wednesday, as Mr. J.G. Reeder was returning across a busy street to rejoin Ranse—after having been to speak with a man he knew to be an informer had signalled for him to go over and receive some news—an attempt was made to run him down with a speeding lorry. Only a *very* prompt evasion, made with what would have appeared amazing speed to

1. *'Their Airships'*: a sobriquet for the Air Members—serving senior officers acting as heads of departments such as 'Plans', 'Operations', 'Intelligence', 'Signals', etc.—of the Air Council, the supeme commanding body of the Royal Air Force.
2. *'Crab-fat'*: derogatory name for a member of the Royal Air Force; corresponding with 'pongo', or 'brown job', particularly when khaki 'battledress' uniforms became standard wear, for a soldier; 'bootneck', 'Joey' or, in the case of an officer, 'bullock major', for a Royal Marine'; 'matelot'—pronounced 'mat-loe'—or 'Jolly Jack' for a sailor in the Royal Navy.
3. *'Wings and Bangs'*: sobriquet, based on the duties performed therein, for the Aircraft and Armaments Experimental Station of the Royal Air Force, at Martlesham Heath, in Suffolk.

anybody unacquainted with the truth about the seemingly aged and frail detective had saved him.[4] His subsequent investigation had exonerated the 'nose' of involvement in the attempt and had established it was organized on behalf of a gang leader operating out of Nottingham and named—with the kind of coincidence no writer of fiction *dare* use as a plot device—Robin Hood.[5] Arrested by the Flying Squad after a hectic chase during which his vehicle knocked down and killed a pedestrian, the driver was induced to incriminate his employer. Added to various other criminal activities revealed by Mr. Reeder's sources of information, this resulted in a lengthy term of imprisonment for the latest seeker after the reward of her deceased father's 'Encyclopedia Of Crime' offered by Olga Flack.

Yet other sources had determined that the thwarted assassination attempt by Herbert McPriest at Waterloo Station had been carried out via the instigation of Louis 'Lou' Birkstone. Unfortunately, on this occasion, the requisite confirmation was not available to allow criminal proceedings to be instituted against Birkstone in a court of law. Instead, the police had commenced an operation against him similar to that mounted in Texas by Major Benson Tragg in order to gather information which would, hopefully, lead to the Chopper. This proved so costly to Birkstone, he soon had cause to regret even having thought of attempting to earn the 'bounty' placed upon Mr. Reeder's head.

Following the usual investigatory procedure, Chief Inspector Oliver Rater had adopted the most obvious course by starting to seek out from among the associates of Frederick Manton in the theatrical world those with a motive for killing him. Even though the entertainer had generally been liked, there were several suspects and testing their respective alibis

4. *The reason for the apparently surprisingly agility, seemingly so at odds with the appearance presented by Mr. James Garfield Reeder, is explained in:* APPENDIX ONE.

5. *Neither we, nor the world's foremost fictionist genealogist, Philip Jose Farmer—author of, in addition to* numerous *other works,* TARZAN ALIVE, The Definitive Biography Of Lord Greystoke *and* DOC SAVAGE, His Apocolyptic Life—*with whom we consulted, have been able to trace any connection between the 'Robin Hood' referred to in this narrative and the distinguished lineage of an earlier, more famous, bearer of the name.*

144

was proving a lengthy process. It was still in progress, but the Orator was already considering he should spread his net further in the hope of finding the solution.

Learning of the failure to prevent the body of Molly Nickerson from being examined by the eminent pathologist, Olga Flack had concluded there was no longer any point in continuing the pretence that she had been killed in the crashed ambulance. Furthermore, on discovering informers had already started to spread the story of her offer to present her father's much sought after 'Encyclopedia' to whoever killed Mr. Reeder, she had seen the advantage of letting it be known she was still alive. Such was the strength of close to superstitious awe and dread still inspired among the denizens of the underworld by the surname she bore, the 'noses' quickly resumed their previous reticence regarding anything even remotely connected with her affairs.

However, before the silence had descended, one significant piece of news reached Mr. Reeder!

The continued failure by the expensive hired killer imported from America to take the required action against the main recipient of Olga Flack's hatred was becoming irksome to William Maxwell 'Billy' Churgwin. According to rumours from the underworld, in spite of having expended a considerable sum of money to bring the Chopper across the Atlantic, Churgwin's dissatisfaction was increased because he had no way of contacting him and demanding an explanation for the delay.

Despite its considerable potential as a news item, the incident at Stivinn's Wharf had continued to be given little coverage in the press. Even that which did appear was inaccurate and made no mention of the participation by Ranse and Mr. Reeder. This was partly because, aware of how the 'liberal' elements were always eager to seize upon any opportunity to defame the forces of law and order for their own ends, it had been decided at high level to keep what a later generation would term a 'low profile' on the matter. This had been helped by the fact that only the two senior officers in the raiding party had been aware of exactly what took place by the dilapidated weigh-bridge building. By the time other officers were allowed to come over, having been occupied before in dealing with the resistance of the grave robbers, the detective and the Texan were no longer on the scene. Therefore, Chief

Inspector Frank Gaylor and Inspector Jonathan Ambrose 'Johnny' Wade had supported the supposition that the Hamilton brothers had been killed by rivals in the underworld.

The desire for the 'low profile' was helped by more than just the delay in reporters hearing of the incident and by the absence of details which would otherwise have supplied an added fillip. In addition to the murder of Frederick Manton being of considerable interest to the public, something even more spectacular occurred to further divert attention from what happened at Stivinn's Wharf. Making a daring raid on the Aircraft and Armaments Experimental Station at Martlesham Heath, in Suffolk, somebody had stolen the Vickers Vimy bomber modified to test the practicality of employing it as a 'ground attack' weapon if armed with several Thompson submachine guns. It had last been seen flying eastwards towards the North Sea, but there had been no report of it having landed anywhere within its range on the Continent.

Having been at a loose end while awaiting the next developments, Ranse had elected to take up the invitation he had received to visit 28 Squadron. Accompanied by Major John Gray—whose rarely used surname was Reeder—he had been treated most hospitably by Squadron Leader Blandish and the other officers. Pressed for a demonstration, inspired by references to his ability to draw and shoot *very* fast—despite his only having exhibited the former quality at Waterloo Station having featured, prominently in the 'popular' press he had obliged. Taken to the Station's 'clay pigeon' shooting range and using his Webley Fosbery 'automatic' revolver drawn from its shoulder holster—it having been decided by Mr. Reeder that he should continue to go armed in some way at all times, in case he too should be selected as a target for revenge by Olga Flack—he had treated his hosts to an exhibition of frontier style gun handling.

Proving his skill as a pilot next, by taking up the Station's Avro 504 utility aircraft, the blond giant had hinted he would like to try his hand in a fighter to make a comparison between it and the Boeing PW-9 he had flown at the invitation of a friend commanding a Pursuit—as the American Army Air Corps called their equivalent of what the British designated a 'fighter'—Squadron. At first reluctant, Blandish had agreed provided the blond giant won a further shooting test by hit-

146

ting a discharged clay pigeon from the draw. As his host did not stipulate he used the Webley, and being unaware that he had a more suitable weapon in the Major's car, he had agreed. Collecting and donning the Burgess folding riot gun, without anybody seeing him or discovering the substitution beneath his jacket, he had earned himself the flight. Shown the 'taps'—as his host described the controls and instruments—on the little Sopwith biplane, a much less complicated matter than would be the case with later and more sophisticated aircraft, he had accustomed himself to the feel of the machine in the air and given the exhibition of aerobatic flying which had provoked the comments on landing.

'I wonder who did steal the bloody thing?' Blandish said, escorting his guests from the grass runway. 'Or who'd *want* it, if it comes to that. Lumbering along at such a low speed, and with the low level it'd be restricted to by all those Tommy guns, its use would be *very* limited against any enemy able to deploy anti-aircraft guns and automatic weapons. It *might* be safe for dealing with rampaging fuzzy wuzzies, but there wouldn't be *any* hope of survival against the Hun or even those Ruskies who I'm sure will eventually become an even *bigger* threat to world peace.'

'I've heard of "fuzzy wuzzies",' Ranse remarked, knowing this to be the name given to various tribes of primitive and fanatical warriors in the Soudan. 'I'm afraid we won't be able to stay much longer, *amigo*,' Ranse warned. 'I could have a *real* busy night's work waiting for me back in the Big City.'

* * * *   * * * *

'THEY did that quite well.' assessed Rita Yarborough, watching the now scantily clad victress and loser being helped from the open area in the centre of the room after the first bout of the 'Cat Fight Night' at the Pinhole Club. 'In fact, except there was no blood, it looked like the real thing. Of course, those of the girls Jason introduced us to said it's only rarely any of them do get hurt.'

'What we heard tell, though,' Mark 'Comanche Blood' Scrapton corrected. 'Molly Nickerson got chomped, whomped and stomped real good the night before she got made wolf bait.'

'That was by an *outsider* who she'd been told to take it easy with,' Rita pointed out. She was pretending to be a prostitute brought from America by her boy friend so that she could

147

acquire information which would not have been so readily available to her male companions. She had said her boy-friend's interests included watching women fighting and this had produced the details she was seeking. 'Not one of the girls.'

'That's her, with that obnoxious little twister, Snoopy Frithington-Evans' party, at what would be a ringside table if there was a ring,'[6] supplied Jason Grant, whose surname only a few people knew to be Reeder, indicating the appropriate location with a gesture of his right hand.

The days since the arrival in London of Rita and her escort of Texans had been spent establishing all of them, with the exception of Ranse Smith, amongst the underworld as criminals of a particularly dangerous kind from America!

However, one part of the plan had been changed by circumstances beyond the conspirators' control!

It had been intended that Jason Grant would introduce *Rapido* and Comanche as a couple of professional gunmen who would be willing to take on assignments provided the price was right. By doing so, offers might be made for them to remove Mr. Reeder and lead them to the Chopper.

Suspecting Churgwin and Wallace Oswald 'Wally' Marks were the most deeply involved of the underworld, being those most likely to have brought the hired killer to England, the Texans had intended to make their acquaintance. However, the supposition that Olga Flack might still be alive had prevented the meeting with either the gang leader or the solicitor. If she should have engineered her escape, at the cost of four lives, she was sure to ruin the deception by identifying the smaller sergeant as one of those responsible for her father being killed.

Despite it being unwise to continue with the original scheme, the conspirators had elected to go on with the pretence of being American criminals being 'shown the sights' by an Englishman who was believed by the underworld to be a

---

6. *Some information regarding the career of 'that obnoxious little twister',
   Horace Wilberforce 'Snoopy'—sometimes, 'Frithy'—Frithington-Evans and
   his connection with Lady Mary Herban is given in*: Chapter 14, 'Educated
   Evans Declares A Win', GOOD EVANS; Chapter Nine, 'The Freak
   Dinner' *and* Chapter 12, 'The Journalist', MORE EDUCATED
   EVANS, *by Edgar Wallace.*

succesful jewel thief.[7] By doing so, not only might they be approached by less well connected 'customers' with designs on the future well being of Mr. Reeder, but if word of their presence and supposed interest in being hired for the task reached the Chopper, it might induce him to come out of hiding and either warn them off or suggest an alliance. Therefore, they had made the rounds of London's night clubs and the various haunts of the habitual criminals each night, dropping hints which it was hoped would draw the Chopper into the open.

While the scheme had not produced the desired result, the party had acquired information on other subjects as well as that in which they were most interested. Scotland Yard was able to clear up three cases and make several arrests as one result of their efforts. However, the most important data had been concerned with the events which led to the murder of Molly Nickerson. Procured mostly by Rita, it was revealed how the prostitute had suffered a bad beating at the hands of Lady Mary Herban which, they all agreed with Mr. James Garfield Reeder's supposition, had caused her to attempt the betrayal from inside the Pinhole Club thus, because of the monitoring of the telephone, subsequently losing her life.

Discovering a 'Cat Fight Night' was arranged for Friday evening, the conspirators had concluded it might be turned to their advantage. Therefore, Jason Grant had obtained the requisite means of entry for himself and his American companions. Dressed in a manner suitable for such an occasion, but not carrying firearms, apart from a Remington Double Derringer pistol—an effective weapon in spite of its age, and easy to conceal in Rita's reticule, they arrived at the club hoping to put their plan into effect.

On their arrival, the party had discovered everything they wanted for their purpose was present!

Looking around and seeing that conditions were in their favour, one member of the group decided their plan might possibly be amended to its added advantage!

'Looks like "old home week",' Alvin Dustine '*Rapido Clint*' Fog commented dryly, making a surreptitious gesture

7. *Until having commenced upon this narrative and requested that certain details be clarified by Mr. James Garfield Reeder, neither we nor our predecessor as biographer had heard of this facet of 'Mr. Jason Grant's' activites.*

towards where Wallace Oswald 'Wally' Marks sat with his two private and confidential secretaries at another of the ringside tables. 'Could be we'll get us a bonus out of it, them being here.'

'You watch Sylvia and, more particularly, Nina if you have in mind what I *know* you have, *Rapido*,' the Englishman advised, conforming with the precaution of always referring to the two Texans by their aliases. 'I know you're *good* but she's tough like a lot of so-called hard men *think* they are.'

'First sight I got of her,' Comanche drawled, studying the massive and unprepossessing bulk of Nina Tanner with a less than flattering gaze. 'I thought, now there's either a *fairly* pretty monster, or one real *ugly* lil ole gal. Man, is she ever *big* and *mean* looking?'

'It's not any of *them*, but *her* I'm interested in,' Rita declared nodding towards the table occupied by Frithington-Evans and his party. A grim timbre came into her voice as she continued, 'And I'm quite looking forward to *meeting* Lady Mary Herban.'

'Are you *sure* you want to go through with it?' Jason Grant asked, having harboured misgivings where this particular portion of the scheme was concerned.

'*We* are!' the girl declared, before either Texan could express a point of view.

'And, should you know her the way we do, *amigo*,' *Rapido* declared, although he too wished their purpose could be achieved without Rita playing her part in it. 'You'd know she's one gal who's real set in her ways when she's made up her Down-East-Yankee mind to do something.'

'There's just *no* way of talking her out of it at all,' Comanche supported, sharing the sentiments of his male companions in spite of the apparent levity in his drawl 'So all any of us can say is, go get her, Rita-gal!'

'Yes,' the girl replied, starting to ease back her chair in a manner redolent of grim determination and not a little anticipatory satisfaction. 'I think I *will*!'

CHAPTER FOURTEEN

SCRUM DOWN, BOYS!

HAVING risen without troubling to look around, the blonde who was the youngest and far the most striking member of the group around the table hosted by Horace Wilberforce 'Snoopy' Frithington-Evans intended to propose a toast. Before she could speak, she felt herself brought into unexpected contact from behind with what she realized could only be another woman. The bump was sufficiently hard to cause the brimming glass of a bright pink concoction, described as a 'Singapore Stinger' by the member of the so-called 'smart set' who had devised it, to jerk sharply. This in turn sprayed its contents over the most expensive—considering the scanty amount of material used to make it—low cut, sleeveless, backless and almost 'frontless' to waist level dress which had excited interest from everybody and a few disapproving sniffs, or *sotto voce* comments of disapproval from others of her sex, on her entrance into the main dining-room of the Pinhole Club to attend the 'Cat Fight Night'.

Some people might have claimed she was *most* inadequately attired in her daringly revealing Paris creation, selected as serving to display her figure to a point approaching *very* close to immodesty, even by the standards of that section of society to which she belonged. Her worst enemy—and there were several women present who might have cared to lay claim to that distinction—could not deny Lady Mary Herban was both extremely shapely and beautiful. On the other hand, even those who regarded themselves as sufficiently broad-minded to accept her lack of moral scruples and liked her conceded—if not openly—that she had her faults. Not only was she disloyal to a very wealthy husband whose work kept him out of the country for long periods, but she was also arrogant and, without the saving grace of being equally quick to forgive, had a temper which was frequently bad and always quick.

Therefore, although she was just as much to blame for the mishap, Lady Mary was not likely to accept with equanimity or Christian forbearance being bumped into and having a cocktail spilled over her expensive evening gown. Nor, on swinging around with a vigour which overturned her chair, was her temper improved in the slightest by discovering the cause of the accident was the extremely curvaceous red head whose attire—as she had noticed with annoyance on her arrival—alone came close to matching the deliberately sought eye-catching brevity of her own.

'You *clumsy* bitch!' the blonde beauty screeched, flinging down the glass so it shattered on the table.

Which was just the kind of response Rita Yarborough had hoped to elicit!

'God damn it, *blondie*!' the female member of Company 'Z's' contigent ejaculated, deliberately broadening her American accent with what appeared an equal wrath. 'Isn't this place big enough for *you* to jump up like a gold-durned drunken Red Indian without having to bump into *me* like that?'

It was not, the red head concluded from what she had learned about the arrogant natured aristocratic blonde, the most tactful way of speaking, even though their collision was supposed to have been accidental!

In fact, Rita realized, many people would have considered her behaviour most ill-advised under the circumstances!

When making her plan of campaign for the night's activities, learning that Major John Gray's valet was on intimate terms with a woman who suffered as maid in the service of Lady Mary, the red head had seen how this might be turned to the advantage of herself and her companions. Asking him to try and discover what the blonde would be wearing at the Pinhole Club, on receiving the information, she had searched London until finding attire of a similarly revealing and attention-drawing nature. On noticing the annoyance which Lady Mary did not trouble to conceal when she caught sight of the resemblance between their less than decorous attire, she had concluded she was correct in her assumption and thought it would prove beneficial to her intended strategy.

As Rita had anticipated and counted upon, having crossed from her table with the intention of 'accidentally' bumping into the blonde, her task was made easier by the other having risen while she was approaching. Causing the collision had aroused annoyance and the discovery that the attractive red head was responsible had added fuel to a very quick temper.

Watching for any hostile reaction her words might provoke from Lady Mary, the red head became aware that—as she had concluded would be the the case—others were starting to take notice of what was happening.

Although the party with whom the blonde had been sitting were watching, none of them spoke or made any other kind of attempt to intercede in the interests of avoiding a 'scene'. Rather, if their expressions were any indication, they harboured hopes to the contrary over the way in which the situation might develop. Knowing her, in fact, they were wondering whether she had arranged for the incident to help pander to her exhibitionistic tendencies. Attracted by the loudly spoken and clearly irate comments, the occupants of the most adjacent tables also began to suspend their conversations and look on with unconcealed anticipation. Soon, as interest in what was taking place spread rapidly, a silence composed of eager expectation began to descend on the room.

In the interests of creating an appearance of realism, prior to each of the pre-arranged 'bouts' on a 'Cat Fight Night', the 'combatants' would enact a similar brief scene to convey the impression that there was a genuine reason for the forthcoming tussling and tearing off of clothing in which they would indulge. Therefore, being aware of this, the less regular attendants who did not know Lady Mary and had missed her earlier participation believed something of the kind was occurring. Those who recognized her, whether they had seen her clash with Molly Nickerson or not, had hopes along the same lines.

For her part, starting to share Rita's realization of what was going on all around, the arrogant blonde was neither disturbed nor alarmed at finding herself at the centre of attraction. While there were limits to just how far she would go, certainly being unlikely to, 'raid herself into a vice den just to get her name in the papers', as had once been suggested, albeit not when she was present,[1] she had never been averse to being noticed and, provided it was along lines she considered acceptable, supplying a topic of conversation. Therefore, she not only had no objections to being seen engaged in a 'slanging match' with another woman, she also realized how it might be turned to an even more satisfactory attraction.

After having made a number of derisive comments about the less than convincing efforts of two inexperienced 'combatants' during the previous 'Cat Fight Night', Lady Mary had been provoked by another female member of her party into betting she could give a more impressive display. However, in spite of having taken lessons in self defense—which included learning several wrestling holds and throws—being determined to win the wager, she had sought to gain an advantage. Making arrangements without the other participant in the wager knowing, she had induced William Maxwell 'Billy' Churgwin to persuade the opponent she selected to believe it was only going to be a friendly tussle and not to be too rough.

As he had no desire to see a wealthy customer suffer an injury likely to make her and her friends take their custom elsewhere, the owner of the Pinhole Club had been only too willing to go along with the blonde's suggestions. Therefore, she had been able to inflict some weakening punishment before her true intentions became apparent to her opponent. Even when Molly Nickerson realized what was going on and started to retaliate in earnest, not only had her injuries lessened her ability to fight back, but she found herself up against an antagonist far stronger and more dangerous than she had anticipated.

Winning, after a considerably harder struggle than she anticipated, Lady Mary had not escaped unscathed as she had hoped would be the case. Nevertheless, she found the pain she was experiencing considerably eased by the enthusiastic response from the spectators. Their applause had also proved most pleasing to her ego. Furthermore, having once been sued by a maid whose head she had cut open with a vase she

---

1. *The maker of the comment was Detective Sergeant William Arbuthnot Challoner of the Selbany Street Police Station in Somers Town who was known to the denizens of his 'manor' as 'the Miller' because of his habit of chewing on a piece of straw. See*: Chapter 14, 'The Freak Dinner', MORE EDUCATED EVANS, *by Edgar Wallace.*

had thrown, she had also derived satisfaction from being able to vent her aggressive tendencies without incurring a similar response from her latest victim.

Glancing swiftly about her, the arrogant blonde beauty sensed everybody was anticipating her taking some form of more than verbal action against the red head. Studying the attire worn by the other, she was given an added inducement by resentment over them both being dressed in such a similarly daring and attention-seeking fashion. Nor did the realization that the spilled Singapore Stinger would ruin her dress do anything to dissuade her from what everybody present clearly expected of her.

'*Blondie*?' Lady Mary screeched back, never one to disappoint an audience. Having made a correct deduction from the accent of the red head, she went on, 'It was *you* who bumped into *me*, you *American* barbarian!'

'What did you call me?' Rita demanded, seeing a couple of men who were obviously the club's bouncers moving forward as they did when the regular 'combatants' were making the comments supposed to cause a desire to fight with one another.

'An *American* barbarian!'

'*That's* what I thought you said!'

Having provoked the required provocation and made her response, Rita did not wait for the bouncers to arrive!

Knotting her right fist in its elbow long blue cotton glove, the red head swung it around!

Taken completely unprepared by such a sudden and not yet expected hostile physical reaction and caught on the jaw with considerable force, the aristocratic blonde was sent spinning past her party's table. Losing a high heeled shoe did nothing to help her halt the helpless twirling stagger which was taking her into the centre of the open area prepared and left vacant for the 'combats'.

Alighting on hands and knees Lady Mary found her troubles were far from over. Darting after her, her assailant delivered a kick to her ideally presented rump and it precipitated her forward to land face down in an untidy sprawl. Before she could recover her wits, much less think about responding to her treatment, she felt the back of her flimsy dress grasped by two hands. Then it was given a wrench which tore it from her, even though, unlike the garments worn by regular contenders, it had not been weakened at the seams to facilitate the destruction and loss. Next, her assailant sank both hands into her stylishly short cropped hair and began to haul her upwards in a most painful fashion.

'Look at *that*!' Frithington-Evans ejaculated, watching the blonde reduced to undergarments—as insubstantial as the forcibly removed dress—silk stockings and one shoe. Plump and porcine of features, he would never have thought of making such a suggestion if things had been going in the blonde's favour. However, realizing events were not going as she planned, he shoved back his chair and went on, 'Come on. Let's stop *her*!'

'We'd better!' seconded the Honourable Claud Messinger —who was tall, painfully thin and weak chinned—also rising and thinking how pleasant it would be to lay hands upon the shapely and far from excessively clothed red head.

Big and burly in a similar fashion, their bulk more attributable to a mutual addiction to the 'pleasures of the flesh' rather than from hard work or strenuous exercise, Randolph Tooks and Saul Siniter shared Messinger's motivation for leaving the table. Patrons of the 'sport of kings' often spoke of them in the same breath as the 'Hon. Claud.' and their host. In all four cases, the terms employed were hardly of endearment and, depending upon the extent of losses incurred as a result of one or another of them manipulating the way their respective horses ran in races, mostly the comments were comprised of numerous profanities. Striding away from the table, without realizing Frithington-Evans was falling behind—although, knowing him to be *very* cautious by nature, neither would have been surprised by the discovery—each wanted to be the first to reach Lady Mary's assailant and have the privilege of taking hold and restraining her.

'Get your cotton picking hands offen my woman, you Limey sons-of-bitches!'

Hearing the command from close behind, 'Snoopy' concluded it was addressed to his companions and himself by an irate male American. However, the sensation of alarm created by the hostile tone and words diminished as he turned and took in the appearance of the closer of the two young men wearing tuxedos—as opposed to the more formal 'white tie' attire of his party and the majority of male customers—who were approaching. Deciding it would be safe to prevent by physical means what was clearly intended to be intervention on the part of the small 'Yankee', he stepped forward to do so.

Like others who had been misled by the small stature of Sergeant Alvin Dustine '*Rapido* Clint' Fog, Frithington-Evans was not left for long in ignorance of his error!

Starting to reach out, the dishonest race horse owner suddenly wondered why he had imagined the man in front of him was small. In some inexplicable and alarming way, he found he was up against what struck him as being a most massive and dangerous proposition. However, he was given no opportunity to revise his intentions. Before he could draw back, although his hands fell limply to his side rather than merely being withdrawn, a sensation which felt like he had received a kick from a mule impacted against his stomach. Letting out a strangled belch of agony, he clutched at his mid-section and, starting to fold over, stumbled backwards.

Snoopy was in no condition to appreciate the fact, but he might have considered himself fortunate in his treatment!

Although *Rapido* was grasping the *yawara* stick in his right hand, he used his knuckles and not one of its even harder rounded ends to deliver the blow. Nor, having been told of the unscrupulous activities of his victim, had he any compunctions over the way he acted. Furthermore, aware that such behaviour was characteristic of the other three men, he did not feel the slightest qualms over employing whatever means he might consider would be required against any of them.

Glancing around, annoyed at having been outdistanced by the other two in making for the red head, Siniter let out an imprecation more suited to the stable yard in times of stress than his present elegant surroundings. Wanting to vent his disappointment upon somebody, but being a bully imbued with a streak of caution, he lunged towards *Rapido* as his selection for being the most suitable and easy recipient.

The burly man was moving too swiftly to be impressed by the transformation seemingly produced by the strength of the small Texan's personality. Nevertheless, he fared even worse than his host. Side stepping the rush he was making, with the ease of a mongoose avoiding the strike of a much larger snake, *Rapido* snapped a kick into his stomach and, as he blundered helpelessly past, sped him on his way by driving an elbow against his shoulders. Propelled forwards at an increased rate, he sprawled across and overturned a table to the accompaniment of loud spoken protests from the people sitting around it.

Darting by his *amigo*, Sergeant Mark 'Comanche Blood' Scrapton went to where Tooks and Messinger had each grabbed Rita by an arm with the intention of making her release the blonde who she was dragging from the floor by the hair. Caught by the shoulder with a grip so painful it caused him to let go and turn upon his unexpected assailant, the former gave a snarl of rage. Snatching himself free of the grip, he swung a roundhouse punch at the deeply bronzed faced of the red haired young man who had intervened.

In spite of what happened to him, like Frithington-Evans, the burly dishonest racehorse owner might have considered himself fortunate his fate was not *far* worse!

Although the illustrious grandfather of the Indian dark Texan had had a Comanche-trained indifference to using nothing other than bare hands when dealing with antagonists, preferring more lethally effective measures, the changed circumstances of his generation had caused him to acquire competence in fighting without relying upon weapons.

Ducking beneath the comparatively slow moving blow without difficulty, its intention having been 'telegraphed' to his trained sensed, Comanche quickly straightened and caught Tooks by the lapels of a well cut Savile Row tail coat. Jerked forward, the bulky man was brought into a position where he could receive something which would have gladdened the heart of many a 'punter' disgruntled by having lost money as a result of his chicanery in a horse race. Rising with speed and power, a knee caught him at a most vulnerable portion of his anatomy and would necessitate a temporary suspension of his less than honourable intentions towards the young woman who he had invited to be his guest. Even as he gave vent to an agonized gurgling profanity and tried to bend over in the hope of relieving the nauseating agony assailing him, he was subjected to a surging swing and heave. Sent reeling in the opposite direction to Snoopy, he too had his progress halted by crashing into a table.

On feeling her arms grasped from behind, concluding she would be advised to turn her attention elsewhere, Rita removed her fingers from the blonde's hair. Fortunately for

Lady Mary, being shoved back flat on the floor by a vigorous jab from her left foot, she had taken the precaution of gaining extra mobility by kicking off her high heeled shoes prior to entering the open area. By the time the thrust was carried out, the arrival of Comanche had removed one impediment to her freedom of movement. Twisting to face the other, she treated him as she had Beauregard Wiggins at the Turtleback Cottage in Brownsville. Although her tactics proved just as effective where the 'Hon. Claud' was concerned, her part in the affair was still not ended. The blonde rolled over and, grabbing her by the legs, caused her to fall. Spluttering furious profanities, Lady Mary swarmed on to the red head and as spirited a brawl as had ever been seen on a 'Cat Fight Night' was commenced.

Despite what would undoubtedly have proved a major attraction taking place in the centre of the floor, there were few spectators able to enjoy it!

Commotion was erupting amongst the occupants of the room!

Despite having been employed for brawn rather quickness of wit, the bouncers, realizing things were not going as intended, moved forward more quickly!

Neither was allowed to carry out his intention of intervening!

Having remained at their table instead of accompanying the Texans, Jason Grant Reeder deftly inserted a foot between the legs of one passing bouncer and tripped him up!

At the opposite side of the room, Major John Gray Reeder sprang to his feet. Giving a bellow of, 'Scrum down, boys!' he tackled the second bouncer as if upon a rugby field. They went sprawling into and smashed beneath them a nearby table. Leaping out of the way, the three men who had sat at it elected to retaliate. As they were starting to do so, others joined the fray. Nor was the involvement of some of them purely by chance. Alerted by the pre-arranged signal, several officers of the Rifle Brigade—wearing civilian evening dress and there at the instigation of the Major—showed the rapidity of movement for which their regiment was famous by leaping up and rushing to his rescue.[2] While doing so, some of them

---

2. *Unlike units of the British Army, which drilled at one hundred and twenty paces per minute, the rate employed by the Rifle Brigade was one hundred and eighty.*

contrived to charge into others of the clientele or waiters and spread the conflict even wider.

The increase of hostilities did not remain for long a purely masculine province!

There were half a dozen intended 'combatants', three of whom had become on good terms with Rita, present and awaiting the signal to start their respective 'bouts'. Seeing the women belonging to Snoopy's group going towards the embattled feminine duo, and having no liking for Lady Mary after her treatment of Molly Nickerson, the trio hurried forward to prevent them attacking the 'nice Yankee bird'. Aroused by the excitement, the other three and several of the female customers began fights of their own.

For the first time since starting to put on the 'Cat Fight Nights' Churgwin was not in attendance. He had been summoned for a conference with Olga Flack at her hiding place. If he was present, he would have been furious at what was happening to the Club which was his particular pride and joy. The fixtures and fittings upon which he had lavished a lot of money were soon suffering what was generally irreparable damage. In addition, every table and chair was broken. One of the latter was thrown deliberately by Jason Grant through a window after the heavy drapes which would otherwise have protected it were torn down in an equally predetermined fashion by Major John Gray.

Despite having disposed of Frithington-Evans and his male companions, *Rapido* and Comanche were not content to rest upon their laurels. Nor were they allowed to do so, or even to try and separate Rita and the blonde if that had been their intention. Sharing the bouncers' appreciation of the situation, some of the waiters had come on to the open space. Their number was augmented by occupants of the overturned tables seeking vengeance. Fortunately for the Texans, however, there was no concerted action against them and the fighting which commenced quickly became general amongst the new arrivals.

Regardless of being occupied in protecting himself against various would be assailants, without making use of the *yawara* stick he was still grasping, *Rapido* was far from being oblivious of what was happening elsewhere in the room. Therefore, he noticed something which posed a threat to a subsidiary part of the scheme upon which his party were engaged.

There was a man present who, in addition to almost certainly

160

having been responsible for the Chopper leaving the United States, had consistently and knowingly assisted guilty criminals to evade the consequences of their often far from minor misdeeds.

One of the functions for which Company 'Z' of the Texas Rangers had been created was to deal with situations of this kind!

Fortunately, the small Texan was close enough to his *amigo* to decide what he considered might offer a solution!

'Send me over *there*, Comanch'!' *Rapido* requested in a sibilant hiss, blocking a blow coming his way and propelling the waiter trying to deliver it to one side with a power packed counter punch.

'Yo!' responded the Indian dark sergeant.

CHAPTER FIFTEEN

YOU'RE GOING FOR A *RIDE*!

ATTENDING the Pinhole Club at the expense of its owner, having a penchant for the kind of entertainment offered on a 'Cat Fight Night', Wallace Oswald 'Wally' Marks looked far more cleanly and better dressed than was ever the case—due to his pose of being a poor and less than successful member of the Bar—during 'office hours'. Sharing his table, as they always did on such occasions, were his two private and confidential secretaries. Sylvia Cornelius was attired in a most attractively feminine fashion as usual and had been one of the women present who expressed disapproval over the less than decorous appearance presented by Lady Mary Herban. However, in spite of her *very* close friend's expressed views on how a woman should dress in public, Nina Tanner wore the 'white tie and tails complete' of the opposite gender. Stories were still told in some circles around London about what had happened to a man indiscreet enough to express amusement over her predeliction for masculine attire.

Being a connoiseur of such events, the dishonest solicitor would have enjoyed watching what was obviously a genuine fight between the aristocratic blonde beauty and the equally attractive, scantily dressed and somewhat more shapely red head. However, aware that William Maxwell 'Billy' Churgwin was not present and realizing the danger being created by the situation when the brawl became general, he reluctantly decided it was inadvisable to stay. Making a sign to the two women, he shoved back his chair and got up with the intention of leaving. Sharing his summation, although they too normally took pleasure from watching the 'bouts' between others of their sex, his companions also came to their feet and Sylvia picked up her reticule, one of which she always carried when outside the flat she shared with Nina.

162

Despite having given the traditional assent of the United States' Cavalry to the request from his *amigo*, Sergeant Mark 'Comanche Blood' Scrapton gave the impression of having failed to recognize the person who had addressed him, and lashed out with a roundhouse left punch. Although nobody else in the vicinity noticed, being fully occupied by their own activities, this failed to make contact. But it seemed to be propelling the recipient of his 'blow' away from him in an uncontrollable rush. However, having carried out his instructions, he was diverted by the need to protect himself from an attacker.

Appearances nothwithstanding, Sergeant Alvin Dustine '*Rapido* Clint' Fog knew exactly where he was going and what he meant to do!

Crossing the room precipitately and apparently with no control over his movements, the small Texan contrived to run up against Marks. Responding as if he believed he was about to be assaulted in return, he spun around and swung his right arm with all the power of a body muscled like a Hercules in miniature. What was more, aware of the nature of the man at whom he was striking, he did not restrict himself to relying upon merely flesh and bone. Caught by a rounded end of the *yawara* stick wielded with skill and precision, there was an audible crack as the solicitor's jaw bone broke and he was pitched sideways to fall huddled in a corner of the room.

However, having delivered what was meant as only the preliminary to more punishment than the law had ever been able to inflict for Marks' many transgressions, *Rapido* was not allowed to continue it anywhere nearly as close to the extent Counsellor Reece Mervyn had suffered at the hands of Sergeant Ranse Smith in the guise of a husband whose jealousy was aroused.

Having followed the example of her employer and Sylvia by lurching to her feet, Nina, seeing him attacked, did not take the action which the latter would have preferred under the prevailing conditions. Instead of accompanying the blonde to help him rise and leave, before the eventuality they—but not she—had envisaged should occur, she rumbled out a profanity in a voice close to bass in its timbre and lunged forward. Taking advantage of the small Texan having been compelled to turn away and deal with an attacker, although she would have preferred to encircle and crush at his rib cage

163

without impediment as being more effective, she threw her arms around his biceps and pinioned them against his sides.

Feeling himself ensnared in a grip more powerful than any he had ever experienced except one, *Rapido* tried to free himself!

In spite of his far from inconsiderable strength, the small Texan found he was unable to do so!

Before *Rapido* could resort to other measures, help was at hand!

Seeing his *amigo's* predicament, Comanche knocked aside his current assailant and darted forward. He had been warned of the massive woman's great strength and proclivity for employing it violently, so realized severe methods would be required to deal with her. Regardless of this, he was unable to entirely restrain his inhibitions over mishandling a member of the other sex no matter how unprepossessing and potentially dangerous she might be. However, although he refrained from applying his full power to the kick he sent into her kidney region, it proved sufficient for his purposes.

Feeling the impact, a squawk of pain burst from Nina and she inadvertantly relaxed her grip. Before she could reapply its previous constriction, her arms were thrown apart and her captive was free. Taking an elbow driven to the rear on to her imposing bosom, which hurt regardless of it being covered by something more substantial than the current trends in feminine attire, she was driven back a couple of paces. Seeing the small Texan being tackled by another man, she started to go towards him.

'Bossy-love!' Sylvia squealed, using the term of endearment she always employed despite being the dominant member of their association. Jumping forward and catching the massive woman by the bicep, she went on urgently, 'Leave him alone and help me take Wally-kins out of here!'

Nobody else in the world could have dissuaded Nina from seeking revenge without employing physical force, but the wishes of the petite platinum blonde were law to her. Putting aside her desire to attack the small Texan, or the man whose kick had caused her to release him, she accompanied Sylvia to where Marks was huddled in the corner.

Although hurt and with blood flowing copiously from his mouth, the solicitor was still conscious. Helped to his feet, he was able to stumble along with the women supporting him on either side. Nor, possessing far more strength than her seemingly frail appearance suggested, was Sylvia's assistance to be despised while they were making for the door as quickly as he could manage. In spite of being burdened by him, the women knocked or kicked aside everybody regardless of sex who showed signs of trying to impede their departure. In this too, using her tiny feet with the skill of one trained in *savate*, the platinum blonde proved almost as effective as her companion.

Leaving the room, the trio found themselves confronted by two men and, slightly to the rear, a woman almost matching Nina in bulk!

Although Sergeant Ranse Smith had discarded Western attire in favour of a well cut tuxedo, Mr. J.G. Reeder was dressed in his usual fashion and carried the inevitable umbrella grasped in his right hand. Behind them, also having made little change to her everyday attire, Mrs. Jane Amelia Grible was looking just as grimly determined.

The housekeeper had accompanied the two men when, using a key acquired by the elderly seeming detective from a member with whom he was acquainted, they had gained admission to the Pinhole Club. Having silenced the doorkeeper, they had not waited for the arrival of the policemen assembled in the vicinity of Leicester Place who were waiting for the commotion as the required excuse to make a raid. Instead, they had hurried upstairs, listening to what was obviously a large scale brawl taking place, to find out how their friends—who were almost certain to have caused it in accordance with their well laid plans—were faring.

'Going -um- *somewhere*?' Mr. Reeder inquired, with what appeared to be an air of genuinely solicitous interest.

Spitting out a profanity, Nina unwound the arm she had draped across her shoulders and left the supporting of Marks to Sylvia!

Springing forward, the massive woman was reaching for the detective when she became aware that the larger man had stepped between them!

What happened next was so rapid and unexpected Nina had only a hazy impression of the events. Her hands were knocked aside with no more discernible effort than if a troublesome insect was being swatted. Then the top and bottom of her white masculine waistcoat were grasped in a grip like steel. Subjected to a surging heave, with a strength exceeding

165

any she had previously encountered, she was swung away from Mr. Reeder by her captor. Released, she could not prevent herself being sent across the landing to plunge down the stairs. Reaching the bottom, she went just as hurriedly and unavoidably onwards to crash into the wall of the reception lobby. Rebounding, as the first of the main raiding party made their appearance through the front door left open by their predecessors, she toppled unconscious to the floor.

Upstairs, as the massive woman was disappearing, Sylvia gave vent to a screech of close to bestial rage. Thrusting aside her employer without a thought over whether he was able to stand unaided, she snatched a wicked looking and razor sharp little *stiletto* from her reticule. Continuing to display the skill of long practice, the lunge she commenced was just as fast and capable, seeming even more menacing due to the expression of primeval fury distorting her beautiful features.

Having swivelled around to fling Nina down the stairs, Ranse had his back to the platinum blonde and could not have avoided the attack!

Nor, despite knowing something about Sylvia's true nature, could Mrs. Grible have moved swiftly enough to intervene!

Fortunately, as he had on many previous occasions, Mr. Reeder proved equal to the situation!

Pressing the catch as he raised the umbrella, the detective caused it to perform its designed function by springing open. Deftly interposing it between the forward thrusting *stiletto* and the blond giant, he averted the attack. The blade sliced through the material of the canopy and a shriek of even greater fury burst from Sylvia as her arm became entangled by the supporting metal ribs. Before she could extricate herself, stepping forward swiftly, Mrs. Grible drove a punch to the side of her jaw which rendered her unconscious.

'And that is -um- *that*!' Mr. Reeder exclaimed in a mildly satisfied tone, drawing free his umbrella as the platinum blonde crumpled flaccidly at his feet. Glancing to where Marks had stumbled against the wall, clearly in considerable agony, he nodded with what seemed a most gentle approval and went on, 'Shall we go -um- into the Club and see whether our friends are -um- *enjoying* themselves?'

*   *   *   *   *   *   *

'I'M *pleased* nobody was in the lobby to see us coming in looking the way we do,' Rita Yarborough stated, as she walked along the dimly lit corridor of the Sunbury Private Hotel's first—although as an American, she would claim second—floor with the three men who had accompanied her on the hectic visit to the Pinhole Club.[1] Glancing down, with vision impaired by an almost closed and discoloured right eye, at the ruined silk stockings which emerged from beneath the cloak she had wrapped about her from neck to knee level, she went on, 'You must admit I'm not *quite* at my *best* just now.'

'Beauty is in the eye of the beholder, my dear,' claimed Jason Grant Reeder, whose face bore a similar adornment as testimony to his participation in the fighting. 'A *black* eye in your case.'

'And as good a one's I've ever seen,' supported Sergeant Mark 'Comanche Blood' Scrapton. Retaining full vision through both eyes, his speech was a trifle distorted from coming through a badly swollen top lip. 'Anyways, Rita-gal, you look a whole heap better than that high-toned white-haired gal did when they hauled you, kicking 'n' squalling fit to bust, off her. And, should you get asked who gave you the black eye, you can always say—!'

' "*Nobody*, I had to fight for it",' the red head interrupted. '*Really*, Comanch', your jokes are almost as old as the ones Jimmy Reeder tells us.'

'I'm glad you said *almost*, dear girl,' Jason Grant asserted, determined to uphold the family honour. 'Because *nobody*, not even Uncle Jeremiah Golden, tells jokes as *old* as Jimmy's.'

'If they do,' Sergeant Alvin Dustine "*Rapido* Clint" Fog declared, marks on his face indicating he too had not emerged from the brawl unscathed in spite of his *yawara* stick and equal mastery of other Oriental fighting techniques.[2] 'I've surely never come across them, nor *want* to.'

'*Philistine!*' Jason Grant accused and, having reached the door of his room, continued, 'Well, goodnight, all of you. I'd like to say how *enjoyable* it's been, but—!

---

1. *Although the Americans number the successive levels of their buildings consecutively from the street, the British commence with the 'ground' and continue upwards with the 'first' floor.*
2. *How Sergeant Alvin Dustine 'Cap' Fog acquired his knowledge of the* yawara *stick and the other Japanese martial arts* ju-jitsu *and* karate *is explained in:* APPENDIX TWO.

167

'But it *hasn't*, so you *can't*!,' Rita offered, before the comment could be concluded. 'You *Reeders*—!'

'Are innocent of all offence on that one,' Jason Grant declared, with an air of conscious virtue. 'I was merely going to say, when I was so *rudely* interrupted, "But not *all* of it was *over* enjoyable." So, once again, dear friends, goodnight.'

'Hot damn if Jas' isn't *right* on that,' Comanche declared with feeling, after the Englishman went into his accommodation. 'There was times back to that old Club, like when those two big jaspers jumped me, when I wasn't *enjoying* it over much at all.'

'Do you know *something*?' Rita inquired, dropping her voice as if meaning to impart a secret of *great* importance. 'I got the feeling dear Lady Mary felt that way before we *agreed* to part company.'

'What I saw,' Comanche drawled sardonically, taking the key to his room from his pocket. 'It took three good ole British bobbies *and* Mrs. Grible to get you to *agree* to stop whomping that gal.'

'I just got a mite carried away,' the red head asserted, although the estimation of the restraining influence required had been exaggerated, her manner suggesting complete exculpation for her behaviour.

'Now to a half-smart lil ole Texas boy like me,' the Indian dark sergeant drawled. 'The only one got "carried away" was *her*. Goodnight, you-all.'

'Goodnight, Comanch', Rita and *Rapido* responded in the same breath and continued walking hand in hand along the corridor towards the suite they were occupying.

Entering the main room of the Club after having dealt with Waly Marks' party, Mrs. Grible, Mr. James Garfield Reeder and Sergeant Ranse Smith had found it in a complete shambles. Still without waiting for the police reinforcements summoned by the chair thrown through the window, they joined the fray. However, their participation had been to lend such assistance as was required by the members of their party already there.

It had been the blonde giant who relieved Comanche from the difficulties caused by a combined attack from two of the bouncers to whom he had referred before retiring to his room. In spite of his aged and frail appearance, as he had done with Sylvia Cornelius, the detective had proved equally effective when intervening to rescue *Rapido* from the attentions of three members of the 'smart set' out to avenge the rough handling of Frithington-Evans.

Deciding that—although the attire of both was reduced to only French knickers and ruined stockings—Rita had the upper hand against Lady Mary Herban, who was being straddled and held supine to receive drubbing which would have gladdened the heart of Molly Nickerson, the housekeeper had ensured nobody else interfered until the police came in. Then, without requiring any assistance regardless of the claim made by Comanche, she had persuaded the red head to rise from the unconscious and battered blonde. Having done so, Rita was taken downstairs. In addition to rendering first aid, the housekeeper had retrieved her cloak to cover the loss of clothing she had suffered.

With the fight brought under control, Mr. Reeder had left Chief Inspector Frank Gaylor—ever a willing participant in his operations—to take care of the situation in the main room while he conducted an examination elsewhere on the premises. To his disappointment, he had failed to find anything which might offer even a suggestion of how to locate Olga Flack or where the Chopper could be found. However, even though it did not supply evidence of what happened to Molly Nickerson, the room housing the man who monitored telephone calls proved more fruitful. It had recordings of conversations, some of which were subsequently proved to have been used for the purposes of blackmail. Furthermore, realizing he would be considered an accessory in the eyes of the law, the operator had sought to reduce his sentence by telling how he believed his employer had murdered the prostitute after learning of her attempted betrayal.

To help support Jason Grant's pose as being a successful jewel thief, although the other participants in the brawl had been allowed to go home after having names and addresses taken, Gaylor had escorted him and the Americans to the local police station ostensibly for questioning. Before leaving the damaged room, however, he had retrieved and returned Rita's vanity bag to her. Kowing it contained the Remington Double Derringer pistol, he had also ensured it was not searched by any other police officer.

Keeping up appearances had occupied Rita and her companions until shortly after midnight!

169

Entering their suite and, having closed the door, switching on the lights, the red head and *Rapido* found somebody had made the most of their absence!

'Get your hands up, Yank!' commanded Billy Churgwin, stepping out of the bathroom with a revolver in his hand. He was followed by two of his men, but only the older of them was armed. 'And don't you scream, tart!'

Although the gang leader did not know it, Rita and the small Texan were aware that raising an outcry would be useless. One of the Hotel's well justified boasts was about the privacy it offered to its residents. This included having had all its accommodation for guests most effectively sound-proofed. Only a far greater noise than could be produced by a human voice could penetrate beyond the walls.

'If this's a *stick-up*—!' *Rapido* commenced, despite realizing it was far from that.

'You *know* it's not,' Churgwin growled.

'Then what in hell do you want?' the small Texan demanded, standing very still yet as tense as a coil-spring under compression.

'*You*!' the gang leader stated. 'And don't try to give me any of that shit about being a Yankee hired gun. Olga Flack told me you're a Texas Ranger and helped that old bastard, Reeder, kill Mad John.'

'Olga always did talk a mite too much,' *Rapido* claimed, glancing at Rita. Although she gave the impression of cowering in terror, huddling the cloak around her and clutching the vanity bag with her right hand inside it, he knew she was just as alert and ready for any opportunity as himself. 'So what're you figuring on doing now you know who I am?'

'You're going for a *ride*,' Churgwin replied, curiosity having caused him to discover where the supposed American "hired guns" were staying before he had been informed of their true capacity by Olga Flack.

'The boss was over in America showing them how to do things right,' boasted the unarmed criminal. 'He knows how Yankee gangsters do it.'

Studying the trio with experienced eyes ever since they came from the bathroom, *Rapido* had formed an assessment of the danger they posed. His conclusions suggested the situation was bad, but could have been worse. For one thing, he felt sure neither Churgwin nor the older criminal were anywhere near as competent with firearms as the kind of criminals with whom he was accustomed to dealing in Texas. Nevertheless, he realized this was only marginally advantageous as he was unarmed except for the *yawara* stick. Effectively as he could wield it, he knew he would only be granted an opportunity if there was some form of distraction. On the other hand, in his favour, the Englishmen did not know of the Remington already in Rita's grasp and they clearly discounted her as a factor.

Having drawn his summations with regards to the gang leader and older man, the small Texan turned his attention to the other man and recognized the type. Young and inexperienced, he exuded a cockily aggressive self assurance when not being sycophantic to his boss. Clearly he wanted to establish he was as tough and competent as his older companion.

Unless *Rapido* missed his guess, the younger underling was the weak link in the chain!

'He does, huh?' the small Texan inquired and turned his gaze to the gang leader. 'Then, seeing's how you've got me and're taking me for a ride, I hope you'll do it the way the boys over to home do and grant me a last request. You've heard they do, haven't you?'

'Of course I have,' Churgwin lied, his acquaintance with American gangsters having been far less extensive than he liked to imply as a means of impressing his underlings. Being unwilling to admit he was unaware of the protocol required when taking a victim for a 'ride', he went on, 'What do you want?'

'To be shot with my own gun,' *Rapido* answered and gestured with his left hand. 'It's in the top drawer of the bedside table.'

'Get it, Bernie!' the gang leader authorized.

'Sure, boss,' assented the younger underling. Crossing to the bedside table, he opened the drawer and lifted out the Colt Government Model of 1911 automatic pistol with a close to rapturous expression. 'Isn't this a beau—!'

'Watch *out*!' Rita yelled in a tone of urgency. 'He always keeps it loaded and ready. Push the safety catch *down*!'

Looking at the weapon, Bernard Copley discovered the hammer was at what he realized must be the fully cocked position. Knowing little about firearms, but eager to display a non-existent competence, he took the measure suggested by the red head with the intention of rendering it safe. Having done so, he snapped the pistol forward as he had seen William S. Hart do with a revolver in Western movies and pressed the trigger to, he believed, simulate firing it.

What happened next was no mere simulation!

As Rita was aware when making the suggestion, although *Rapido* removed and emptied the magazine to conserve its spring when not required for use, he always kept the pistol cocked with a round in the chamber and the safety catch applied. In addition, as an aid to rapid firing, he had had the pressure required to operate the trigger reduced somewhat.

Lacking the red head's knowledge and being equally in ignorance of the working of the Colt, by following her suggestion, Copley had taken off instead of applying the safety catch. To compound his folly, fortunately without pointing the barrel at anybody, his impersonating of the famous star of Western movies which of all the genre offered by Hollywood most impressed him—the day of 'gangster' films still being in the future—caused the weapon to discharge.

'What the he—?' Churgwin snarled, as he and the older underling snapped around their heads on hearing the detonation.

Granted the opportunity each had known was desperately needed, Rita and *Rapido* instantly set about making the most of it.

Throwing off the cloak, oblivious of how doing so left her most scantily clad, the red head flung the vanity bag away from the Remington she was already holding and had cocked without being detected during the conversation. Raising it double handed, she thrust it shoulder high at arms' length to make the most of its limited potential for accuracy. Even as the small Texan was snatching out the *yawara* stick and moving forward, she sighted and fired at the man she concluded posed the most immediate threat.

Starting to return his diverted attention, Churgwin was granted no chance to cope with the drastically changed circumstances. Spat from the upper barrel of the weapon grasped so competently in the hands of the half naked girl, and propelled by the black powder charge of a rimfire cartridge, a .41 bullet took him between the eyes. Killed outright, he spun and fell with the revolver flying from his hand.

Seeing through the swirling white smoke of the burned powder that her shot had taken effect, Rita did not waste time on self congratulation. Aware the threat was still not ended, she thumbed back the hammer and caused the firing pin to descend until level with the lower of the superposed barrels. Turning the weapon, she saw the shock and consternation which came to the face of the older underling. His revolver was being allowed to dangle downwards, but she knew it could easily enough be aligned if he was granted an opportunity. With that in mind, making the most of his confusion, she sighted and fired in a less lethal fashion. Hit in the right shoulder, he dropped the gun and, without realizing to do so would have been impossible until she had reloaded, he yelled for her not to shoot again.

Just as much alarmed as his companions had been by the Colt going off in his hand, Copley gave a snarl of mingled alarm and fury as he saw the small Texan darting towards him. Bringing the weapon around, he snatched at its trigger when sure the barrel was pointing in the required direction. To his distress, instead of the desired explosion and a bullet being emitted, nothing happened. Before he could appreciate the full implications of this phenomenon, he found himself in even more serious difficulty.

Bounding into the air, performing what a connoiseur of Japanese *karate* would have identified as a perfectly executed *yoko tobi geri* side jumping kick, *Rapido* sent the ball of his right foot into the centre of the criminal's chest. Precipitated backwards into a corner, Copley remained on his feet. Only for a moment, however. Following him, the small Texan swung the *yawara* stick into contact against the top of his head and he collapsed unconscious with a fractured skull.

'Go fetch Jason, honey!' *Rapido* commanded, retrieving the Colt dropped on to the bed as he passed his victim.

While Rita was redonning her discarded robe and leaving, the small Texan collected and started to feed rounds into a magazine. Sliding this into the butt slot when ready for use, he snapped back and released the cocking slide to charge the chamber. Such was his competence, he had done practically all the reloading without more than glancing momentarily away from the criminal now kneeling and holding the wounded shoulder.

There was a delay before Rita returned, but the effect

which resulted from this made it well worthwhile!

Accompanying the red head, was Mr. J.G. Reeder!

Having following his usual precaution of having what he needed available, Jason Grant had been able to transform himself into looking sufficiently like the occupant of Daffodil House to satisfy the one conscious criminal whose injury had rendered him less discerning than might otherwise have been the case.

'Carrying a -um- *shooter* now, are you, Jesse?' the newcomer inquired, in the appropriate tone. 'That's good for another seven -um- years on your sentence.'

'Billy made me do it, guvnor!' the underling claimed, glancing to make sure his boss was in no condition to refute the statement or take reprisals for it having been made. 'And, if you'll make it easy for me with the Wig, I'll give you something that'll make it worth your while.'

'Well, well, well!' Mr. Jason Grant Reeder breathed, with none of the usual hesitancy, after having heard the information imparted by the criminal in the hope of reducing the added sentence always given in Britain at that time for the carrying of a firearm in the commission of a crime. 'Now I *know* why the Vimy was stolen!'

CHAPTER SIXTEEN

LET'S GO TO THE PALLADIUM

SITTING in the rear of the Vickers Vimy bomber as it lumbered on a warm and otherwise clear Monday afternoon, at close to its 'ceiling' of seven thousand feet through the scattered clouds towards Brockley, Kent, Olga Flack was filled with a sense of wild elation!

Of slightly more than medium height, the daughter of Mad John Flack was a strikingly beautiful brunette whose features only rarely gave an indication of the evil which was her true personality.[1] Nature had imbued her with a beautiful face, concealed at that moment beneath a flying helmet and goggles, which gave an impression ideally suited to the winning over of such susceptible male victims as were required to serve her unlawful needs. What was more, not even being clad in a long leather jacket, riding breeches and boots, could entirely conceal the fact that she had a shapely slender figure. She never hesitated before employing its attractions sexually to achieve her illicit ends.

People often wondered how the mentally deranged master criminal could have sired such an outwardly beauteous woman as his only known offspring!

Those better informed about Olga claimed she was very much her father's daughter!

Some even went so far as to assert that the delicate seeming brunette exceeded old Mad John in her cold blooded

---

1. *We realize our description of Olga Flack is far from in keeping with that given in a much earlier biography. Although neither Penelope Wallace nor Mr. James Garfield Reeder will confirm our supposition, we believe she may have been successful in misleading Mr. Jason Grant as to her true nature and this, in addition to his having suffered the trauma of recovering the woman he loved and had believed dead, caused his failure to institute criminal proceedings against her after the events Edgar Wallace recorded in:* TERROR KEEP.

disregard for any human life except her own!

Even though confined in Holloway Prison For Women, albeit already planning for her escape, Olga had been hired to organize the theft of the unconventionally modified big biplane from the Royal Air Force's Aircraft and Armaments Experimental Station at Martlesham Heath. Not only had her arrangements—made through Wallace Oswald 'Wally' Marks on his frequent visits, ostensibly to discuss the progression of his attempts to obtain an appeal against her sentence—proved successful in procurring the Vimy for her principals, but they were sufficiently thorough to have ensured it remained concealed when she modified the original plan for her own benefit.

Throughout the whole period of her incarceration, the brunette had sought to bring about the death of the man she hated more than any other in the world. That was why she had made the offer of presenting her father's already legendary 'Encyclopedia Of Crime' to whoever killed Mr. J.G. Reeder. Making his regular visits, Marks had had to admit there were only failures to do so. Therefore, she had decided to take the matter in hand personally once she had acquired her liberty. With this achieved, discovering Louis 'Lou' Birkstone was organizing an attempt shortly after she had attained her freedom, she could not resist the temptation to accompany Herbert McPriest to Waterloo Station and see what happened. It had been she who killed the failed assassin as he approached her car in the belief that she would carry him off to safety.

The latest abortive effort had served to strengthen Olga's determination to arrange for the detective to be dealt with herself!

It was only shortly before the theft was successfully perpetrated that, learning something she considered of *great* interest, the brunette had envisaged the purpose to which the stolen biplane was now being put. On announcing the change of plan, she had found need to be grateful once again for having a face and body so pleasing to men. It had only been by exerting all the charm she could employ so effectively that the Russian pilot supplied by the sponsors of the acquisition was induced to delay his departure from England—although he had given the impression of having done so when flying away from 'Wings and Bangs'—and carry out her wishes.

While Olga had had little liking for the sexual recompense demanded by the uncouth Russian as a bonus to the monetary payment involved, she considered the aeroplane would never be employed for a better purpose. Within less than ten minutes, the organization built up by the man who had first caused the confinement in Broadmoor Asylum For the Criminally Insane and later killed her father would be ruined. Even if Mr. J.G. Reeder should survive the onslaught of the strafing attack she planned to make upon the chicken farm which served as his, she felt sure he believed, secret headquarters, the British people would never allow him to operate again after having endangered—perhaps even cost—the lives of his Royal visitors.

Being informed that William Maxwell 'Billy' Churgwin had been found shot through the head in Hyde Park, the brunette had concluded an attempt to extract vengeance in another direction had met with failure!

Olga had realized at first sight that the 'Sergeant Alvin Dustine Fog' who was met by Mr. Reeder at Waterloo Station was not the same one who had posed as '*Rapido* Clint' and, by successfully hoodwinking her father—having in fact, fired one of the fatal bullets into him—had helped to cause his death. Deducing correctly that the substitution must mean the genuine Texas Ranger had also arrived from the United States, almost certainly to hunt down the Chopper, she had had no difficulty in verifying the supposition with regards to his identity while he was making the rounds of London's night spots and criminal rendezvous. Satisfied on that point, she had seen what she believed to be an opportunity to extract vengeance upon him as well as the British detective.

Being fully occupied with her plans for the attack upon the chicken farm, the brunette had assigned the removal of the genuine Sergeant Fog to Churgwin. Despite having given an impression of developing a strong romantic attachment for him, she had never considered him as other than a disposable tool to be used and eventually discarded. Nor, even without realizing he had taken an opportunity to remove a threat to himself while helping her, had her feelings changed when he provided the woman whose body was an essential factor of her escape from Holloway. Therefore, she had felt more relief than remorse—albeit tinged with annoyance at what she felt sure had been his failure to achieve his purpose—on learning he was dead.

Knowing where she had sent Churgwin to find and dispatch

the Texan, Olga had concluded correctly that his body was removed from the Sunbury Private Hotel with the connivance of Mr. Reeder so as to avoid unwanted publicity for the American peace officer who was responsible for his death. For once, her generally effective sources of information had been unable to find any trace of either of the underlings who had assisted the gang leader. She was aware that, if they too were killed, their bodies would have been left with him. As this was not the case, she concluded they were in the hands of the authorities and hidden away to suit the needs of the detective. Nevertheless, disturbing as the prospect was, she had drawn consolation from her belief that neither knew anything about her affairs and would be unable to seek a reduction of punishment by betraying her.

Satisfied that she had nothing to fear because of the latest failure of those upon whom she had to depend for implimenting her schemes, the brunette turned her thoughts to the vengeance she was soon to extract upon the hated Mr. Reeder.

Even though the clouds were far too scattered to permit an approach to be made unseen, Olga considered there was no danger of being detected by her intended victims. While the aircraft in which she was flying had been stolen, she saw no reason why its appearance over the chicken farm should arouse suspicion. There was no external sign of its modifications for a 'ground attack' role and it was the standard drab colour scheme, given to all its kind by the Royal Air Force's Bomber Command, lacking the distinctive and eye-catching decoration of fighters. Her sources of information had indicated the ploy of having it flown off over the North Sea and, when out of sight of land, circle back across a thinly populated section of the East Coast to come down at a place she had prepared for it to be hidden—the landing area already having been made ready for another scheme upon which she was engaged.[2] Everything had been successful in so far as all

2. *When we queried the possibility of a Vickers Vimy bomber being able to land anywhere other than on a full sized and equipped airfield, Mr. James Garfield explained it needed far less of a runway than even the twin engined aircraft used in World War II. He also pointed out that, as late as into the mid-1930's, pilots of airliners such as the Armstrong Whitworth Argosy always made a habit of studying the terrain ahead whilst in flight to select ordinary fields of suitable size in which to land should the need arise and such descents were, in fact, not infrequently carried out safely.*

178

the searching for it was being concentrated upon the Continent. Therefore, she felt sure the detective would suspect nothing of the danger when it was coming towards him until too late to avoid the consequences.

A piercing whistle diverted the brunette from her reverie!

Picking up her end of the Gosport tube,[3] Olga heard the voice of the Russian pilot and realized from its tone he was in a state of consternation!

'Look to your right!'

Turning her gaze in the required direction, Olga saw that three small aircraft painted white and with the red, white and blue roundels of the Royal Air Force were diving towards them. Each upper wing and fuselage was also decorated by two crossed scarlet bolts of lightning which, although she was not aware of their meaning, was the insignia used to offer more easily discerned indications of 'ownership' by 28 Squadron than the usual registration letters and numbers. Single seaters, even without the assistance of the momentum acquired in the angled descent, they were considerably faster than the Vimy. Retaining their 'arrowhead' formation, they closed in to range alongside the bomber. Waggling his wings to attract the attention of its occupants, the pilot of the leading aircraft made gestures with his hand which clearly meant they should turn around and land.

'They're on to us!' the Russian screeched, being better informed than his passenger, recognizing the newcomers were flying Sopwith F7.1. Snipe fighters and reverting to his native tongue in his panic.

'To hell with them!' Olga replied in the same language, hoping by using it to lessen the close to panic assailing the man ahead of her. 'Keep going!'

A competent enough aviator, albeit very much a 'man of the people' and lacking the social graces of his contemporaries in the Royal Air Force, Lieutenant Boris Andropov was silently cursing himself for having left his homeland. From the beginning, he had not wanted to be sent to pilot the aircraft stolen for his Government with the connivance of

---

3. 'Gosport tube': a simple device, much like the 'speaking tubes' employed in large houses before the development of telephones, used to permit conversation between the crew of an aircraft before more sophisticated 'inter-com' systems became available.

some British 'liberals' and Communists active in the trade union movement. Unfortunately, he lacked the requisite influence with the *Commissariat* to have the assignment given elsewhere and was all too aware of the extremely unpleasant fate meted out to anybody who refused the dictates of those in higher authority.

Despite the Russian's serious misgivings, the theft had proved so easy he had wondered why he felt concerned in the first place. Instead he had been eager to fly such a potentially lethal device when the time came to invade Finland, Poland and other East European countires as the start of spreading the blessings of Communism all over the world. However, his lust for money and the sexual benefits which went with it had caused him to delay making the delivery as originally intended. To ease what passed as his conscience, he had accepted the assurance of the prominent 'liberals' to whom he was introduced by Olga that—due to the quality of some of the intended victims—his actions would bring high acclaim from his superiors on his delayed return.

Now, faced with the almost certainty of capture, the pilot was wishing he had been more circumspect and followed his orders to the letter. Regardless of that, accepting that he had disobeyed, he was equally aware there was no way he could escape from the trio of fighters. Even without being burdened by carrying so much extra equipment, the bomber lacked the performance required to lose them by speed or powers of manoeuvrability.

'We *have* to do what they want!' Andropov wailed, having drawn his unpalatable conclusions and wondering whether he possessed any military information with which he might reduce the consequences of his actions.

'Like hell we do!' Olga denied vehemently.

While the original Larsen All-Metal Attack Plane was armed entirely by Thompson submachine guns, as an inducement for financial assistance by their manufacturers, the Vimy still retained a portion of its earlier armament.

Knowing how to operate them, hoping there might be an opportunity to use them on Mr. Reeder if he should evade the volume of fire pouring from beneath the aircraft, the brunette had had the twin Lewis guns on the Scarff ring in the rear cockpit loaded prior to taking off. Spitting out the words in English, she slipped into position and swung the weapons on

180

their efficient mounting.[4] Sighting on the leading fighter, which was sufficiently close for her to feel confident of making a hit, she set the light machine guns working. As flame spurted from the muzzles and empty cartridge cases were ejected, she saw the man who had given the command to turn and land suddenly jerk and his aircraft spun away. To her added delight, although she had not fired at it as yet, the nearer of the other two machines immediately followed her victim downwards.

*　　*　　*　　* 　　 *　　*　　*　　*

WEARING the mandatory flying helmet and goggles and the largest pair of white overalls available in the Quartermaster's Store at the Station of 28 Squadron, Sergeant Ranse Smith was sitting in the cockpit and piloting a Sopwith F7.1. Snipe for the second time!

However, on this occasion, the blond giant was not flying for pleasure!

With the assistance of Scotland Yard, who were delighted to see the end of such a dangerous and successful criminal, Jason Grant Reeder had disposed of Billy Churgwin's body so it could be 'found' in Hyde Park. He had also arranged for the two injured criminals to be taken to an outlying police station and held *incommunicado*. Then he had wasted no time in acting upon the information received from the less seriously injured of the pair. However, despite the search he had set into motion, the missing Vickers Vimy bomber had not been located on Sunday. Called into conference with the Prime Minister and Home Secretary, having temporarily resumed the *persona* of the occupant of Daffodil House, he had suggested measures for the protection of the Royal visitors to the family's headquarters the following day.

The precautions had resulted in Ranse becoming a far more active particpant than he or anybody else envisaged!

It having been considered impolitic under the circumstances for the contingent from Company 'Z' to be presented to the Royal Family, they had been invited as guests of the officers' mess at 28 Squadron's Station. Although Major John

---

4. *'Scarff ring': a metal frame carrying a movable arm to which one or two light machine guns such as the Lewis could be attached, fitted as armament in the crew's cockpits on aircraft. Named after the designer, Warrant Officer F.W. Scarff.*

Gray Reeder was at the chicken farm, Colonel Brian Besgrove-Woodstole was with them. In his capacity as the current head of British Military Intelligence, he was assigned to co-ordinate the defensive patrols of fighters from the base and, hopefully, take charge of any prisoners should the Vimy put in the anticipated appearance and possibly be compelled to land on the airfield. However, if the people aboard it refused to follow the orders, the pilots had been authorized to take whatever other action proved necessary to prevent them from reaching their objective.

To avoid attracting too much attention, which was also considered politically undesirable, it had been decided that the task of protecting the Royal Party against an attack from the sky was to be handled by only the nearest available single squadron. Therefore, on being assigned the duty, Squadron Leader Arnold Blandish had insisted that every available pilot and aircraft must be employed to ensure as complete a cover as possible was maintained over the vital period when the attack would have to take place. Having one man absent on leave and beyond recall, and remembering the display of flying he had seen during the previous visit, he had asked Ranse to make up the number.

Taking off as the third member of the 'vic' led by Blandish, the blond giant had ascended to the ten thousand feet 'ceiling' of the Snipe. From this position, higher than the Vicker Vimy could attain, the arrowhead formation had been ideally positioned when—by a turn of fate which would be discarded by any author of fiction as being too improbable to be used as a plot device—it came into view from amongst the clouds. Acting upon the signal from the Squadron Leader at the point of the 'vic', the fighters descended to make their interception and, in accordance with his orders, he had indicated the course of action expected from the pilot of the stolen bomber.

Although he had received training in how to cope with similar conditions and far from being a coward—he was later to distinguish himself, in particular, throughout the Battle of Britain during World War 11—seeing his commanding officer hit by the Lewis guns in the Vimy, the young pilot officer nearest to it could not prevent himself from following Blandish's involuntary dive.

Equally startled, although from his position in the 'vic' Ranse was unable to observe what had caused the departure, he guessed what had happened and reacted in a way which any experienced fighter pilot would have admired. Thrusting on the throttle, he caused the Snipe to gather speed and kept it in level flight. Going past the bomber, his supposition over the departure of his companions received confirmation. Bullets from the bigger aircraft slashed through the fuselage of the Snipe, fortunately without hitting him or any vital part. Once clear, he twirled the manoeuvrable little fighter around and returned head on.

Like Olga Flack, the blond giant was conversant with the armament of his aircraft. The two Vickers machine guns mounted on top of the engine cowling, being synchronized to send their bullets through the arc of the whirling propellor without striking its blades, were operated in much the same fashion as those of the Boeing PW-9 'pursuit' fighter he had flown on a 'firing run' with the American Army Air Corps in Texas. Aiming the Snipe straight at the Vimy and waiting until his instincts suggested he was within effective range, he cut loose with a twin burst of .303 bullets at a rate of—although he did not continue to fire for that long—about five hundred per minute. One in ten were 'tracers' and, by the smoke-like trail they emitted, he could see he was hitting the front of the fuselage.

Still firing as prudence demanded he turned aside to avoid a collision, Ranse sent more lead into the starboard engine. Its propellor stopped and a spurt of flame erupted from its body. Furthermore, the Vimy was already making a swing in the opposite direction to that in which he was going. Looking over his shoulder as he was bringing the Snipe around to continue the attack if this should prove necessary, he watched the bomber making a slowly spinning dive with the blaze from the engine spreading.

In the Vimy, having swung the Lewis guns as far as the arc of the Scarff ring would allow, Olga glared furiously after the Snipe as it went beyond her line of fire. Looking forward and discovering it was swinging back, she released the weapons and grabbed for the mouthpiece of the Gosport tube. Screaming down it for the Russian to turn so she could aim at it, the bomber having no forward firing armament, her words elicited no response.

Although Lieutenant Andropov heard his passenger, in his present frame of mind he was unable to translate her words into Russian from the English she was using in her stress. This was the first time he had encountered danger to himself. He had gained his training as a pilot and rank as a reward for having helped with the 'removal'—a polite name for murder —of several families considered by the *Commisariat* as undesirable 'enemies of the State', but they had always been unarmed and entailed no threat to his well being. Faced with the possibility of *very* grave personal peril, his thoughts were too numbed to listen to Olga or even think of taking evasive measures.

Just as an instinct for self preservation was belatedly forcing the pilot to consider making some move, it was too late. His last living sight was of spurting jets of flame coming from the machine guns on the cowling of the rapidly converging fighter. Then bullets were ripping into him. They were a dead man's hands which involuntarily jerked at the control stick to make the Vimy swerve as if wishing to escape the damage being inflicted upon the front of its fuselage.

To her horror, Olga watched the earth seeming to revolve as the aircraft went into a plunging spin with the flames from the engine spreading to the upper wing. There was nothing she could do to save herself. Having claimed it would be unnecessary, she had refused the offer of a parachute. Even if she had had one, the realization of her terrible predicament produced such a freezing effect upon her normally lightning fast senses that she could not have tried to quit the rear cockpit as a means of escaping. She could do nothing more than scream much as Molly Nickerson had done while being killed by Churgwin, although she had not been present to hear it, as she watched the ground rushing nearer at an ever increasing speed.

Circling and following the Vimy in its uncontrollable descent, Ranse watched it disappear into thick woodland which he knew to be about three miles from its chicken farm objective. Pulling out and passing over, he felt the shock wave as it struck the ground and, gazing back, saw an ever growing mass of flame arising from amongst the trees. Then, turning his gaze upwards, he discovered the other two Snipes were approaching. Relieved by the implication that Blandish had escaped serious injury when fired upon from the Vimy, he concluded the same was unlikely to prove the case with its occupants.

*   *   *   *   *   *   *   *

'WHAT with the fire setting off all those drums of ammunition, the aircraft and everything in it was blown to fragments and burned beyond recognition before we arrived,' Colonel Besgrove-Woodstole informed a most attentive, small and formally dressed, audience. 'But I think we can safely say that this time Olga Flack is really dead.'

'At the risk of appearing -um- callous,' Mr. Jeremiah Golden Reeder declared. 'I'm afraid I, for one, can't say I'm deeply -um- grieved by hearing that.'

The owner of the chicken farm received nods of agreement from his assembled relatives and the contingent from Company 'Z'.

As a precaution, the Royal Party had delayed Their arrival until the Vickers Vimy had been reported destroyed and the danger was over. Nevertheless, the visit had been a great success. Among other things, Mr. Jeremiah Golden was informed that he was to be gazetted a Knight Commander of the Bath in the forthcoming New Year's Honours List. After They had taken Their departure, he had invited his nephews, the wives of two and fiancee of the third, and the Americans to a celebratory dinner. On being joined by the Colonel, who he had asked to come as an old friend and fellow chicken raising enthusiast, he had been as eager as all the others to learn of the latest developments in the affair.

'By the by, before we go on with the festivities,' Besgrove-Woodstole said. 'It slipped my mind with all the excitement, but do any of you know a black chap who's a burglar?'

'I can't bring -um- one to mind,' James Garfield Reeder declared.

'Really, James,' Mr. Jeremiah Golden protested, before his youngest nephew could continue. 'You do a good job of being me, but I -um- never say *-um-* nearly as often as you do.'

'Sorry, -um-, sir,' the current occupant of Daffodil House apologised with a grin. Becoming serious, after his relatives had also disclaimed knowledge of the matter raised by the Colonel, he continued, 'If it isn't an *indiscreet* question, Brian, why this sudden interest?'

'The butler at General Anstruther's place in Hampshire saw a black chap lurking in the bushes,' Besgrove-Woodstole explained. 'He ran off and got away in a fast car, but he left a jemmy behind. Which made me wonder if he was a burglar.'

'Wasn't the General your predecessor?' James Garfield inquired.

'He was,' the Colonel confirmed. 'And he did such a good job of it all through the Great War, it's not an easy post to fill.'

'Yes, I thought he was running your office in the War,' James Garfield said pensively. Then, swinging his gaze to the Americans, he went on apparently at a tangent, 'Let's go to the Palladium tomorrow evening.'

'I thought your taste in entertainment ran more to a Drury Lane melodrama.' Rita Yarborough commented, despite concluding from the absence of the word "-um-" there must be something *far* more than a mere desire for entertainment behind the suggestion.

'It is, my dear -um- young lady, hoping I've got it *right* this time,' answered the current occupant of Daffodil House. 'However, I think it may prove sufficiently -um- melodramatic to satisfy us all.'

CHAPTER SEVENTEEN

YOU ARE THE -UM- CHOPPER

'WHAT the hell're you doing, coming in here?' the man billed as 'Haysoff Spades' demanded coldly, glaring at Mr. James Garfield Reeder and Sergeant Alvin Dustine '*Rapido Clint*' Fog as they entered and closed the door of the 'star's' dressing-room at the Palladium Theatre. 'Didn't they tell you I don't see *nobody* backstage?'

'I'm afraid I told a -um- *fib*,' the elderly seeming detective replied, in a tone seemingly hushed by the enormity of his misbehaviour and disregarding the fact that he had produced official authorization for the visit when seeking admission. 'I led the -um- stage manager to assume you had summoned Sergeant Fog and myself to -um- see you upon a matter of some urgency when, in fact, it is we who wish to see your good -um- self.'

'Then get the hell—!' the entertainer commenced, sitting in his shirt sleeves—albeit with the 'blackface' make up and white cotton gloves he always wore in public—at his surprisingly uncluttered dressing-table. The angry words died away and he stiffened slightly as he noticed the silver star-in-a-circle badge suspended on the left breast pocket of the smaller visitor. To men as watchful and discerning as they were, the hostility in his invariable stage stereotype 'poor Negro' voice became tinged with perturbation as he continued, 'Just who th—*what* the hell are you, *cops*?'

'I am a mere -um- dilettante, with scarcely any *official* standing,' Mr Reeder claimed, with little justification as he had a status equivalent to a superintendent of police and although the first part of the question at least had been directed at the small Texan. 'But my colleague could correctly if inelegantly be classified as a -um- "cop", being, as you undoubtedly deduce from his badge of -um- office, a sergeant of the Texas Rangers.'

'I'm always pleased to do a benefit for a cop,' Haysoff Spades declared, but his tone conveyed little conviction of him being at ease to either experienced visitor. 'If that's what you've come about.'

'It is *not*, as you have doubtless already also -um- deduced,' Mr. Reeder replied in his most apologetic and, to those who knew him well, therefore his most dangerous fashion. 'We have come to ask you to accompany us to the nearest police station.'

'*Accompany* you to the—!' the entertainer began, dropping his gaze briefly to a drawer of the dressing-table that he always kept locked when absent, and open while in occupation of the room. Then, letting his left hand go into it with what appeared a casual and unthinking gesture, he went on with what seemed to be a complete lack of comprehension. 'What for?'

'Because,' Mr. Reeder answered, like '*Rapido*' giving no sign of having noticed or attached any significance to the apparently harmless yet nervous response his previous words had elicited. '*You* are the -um- Chopper!'

'If that's a *joke*,' the man at the dressing-table snarled, trying a desperate bluff. 'It's in *lousiest* taste I've ever come across!'

'The matter is quite easily settled,' the detective claimed. 'All we have to do is see you without *all* your make up and check the fingerprints of yourself, not those of your -um- *alter ego* is, I believe, the appropriate foreign -um- term!'

Once again the 'criminal mind' of Mr. J.G. Reeder had been put to excellent use!

Always possessed of an exceptional memory—a trait of all his family—the current occupant of Daffodil House had formulated a theory arising out of the request for information about a 'black burglar' from Colonel Brian Besgrove-Woodstole the previous evening. Stimulated by the question, he had remembered what he was told about the night Sergeants Jubal Branch and Hans 'Dutchy' Soehnen were killed. When first hearing the story, knowing of certain social conditions in the United States, he had been reminded of a theory once expressed by his older cousin. However, at that time he had refrained from mentioning the supposition aroused by one aspect of the events. With his interest rekindled, he had explained his reasons for such a belief and found his audience were in agreement that it could explain many puzzling aspects about the Chopper's career.

Despite the concurrence, putting the theory to the test had had to be delayed until that evening as the attempted assassination by Olga Flack had been considered a greater priority!

Although Mr. Reeder eventually unearthed the names of the 'liberals' and Communist trade unionists behind the affair, his efforts to obtain sufficient evidence for an arrest came to nothing. Nevertheless, those in the vicinity of the chicken farm had fled as soon as they saw the Vickers Vimy being shot down in the flames. Being disinclined to trust one another, the majority of the conspirators fled the country to live as 'expatriates' proclaiming constantly their disillusionment and disinclination to remain in a 'capitalist society.'[1] Strangely, in spite of this point of view and their assertions describing it as a paradise on earth, *none* of them went to, much less settled in, Russia.

The death of Billy Churgwin had been explained and the action taken was given approval by the Home Secretary. However, the verdict reached by a coroner's court and the story which subsequently appeared in the press, claimed he had been shot by an American professional hired killer, 'James Bowie "*Rapido*" Clint', brought a second time to England for this purpose. Interviewing Wally Marks in hospital, Mr. Reeder had come away convinced he had not been informed of the true state of affairs regarding the small Texan by Olga Flack. Such reticence, the detective knew, had always been a trait of hers and had led her never to tell her associates any more than she considered absolutely necessary.

Nor had the two injured underlings, on being questioned, been any better informed. Their boss had told them only that they were to assist him to get rid of a 'Yankee gunman' hired by an unspecified 'business rival' to kill him.

A further assumption by the detective, based upon the sour look of the dishonest solicitor when the point was raised, had

---

1. *Some of these 'expatriate' criminals served as mercenaries on the* losing *side in the Spanish Civil War. Returning to Britain at the cessation of hostilities, they took reserved occupations when World War 11 broke out and did not give the country of their birth any support until after Russia went to war with Germany in June, 1941.*

been that he was also in ignorance of the location of Mad John Flack's 'Encyclopedia of Crime'. Nevertheless, in the future, further attempts to earn it would lead Mr. Reeder to assume it was still being sought for by members of the underworld.

With the other details either concluded, or left in the hands of Jason Grant and Major John Gray Reeder—the latter in his capacity as an officer of the Rifle Brigade seconded to British Military Intelligence—the current occupant of Daffodil House and the contingent from Company 'Z' had been at liberty to attend to the other matter. Contacting Chief Inspector Oliver Rater and explaining his theory, James Garfield had asked if he could confront the suspect personally. Another friend of long standing, the Orator had raised no objections even when told that one of the Texans would also be present.

Having had Jubal Branch serve as his guide, mentor and partner during the trial period following his enrolment in the Texas Rangers, therefore having been closer than the other two sergeants, *Rapido* had been accorded the right to accompany the detective. However, arrangements had been made by which it was hoped he could continue to preserve the identity of his *alter ego* for future undercover duties.

Realizing what must be implied by the remark about his own fingerprints and those of his *alter ego*, the man who the world believed to be entertainer and war hero, James 'Haysoff Spades' Ogilby concluded it was almost certain his secret was known to his visitors!

What was more, the peace officers were aware of how easily the assumption that he was the Chopper could be confirmed!

A graduate of the Texas Southern University For Negroes, at Houston, the hired killer was descended—although he was unaware of the fact—from a member of the Lulongo tribe which inhabited part of the so called 'River Territories' of British West Africa and had once been described by the authority who subsequently made the identification of his origins as, 'a bitter, crabbed and beastly people'.[2] His ancestor

2. *The information regarding the 'roots' of the Chopper was supplied by Mr. Commissioner—later Sir—Henry Sanders, K.C.M.G., arguably the world's foremost authority upon the various African tribes. Information regarding his career and about the Lulongo tribe is given in the* Sanders Of The River *series of biographies by Edgar Wallace.*

had been sold into slavery after being captured by another nation in the course of a war. While very intelligent, he had inherited all the worst traits of his ancestry and turned instinctively to crime. Learning of the special dispensation given to Ogilby, seeking to find more lucrative illegal fields than were available to a member of his race in those days, he had seen how this could be done.

Obtaining employment as the entertainer's 'dresser', the Chopper had acquired all the information he required to make work the substitution he proposed to effect. When satisfied this was the case, he tendered his resignation. Two days later, he murdered and took the place of 'Haysoff Spades'. Putting to use his extensive knowledge of the under-world, aided by a masterly skill at disguise and special equipment he had acquired, he had established himself as a professional killer and had built up a network of contacts through which he could be reached without anybody being able to trace the chain from beginning to end.

The popularity of Haysoff Spades, which he had just enough talent to sustain when helped by keeping alive memories of why the blackface make up had always been worn by his victim, allowed the Chopper to be able to obtain engagements to appear at theatres in whichever city he had received a 'contract' for a kill. Such had been his competence in his major line of work, it was not until the night in Fort Worth that he had made a serious error. This was having allowed himself to be found in the alley by the police offi-cers. Knowing they would be upon him quickly, he had hid-den his Thompson submachine gun in an empty trash can and, gambling—as had occurred upon previous similar occasions—upon the peace officers believing a Negro could not be the man they were seeking, allowed himself to be questioned. The problem had arisen as a result of the means he had selected to end the first attempt at pursuit made by the pair of peace officers from near the Interstate Vaudeville Theatre.

Successful though the ploy had been, due to the furore aroused by his having killed two sergeants of the Texas Rang-ers as well as his intended victim, the Chopper had concluded he would be well advised to leave the country until things quietened down. Fortunately, as he had considered it at the time, he had lucrative offers for engagements in both of his forms of employment from England. He was satisfied his disguise would stand up to whatever checks were made upon it, particularly the face masks—upon which the 'minstrel' make up was applied—and the gloves he had had made simulating the effects of the *icthyosis*. As an added precaution, which he had not needed on his arrival at Southampton, he had had the latter given ridges and whorls which exactly duplicated the fingerprints of his *alter ego*.

While the Chopper had never heard of it, he had found there was truth in the assertion by Jason Grant that—like certain good wines and types of tobacco—criminal activities were best confined by the perpetrator to the country of his origin!

It had soon become apparent to the hired killer that, in spite of the considerable success he had attained throughout the United States, he was likely to find things vastly different in England!

In his homeland, the Chopper had always derived two major benefits from his birthright!

Firstly, because the activities of a family were almost always known by any domestic staff they employed, the hired killer generally had a source of information about his intended victims. Particularly in the large cities, which was one reason he would only accept contracts in such a region, servants were predominantly Negroes. Being able to appear charming and sociable when he wished, despite having a disdain for what he thought of as inferior beings, he was able to obtain many useful facts from members of his own race. These were supplied in the majority of cases innocently—not out of hatred for their white employers, as ethnic apologists and professional racists of a later generation would claim—and would have aroused alarm, even distress, on the part of the donor if the true purpose of his inquiries had been suspected.

Secondly and perhaps more important, because of the numbers of his race in the cities, the Chopper had found his true identity offered a perfect camouflage. As had proved the case in other places besides Fort Worth, the natural colour of his skin helped him turn aside suspicion which would have been directed at a white man found in the vicinity of the kind of killing he had made his speciality.

Not until he had settled in his accommodation at the Savoy

Hotel had the hired killer realized what he had found puzzling since landing at Southampton!

Tipping the porter, the hired killer had suddenly become aware that the kind of jobs which were almost the sole province of Negroes in America were being performed by white people. For the first time, he had appreciated that he would not have either his major source of information or what had frequently amounted to something close to a cloak of invisibility. Just how true the latter was had been brought home to him in no uncertain manner on the night of his only killing so far carried out in England.

One of the problems of the pose as being Ogilby had always been meeting with former acquaintances. However, because of the unsightly disability, the entertainer had made no intimate friends since resuming his civilian occupation. Nor had he been a very sociable person prior to enlisting, so he had few friends from the past. What was more, he had had a reputation for possessing a poor memory for faces, names and events, which had enabled his murderer to excuse failure to recognize anybody who claimed his acquaintance at some earlier date.

Nevertheless, there were two men who Ogilby had often claimed were his only close friends. While the Atlantic Ocean had separated them, the Chopper had never been worried by their existence. He had known this state of affairs was certain of change once he reached England and, in fact, this had been his reason for having refused tempting offers of 'contracts' there in the past. Sure enough, shortly after his arrival, he had received telephone calls from both suggesting meetings. Anticipating this, he had taken the precaution of learning how they could be located. Fortunately, both had been too busy with other matters to meet the liner in which he arrived and he had persuaded them to postpone any getting together until the conclusion of his Palladium engagement. His intention to ensure no rendezvous occurred had only met with partial success.

While successful in killing Frederick Manton—with whom Ogilby had been a good friend and enlisted in the British Army—outside the Apollo Theatre, the Chopper had been seen and, according to Wally Marks on being consulted during a meeting similar to their first, the witness had told the police he was black. Furthermore if a shout of, 'Stop, you damned nigger!' was any indication, a similar recognition of his race had occurred when—having been compelled to wait until Sunday because of his commitments at the Palladium—he had tried to remove the second threat to his secret. He had driven in a hired car to the home of General Sir Henry Anstruther with the intention of gaining admission and removing the remaining link with Ogilby's past. Despite having elected to forego the 'contract' even before learning of its sponsor being killed, because of the unexpected problems he had discovered were caused by there being so few Negroes in London, he had decided this must still be done.

While the hired killer had returned the balance of his advance payment for the 'contract', he had known he would still turn a healthy profit by his legitimate earnings!

What was more, until the two unwelcome visitors had arrived, the Chopper had been convinced the truth of his dual personality was no more suspected in England than it had been in the United States.

'I don't suppose it'd be any use telling you you're making the biggest god-damned mistake of your lives?' the hired killer suggested, still feeling surreptitiously inside the drawer.

'None -um- whatsoever,' Mr. Reeder confirmed.

'I thought not,' the Chopper admitted and, confident his intentions were unsuspected as he was using his left hand, he started to bring out the revolver he always kept concealed in a similar place ready for just such an emergency.

Unfortunately for the hired killer, his behaviour had neither gone unnoticed nor its purpose been unsuspected!

At the first indication of his suppositions being correct, his own close to ambidextrous prowess having taught him never to discount the left hand as a potential threat, *Rapido* was ready to deal with it when it materialized!

Displaying smooth co-ordination combined with the sort of speed which in part accounted for the sobriquet he had adopted, the small Texan pulled open the left side of his jacket and his right disappeared beneath it. Grasping the butt of his Colt Government Model of 1911 automatic pistol, he twisted it from the spring retention shoulder holster in which it was carried. Turning it forward, his right forefinger entering the triggerguard and thumb, forcing down the safety catch only *after* the muzzle was pointing away from his body. Lined at waist level, the pistol crashed no more than .6 of a second after the draw was commenced.

Because of the great speed with which *Rapido* moved, before the Chopper could bring his own weapon into action, he was struck in the centre of the forehead by the .45 bullet. Slammed backwards from the chair, he lost his hold on the revolver and pitched lifeless into the corner of the dressing-room.

'*Your* bird this -um- time,' Mr. Reeder declared, having drawn a simlar weapon to that of his companion, albeit not so quickly, and thinking of a similar comment he had made on the night Mad John Flack died at the hands of his companion and himself.

'*Gracias, amigo*,' the small Texan replied. Lowering his voice, he went on, 'We've got the Chopper for you, Jubal, Dutchy!'[3]

---

3. *Contriving to create a confusion in which Sergeant Ranse Smith was substituted for Sergeant Alvin Dustine Fog, Mr. Jason Garfield Reeder had let it be known that the former had killed the Chopper whilst resisting arrest for murder in the United States. The full story of how the hired killer had contrived to operate was given to the coroner's court and appeared in the newspapers of Britain and the United States. With the formalities over and their assignment completed, the contingent from Company 'Z' returned to Texas on a passenger liner and resumed their operations against criminals who evaded the conventional processes of the law.*

APPENDIX ONE

AFTER having attended the 22nd Convention of Western Writers of America in 1975, we were privileged to meet for the first time Alvin Dustine 'Cap' Fog. Amongst the other things we learned was that he had visited England during the mid-1920's, in the line of duty as a member of the Texas Rangers' elite and unpublicised Company 'Z'. The cases brought him into contact with the organization operated by Mr. J.G. Reeder. However, although we had read all the volumes of biography by Edgar Wallace which dealt with the career of this illustrious British detective,[1] we had not seen any reference to his meeting with 'Cap'.

While 'Cap's' official report and other related records were thorough in their coverage of his part in the events we later published under the title, 'CAP' FOG, TEXAS RANGER, MEET MR. J.G. REEDER—albeit with one misconception which we have corrected in this narrative,[2]—they left unanswered a number of points with regards to the participation of his British contemporary.

1 . *Various cases handled by one or another of the Mr. J. G. Reeders are recorded in:* ROOM 13, THE MIND OF MR. J.G. REEDER, RED ACES, MR. J.G. REEDER RETURNS *and* TERROR KEEP.

2 . 'CAP' FOG, TEXAS RANGER, MEET MR. J.G. REEDER *was not our original choice of title for this volume. We selected* KILL MR. J.G. REEDER!, *but Ms. Penelope Wallace said she would prefer some reference to our character in the title, so we suggested* MR. J.G. REEDER, MEET 'CAP' FOG. *For some reason which was never explained, on the advice of their Sales Department, Corgi Books made the longer substitution.*

2a. *We now find we were in error when we were preparing the manuscript for this title, as we suggested 'Cap' had already acquired his sobriquet by becoming the youngest man ever to attain the rank of Captain in the Texas Rangers. He, in fact, at that time was only a sergeant and his promotion came about as a result of the case we have recorded herein.*

On our return to England, we contacted Ms. Penelope Wallace, daughter of Mr. Reeder's biographer and organizer of THE EDGAR WALLACE SOCIETY, requesting this information. Ms. Wallace kindly placed at our disposal all of her father's notes and the relevant case-book which he had received from Mr. Reeder, but had not worked upon. These not only allowed us to fill up the gaps in 'Cap's' story, but also shed light upon several hitherto puzzling aspects relating to Mr. Reeder personally. They enlarged upon the suggestions put forth by John A. Hogan—arguably the world's foremost *serious* student and researcher of Edgar Wallace, in his excel- lent article, *AUREUS HARUNDUM*.[3]

While building his reputation as an exceptionally compe- tent and well informed private detective,[4] Jeremiah Golden Reeder trained his three nephews, Jason Grant, John Gray— who served as a captain, later major, in the Rifle Brigade and was seconded to M.I. 5—and the youngest, James Garfield, to carry on his work. Knowing the superstitious nature of many habitual criminals, he decided the organization could func- tion more effectively and efficiently if the connection between himself and his nephews was kept a secret.

Using the family's chicken farm at Brockley, Kent, as his headquarters, Mr. Golden—as he was referred to by the very few people privy to the secret—maintained the main files of the organization and correlated the information which came from their multifarious sources. When in public, whoever was currently in residence at Daffodil House, on—by a coincidence—Brockley Road in London, spoke, dressed and employed the mannerisms made famous by Mr. Golden when he had lived and operated from there. The resident, or other two when the need arose, wore a wig and make up to give an appearance of being the appropriate age and further

3. AUREUS HARUNDUM: *to quote its author John A Hogan, 'It is the nearest I can get with my memories of Latin to 'Golden Reeder', which seemed rather apt in this case'.*

4. *Mr. Jeremiah Golden was helped greatly during his early days by being the nephew of Major General Sir Patrick Reeder, K.C.B., V.C., D.S.O., M.C. and Bar, details of some of whose career as a member of the British Secret Sevice—to which he was seconded in the rank of captain from the Rifle Brigade—is recorded in:* THE REMITTANCE KID *and* THE WHIP AND THE WAR LANCE.

emphasise the already strong family resemblance of their respective features.

We realize that our description of Mrs. Jane Amelia Grible, housekeeper at the town residence, is not in accord with the occasional references to her in the biographies written—without differentiating between whichever Mr. J.G. Reeder was in occupation—by Edgar Wallace. At the time of their production, the most stringent condition imposed upon our illustrious predecessor when permission was granted for them to be published was that there must be nothing to expose the security arrangements of the organization, nor to identify its employees.[5]

These restrictions have now been lifted and the late Mrs. Grible can be given the credit she well deserved. Our predecessor was allowed to pay only an indirect tribute to her by recording the major part she played in the case he called, THE TRAITOR'S GATE. However, omitting all mention of her belonging to Mr. Reeder's organization—even going to the extent of giving her a non-existent 'son' and claiming she held a post at Scotland Yard—he referred to her throughout as 'Mrs. Jane Ollorby'. Nevertheless, he only changed her description slightly. While her face was 'big, with three chins and a somewhat masculine nose,' her eyes only 'twinkled with amusement' on rare occasions and her expression was not often genial in public.[6]

5. We are subjected to similar conditions when writing about the people we call the 'Hardin, Fog and Blaze' clan. They insist we never disclose their true identity or whereabouts and include sufficient anomalies and discrepancies to prevent either inadvertently being discovered.
6. The only reference Edgar Wallace was allowed to make, giving a suggestion of the true state of affairs at first hand, was on Page 53, RED ACES: quote, 'This lady is Mrs. Grible of my Department,' he—Mr. Reeder—said gravely.

APPENDIX TWO

IN every democracy, the laws framed for the protection of the innocent have loopholes which can be exploited for the benefit of the undeniably guilty—and frequently are!

Although accepting that such a state of affairs must exist in a free society, the serving Governor of Texas grew very concerned over the ever increasing wave of lawlessness which had followed in the wake of the well meant—albeit unpopular, ill advised and difficult to enforce—ratification of the so called 'Volstead Act'.[1] He concluded that only unconventional methods could cope with malefactors who slipped through the meshes of the legal system. Ordinary peace officers, being severely restricted by Federal, State, county and municipal regulations, were unable to take the necessary action in circumstances of this nature.[2]

1. 'Volstead Act', the colloquial name for the Eighteenth (Prohibition) Amendment to the Constitution of the United States of America. This defined intoxicating liquors as those containing more than one half of one percent alcohol and made illegal the manufacture, transportation and sale of such liquors for beverage purposes. Introduced by Representative Andrew J. Volstead of Minnesota, the act was ratified—over the veto of President Woodrow Wilson—on October the 18th, 1919. By the time it was repealed in 1933, it had inadvertently helped finance and pave the way for the rise of 'organized crime'.

2. The jurisdictional authority of a town marshal or police department was restricted to the municipality by whom they were hired and a sheriff's office within the boundaries of the county to which its personnel were elected. As was suggested by the title of the latter, Arizona and Texas Rangers and State Police were restricted to their specific States. Except for Company 'Z' when on 'official unofficial' assignments, in general Rangers were expected to wait until invited by county or municipal agencies before being able to participate in either's investigations. United States' Marshals, their deputies, the Federal Bureau of Investigation and Prohibition agents had country-wide jurisdiction. However, the first three were responsible only for handling 'Federal' crimes such as robbery of the mails and kidnapping.

While pondering upon the problem, the Governor met three prominent European criminologists who were touring the United States and giving a series of lectures on this subject to the heads of major law enforcement agencies. Acting upon the unconventional suggestions of George Manfred, Leon Gonzales and Raymond Poiccart,[3] he had instructed the State Attorney General to select a special group of Texas Rangers who would form—without any mention of it being made public—a new Company given the identifying letter 'Z' and put under the command of Major Benson Tragg. Every man was picked for his courage, skill with weapons and bare handed combat, integrity, specialized knowledge and devotion to the cause of justice. Their purpose was to deal with such criminals as could not be touched by conventional methods, even if the means they employed to do so might be considered as stepping beyond the legal boundaries of the law.

Aware that his men were well known to the underworld, Major Tragg had enrolled Alvin Dustine Fog, Mark Scrapton and Ranse Smith, who he knew possessed all the requisite qualities and one other. Although all had served as peace officers, none of them had previously been connected with the Texas Rangers. Despite this, after a probationary period during which each had proven himself capable of carrying out the duties required of him, they were appointed to the rank of sergeant to give them the necessary authority when on an assignment.

One of the points raised by members of the J.T. EDSON APPRECIATION SOCIETY since we were allowed to start producing the Alvin Dustine 'Cap' Fog series is to question the very close physical resemblance he had with his paternal grandfather, Captain Dustine Edward Marsden 'Dusty' Fog—for whom we also have the honour to serve as official

3. George Manfred, Leon Gonzales and Raymond Poiccart were the surviving members of the 'Four Just Men' crime fighting organization, the fourth having been killed before their first recorded adventure was published. Although none of the following volumes cover their lecture tour of the United States, see chronologically: THE FOUR JUST MEN, THE COUNCIL OF JUSTICE, THE LAW OF THE FOUR JUST MEN, AGAIN THE THREE and THE THREE JUST MEN. by Edgar Wallace.

biographer[4]—except that his hair was black instead of dusty blond.[5] The similarity was increased by Cap having received much the same education where gun handling, law enforcement duties and certain Japanese martial arts were concerned.[6] Furthermore, he had always revered the memory of his grandfather and sought to model himself in Dusty's image. However, due to having served as a peace officer after graduating from college—first as a deputy under his father, Sheriff Jackson Fog of Rio Hondo County[7]—Cap acquired only a minimal knowledge of the cattle raising business. Therefore, although equally competent as a gun fighter and, arguably, the finest combat pistol shot of his day,[8] he never

4.   Details of the family background, career and special qualifications of Captain Dustine Edward Marsden 'Dusty' Fog are given in various volumes of the Civil War and Floating Outfit series.

5.   Alvin Dustine 'Cap' Fog's black hair was inherited from his paternal grandmother. Prior to her marriage to Dusty Fog, she was Lady Winifred Amelia 'Freddie Woods' Besgrove-Woodstole. How she and her husband met and their romance progressed is told in: THE MAKING OF A LAWMAN, THE TROUBLE BUSTERS, THE GENTLE GIANT, BUFFALO ARE COMING! and THE FORTUNE HUNTERS. She also makes 'guest' appearances in: WHITE STALLION, RED MARE; THE WHIP AND THE WAR LANCE and Part Five, 'The Butcher's Fiery End', J.T.'S LADIES.

6.   Alvin Dustine 'Cap' Fog's instructor in the employment of, among other aspects of Japanese martial arts, ju-jitsu, karate and the yawara stick, was a nephew of Tommy Okasi, a samaurai warrior who acted as valet for General Jackson Baines 'Ole Devil' Hardin, C.S.A. Details of the special qualifications of the General and Tommy are given mainly in the Ole Devil Hardin series.

7.   Although as yet no details have been forthcoming with regards to the activities of Jackson Marsden Fog in his capacity of sheriff of Rio Hondo County, Texas, he makes a 'guest' appearance—based upon an incident when he was serving with the American Expeditionary Force in France towards the end of World War 1—in: Case Two, 'Jubal Branch's Lucky B.A.R.', YOU'RE A TEXAS RANGER, ALVIN FOG.

8.   Some authorities give pride of place as the best combat pistol shot of the period to Ed McGivern of Montana, author of—among other works— FAST AND FANCY REVOLVER SHOOTING AND POLICE TRAINING.

excelled as a cowhand as did his grandfather.[9] On the other hand, circumstances had never compelled Dusty to adopt the kind of unconventional measures employed by Cap and Company 'Z' during those periods when he had been required to serve as a lawman in the Old West.[10]

As a tribute to the memories of their paternal grandfathers, Cap and Mark adopted the aliases, '*Rapido* Clint'[11] and 'Comanche Blood' when seeking to establish themselves as desperate criminals, as these had been used on similar occasions by Dusty Fog and the Ysable Kid.[12] Ranse had inherited the looks and physique of his maternal grandfather, Mark Counter who had been a good friend of Dusty and the Kid.[13]

9.   One occasion when Dusty Fog proved his excellence as a cowhand in competition with his peers is recorded in: GOODNIGHT'S DREAM. *Despite there already being an entirely different English volume with the same name, the Bantam Books Inc. re-titled their 1974 edition,* THE FLOATING OUTFIT.

10. *In addition to the first four titles listed in* Footnote 5, *which refer to the early association between Lady Winifred Besgrove-Woodstole and Dusty Fog, further information pertaining to his activities as a peace officer is given in:* QUIET TOWN, THE SMALL TEXAN *and* THE TOWN TAMERS.

11. *Why Dusty Fog used the alias,* Rapido Clint *is told in:* BEGUINAGE *and* BEGUINAGE IS DEAD!

12. *Information regarding the family background and career of Mark Scrapton's grandfather, the Ysabel Kid, can be found in the* Floating Outfit *series. Occasions when he employed the alias, 'Comanche Blood' are given in:* HELL IN THE PALO DURO, GO BACK TO HELL *and* Part Three, 'Comanche Blood', THE HARD RIDERS.

13. *Details of the career and family background of Ranse Smith's grandfather, Mark Counter, are given in the* Floating Outfit *series. As is told in the* Rockabye County *series—which covers the organization and duties of a present day Sheriff's Office in Texas—Ranse's activities with Company 'Z' induced another member of the family, Bradford 'Brad' Counter to become a peace officer.*

APPENDIX THREE

THROUGHOUT the years we have been writing, we have frequently received letters asking for various terms we employ to be explained in greater detail. While we do not have the slightest objection to such correspondence and always reply, we have found it saves much time consuming repetition to include those most frequently requested in each new title. We ask our 'old hands', who have seen these items many times in the past, to remember there are always 'new chums' coming along who have not and to bear with us. J.T.E.

1. We strongly suspect the trend in movies and television series made since the mid-1950's, wherein all cowhands are portrayed as heavily bearded, long haired and filthy arose less from a desire on the part of the productions companies to create 'realism' than because there were so few actors available—particularly to play 'supporting' roles—who were short haired and clean shaven. Another factor was because the 'liberal' elements who were starting to gain control over much of the media seem to obtain some form of 'ego trip' from showing dirty conditions, filthy habits and unkempt appearances. In our extensive reference library, we cannot find even a dozen photographs of actual *cowhands*—as opposed to civilian scouts for the Army, old time mountain men, or gold prospectors—with long hair and bushy beards. In fact, our reading on the subject and conversations with friends living in the Western States of America have led us to the conclusion that the term 'long hair' was one of opprobrium in the Old West and Prohibition eras just as it still tends to be today in cattle raising country.

2. 'Clip' point: where the last few inches of the otherwise

unsharpened 'back' of the blade—when laid in a horizontal position with the 'edge' down and the handle to the left of the viewer—joins and becomes an extension of the main cutting surface in a concave arc. This is the characteristic which many authorities claim identifies a 'bowie knife'.

2a. What happened to the knife of the alleged designer of such a weapon, James Bowie—many claim this was actually his older brother, Rezin Pleasant—after his death during the final attack upon the besieged Alamo Mission at San Antonio de Bexar, Texas, on March the 6th, 1836, is told in: GET URREA and THE QUEST FOR BOWIE'S BLADE.

2b. A 'spear' point, which is less utilitarian than a 'clip', is formed by the two sharpened 'edges' of the blade coming together in symmetrical curves. It was generally used for purely fighting knives such as the 'Arkansas toothpick' or assassin's weapons.

3. 'Riot gun': a single barrelled, twelve gauge, five shot, generally pump action, shotgun used by law enforcement agencies. One of the earliest examples was the Winchester Model of 1897 as modified for use in the trench warfare of World War 1 by having the barrel reduced to twenty inches—'sporting' versions being at least four inches longer—given a radiating cooling sleeve to permit sustained rapid fire and equipped to take a bayonet.

3a. The 'trench gun', as such *weapons*—they no longer classed as sporting guns—became known, proved to be an exceptionally effective device for use at close, or in confined, quarters, especially when charged with nine .32 calibre buckshot balls. One purpose to which it was put was to deflect 'stick' hand grenades thrown by the enemy.

3b. After trench guns had been employed to play a major part in breaking up a mass infantry attack, the Germans—who had already delivered assaults with poison gas, including the vicious 'mustard' variety—complained such use was an 'inhumane and barbaric way of waging war'. Their threat to execute any member of the American Expeditionary Force captured with a trench gun in his possession was countered by a reminder from the United States that a number of German prisoners of war were being held and Congress would know what action to take by way of reprisals.

3c. Between World War 1 and 2, peace officers adopted the trench gun format as an offensive weapon—handguns being primarily issued for defensive purposes—and these were given the name, 'riot guns'. However, during the early 1970's, the management of the Remington Arms Company considered the term 'riot gun' was inaccurate and had an undesirable connotation as such weapons were not confined to coping with civic disorders. The correct purpose, they claimed with complete justification, was to supplement the *defensive* armament of peace officers in all types of law enforcement combat situations. Therefore, the Company designated such firearms of the kind which they manufacture 'police guns'.

4. We consider at best specious—at worst, a snobbish attempt to 'put down' the myth and legends of the Old West—the frequently repeated assertion that the gun fighters of that era could not 'hit a barn door at twenty yards'. While willing to concede that the average person then, as now, would not have much skill in using a handgun, knowing his life would depend upon it, the professional *pistolero* on either side of the law expended time, money and effort to acquire proficiency. Furthermore, such a man did not carry a revolver to indulge in shooting at *anything* except at close range. He employed it as a readily accessible *weapon* which would incapacitate an enemy, preferably with the first shot, at close quarters, hence the preference for a weapon of heavy calibre.

4a. With the exception of .22 calibre handguns intended for casual pleasure shooting, those specially designed for Olympic style 'pistol' matches, the Remington XP100—one of which makes an appearance in: THE LAWMEN OF ROCKABYE COUNTY—designed for 'varmint' hunting at long distances, or medium to heavy calibre automatic pistols 'accurized' and in the hands of a proficient exponent of modern 'combat' shooting, a handgun is a short range *defensive* and not an *offensive* weapon. Any Old West gun fighter, or peace officer in the Prohibition era and present times expecting to have to shoot at distances beyond about twenty *feet* would take the precaution of arming himself with a shotgun or a rifle.

5. The sharp toes and high heels of boots worn by cowhands were functional rather than merely decorative. The former could find and enter, or be slipped free from, a stirrup iron very quickly in an emergency. Not only did the latter offer a firmer brace against the stirrups, they could be spiked into the ground to supply added holding power when roping on foot.

6. The Texas Rangers were to all practical intents and purposes abolished—their functions being taken over by the more prosaic Department Of Public Safety at Austin and the Highway Patrol—on October the 17th, 1935. This was almost one hundred years to the day after their formation.

7. 'Make wolf bait', one term meaning to kill. Derived from the practice in the Old West, when a range was infested by stock killing predators—not necessarily just wolves, but coyotes, the occasional jaguar in southern regions, black and grizzly bears—of slaughtering an animal and, having poisoned the carcase, leaving it to be devoured by the carnivores.

8. 'Mason-Dixon line', erroneously called the 'Mason-Dixie line'. The boundary between Pennsylvania and Maryland, as surveyed from 1763-67 by the Englishmen, Charles Mason and Jeremiah Dixon. It became considered as the dividing line separating the Southern 'Slave' and Northern 'Free' States.

9. 'New England': the North East section of the United States—including Massachusetts, New Hampshire, Connecticut, Maine, Vermont and Rhode Island—which was first settled by people primarily from the British Isles.

10. 'Light a shuck', a cowhand term for leaving hurriedly. Derived from the habit in night camps on 'open range' roundups and trail drives of supplying 'shucks'—dried corn cobs—to be lit and used for illumination by anybody who had to leave the campfire and walk about in the darkness. As the 'shuck' burned away very quickly, a person needed to hurry if wanting to benefit from its illumination.

J.T. EDSON TITLES AVAILABLE FROM CORGI BOOKS

While every effort is made to keep prices low, it is sometimes necessary to increase prices at short notice. Corgi Books reserve the right to show new retail prices on covers which may differ from those previously advertised in the text or elsewhere.

The prices shown below were correct at the time of going to press.

ORDER FORM

All these books are available at your book shop or newsagent, or can be ordered direct from the publisher. Just tick the titles you want and fill in the form below.

CORGI BOOKS, Cash Sales Department, P.O. Box 11, Falmouth, Cornwall.

Please send cheque or postal order, no currency.

Please allow cost of book(s) plus the following for postage and packing:

U.K. Customers—Allow 45p for the first book, 20p for the second book and 14p for each additional book ordered, to a maximum charge of £1.63.

B.F.P.O. and Eire—Allow 45p for the first book, 20p for the second book plus 14p per copy for the next seven books, thereafter 8p per book.

Overseas Customers—Allow 75p for the first book and 21p per copy for each additional book.

NAME (Block Letters) . . . .

ADDRESS . . . .

. . . .